BEACHHEAD

ALSO BY SCOTT JAMES MAGNER

THE FOREWORLD SAGA

Hearts of Iron

Blood and Ashes

THE TRANSGENIC WARS

Homefront

The Homefront trilogy:

Invasion

Landfall

Beachhead

The Reclamation's End trilogy:

Starfarer's Legacy

Red Genesis

Black Destiny

THE HUNTERS CHRONICLE

Seasons of Truth

Empire of Night

Crusade of Shadows

BEACHHEAD

A NOVEL OF THE TRANSGENIC WARS

SCOTT JAMES MAGNER

ARUS
Entertainment

Portions of this book previously appeared in *Homefront*, published by Arche Press, an imprint of Resurrection House.

Published by ARUS Entertainment (Seattle, WA).

This book is catalog #ARUS4003, and has an ISBN of 979-0+9963059-9-0

Edited by Mark Teppo, Fleetwood Robbins, and Darin Bradley

Original *Homefront* cover design by Jennifer Tough and Darin Bradley

Cover art and design by Al'n Duong and Honor Zavatta-MacDonald

www.arusentertainment.com

For the readers. This book is as much your story as it is mine.

And for the writers, who drive me to excellence with every turn of the page.

Voiceover against a black screen: "This recording contains material of a graphic nature, and is not suitable for children or the faint of heart."

The scene fades in on cloudy day, with a modest crowd assembled in front of a wide, raised dais with a podium installed at the front arc. At the podium is a tall man wearing a blue jumpsuit, gesturing behind him at a number of chairs similar to those of the first few rows below the dais.

Seated there are the eight members of the Reclamation Council dressed in their formal robes, a young woman next to Mordecai Harrison with an empty chair on her other side, and a number of uniformed SDF officers. Harrison's head is bent in conversation with the woman, and he looks up at the podium as the speaker concludes his remarks.

"And without further delay, please welcome my uncle, whom I had to remind several times this morning to put on his clothes so he could attend his own inauguration!"

The crowd applauds, and a smiling Mordecai Harrison steps up to the younger man and shakes his hand, pulling him in close for a quick exchange. Harrison then approaches the podium, arms held high and waving at the crowd. His black and green councilor's robes are being whipped about by a strong wind, and he grabs the sides of the podium for support as a particularly strong gust whips his hair around.

. . .

The crowd noise dies down as the front of the podium lights up, then Harrison and the podium rise up on a null-grav saucer to a height of three meters. A shimmering force screen appears in front of his face, which is in turn projected above him at least twenty meters high. As he speaks, his strong voice flows from speakers around the plaza.

"Thank you Paul, for that lovely introduction. I'll be sure to put a little something in your pay envelope next week.

"People of North America, people of Earth, Luna, Mars, and whoever else is bored enough to listen to this speech. I'm so happy that you've joined us here, on what's perhaps the most miserable day in the last hundred years. I know old men aren't supposed to complain about the weather, but I don't get to see it that often, so I've got a bit of catching up to do.

"My wife, Almira, says that shared experiences are the only ones worth having. That's her down in the front row, fretting about my hair and wishing I'd give up this notion of worldwide prosperity and just come home."

The focus shifts briefly, centering on a woman approximately the same age as Harrison, dressed primly in a blue jumpsuit and a flowing black and green wrap. She cocks her head back and laughs, then nods forward, eyes downcast, and waves away his joke with two quick downward strokes. The reporter sitting to her left says something which makes her laugh even harder as the focus returns to Harrison.

"But that's the one thing we both know I can't do. The Reclamation asks a lot of us all, and rebuilding our wasted world is a goal my family has worked toward for centuries. Mind you, I've only been around for a few of them, but in that time I've seen many positive changes in our world, and my hope is that they'll keep on happening long after we're gone."

. . .

Harrison's podium drifts back and forth in front of the gleaming stage, and as he does, the projection of his face turns to address different parts of the crowd of several thousand people assembled below.

"In the last four years, it has been my honor to serve on the Reclamation Council. It's a much more daunting task than I'd first imagined. But also a most rewarding one.

"As a doctor--as a scientist--I've spent my life addressing the needs of the people of Earth and the habitats as best I could from within the walls of my Institute. When my predecessor proposed that we end the Reclamation, abandon our dream of a green and prosperous Earth and return to an Earth-centric government, I could not sit idly by and allow us to turn away from that progress."

The crowd applauds, and music plays for a few seconds as Harrison motions for them to subside. His podium floats back to the center of the plaza, and he speaks again when noise level drops

"Thank you, thank you. Please let me get through these prepared remarks, so we can all get out of this weather and have some cake!"

There is more cheering, but Harrison waves a finger and it dies down.

"That's the thing about science, you see, and I hope you'll forgive me for talking about my second favorite topic. Science makes the world-- the universe--accessible to everyone. It's a tool that responds to its user with measured, predictable effects. And like all tools, it is not respon- sible for those outcomes.

"Science did not ruin our world, humans did. Our planet, our beautifully fragile home, was already in an ecological crisis when we first went to the stars. We built domes on Mars, hollowed out our moon, and created gateways to other parts of the galaxy looking for the answers to our problems.

"And in the end, all we found were more questions. We took our problems with us, along with our worst natures. Anger. Jealousy. Fear. We took War out with us into the universe, and when we came back, it was still waiting for us."

Harrison closes his eyes for a moment. The crowd is silent following his unex-pected shift in conversation, and for a few moments there is only the sound of flapping flags behind him, one for each of the Reclamation zones. When he speaks again, it is with tears in his eyes.

"The truth is...the truth is we are a divided people, holding on as hard as we can to this shell of a barely healed world. The same forces that split us apart, that scorched the sky and burned our cities and destroyed our home, are what keep us apart.

"This division not only stops us from moving forward, but mires us in the past. We resent the people of Mars for their success in conquering an inhospitable world, but at the same time happily help them with their basic needs. We envy the Corridor colonies their virgin worlds, and dream of escape from the ruined one we must fight for with every fiber of our being.

"I come to you with a simple request. A call for unity. Let us set aside our differences and take our next step forward as one people. Let us end the Ex--wait, what are you doing? No, Stop!"

A flash of light fills the screen. The holo's focus shifts from Harrison at the podium to three views of the front row, as the woman sitting next to Almira

Harrison stands up and removes her jacket. Armed troopers rush in from the sides, but are tackled by a handful of attendees shouting "Earth First!"

The woman smiles up at Harrison and mouths the same slogan. Her face and arms are glowing from within, and then she explodes in a blinding ball of light.

The focus shifts again, showing the woman as she stands from behind, from a great distance away, then rushing forward immediately from the edge of the plaza after the explosion. A remote camera captures the crowd as it moves, screaming and fighting to get away through a billowing cloud of smoke and flame.

On the dais, the tall, jumpsuited man and a fleet officer are pulling Harrison from the shattered and burning podium. Fragments of ceroplastic are embedded in Harrison's face, and his legs are on fire. As the fleet officer tries to smother the flames with his removed tunic, the camera pushes in on Harrison's face to record his last words.

"Why? Why ... "

19 JULY, 2640 OER

MORDECAI

MORDECAI HARRISON WOKE UP TO AN URGENT KNOCKING AT HIS BEDROOM door. He gave what he felt was the only proper response: burying his face in his pillow and pretending he didn't hear anything. When the knock repeated, even that pleasure was denied him.

"Doctor Harrison. Doctor Harrison. There's something you need to see. Doctor, are you in there?"

"G'way. M'sleeping. Leave an old man alone, why don't you?"

When a third round of knocking started, Mordecai gave serious consideration to hiding under his bed. Paul Czgeny was an able assistant, but as the husband of Mordecai's grandniece he enjoyed a few privileges most students did not.

Like the key sequence to my private quarters. Go away, Paul. I'm tired. Damned if I know what Chrissia sees in you anyway.

Tired was perhaps too mild a term for his deep exhaustion. Four straight days of hearings, posturing, and screaming fits by the senior captains of the fleet was enough to wear down a man half his age, and that was without the daily trips up the elevator to the orbital habitats. Floating back down on whatever shuttle was flying near Old Chicago was the best part of his day now, if you took out the increasingly rare hours when he could sleep in his own bed.

"Mordecai, are you going to get out of bed or not? You're not going to want to miss this."

Surrendering to the inevitable, Mordecai rolled over and opened his eyes. When he swung his real leg off the bed and reached for his prosthetic, the room sensed his motions and brought up the lights just enough to aid his search but not enough to dazzle his remaining eye.

I should just let them replace the rest of me next time. It's getting harder and harder to get though the day without squinting. I hear the new model eyes can read signs on the moon, if the comsats are in the right locations.

"Mordecai?"

"I'm awake, Paul. What time is it in your universe?"

The artificial leg warmed at his touch, a feature he'd come to appreciate over the last year. He fitted it in place and waited for the pseudo-nerves to reacquaint themselves with the real ones in his stump.

The leg they'd fitted him with during his rehabilitation was a cold and lifeless half-measure, little more than a jointed crutch. Once he'd learned to walk again, a "real" prosthetic was manufactured and calibrated to his gait, and there were almost five minutes every day when he didn't hate everything about it.

Almost everything. At least it's warm.

"Enter."

The door slid back into the wall, and light from the other side framed Paul waiting with a data cube in his hand.

"That couldn't wait? I've got a full day ahead of me chairing oversight committees and babysitting idiots with guns."

Paul took a step back while Mordecai stood up and shrugged into an old sweater he picked up from his chair. It hung low enough to hide the top of his prosthetic, but more importantly, it had a packet of stims in one of the pockets. The older man popped one in his mouth and chewed it as he shuffled out of his sleeping chamber. When he entered the main living area, the smart room obediently dimmed the lights and began disinfecting the bed.

Yawning, Mordecai looked at Paul's tired face. His assistant was usually impeccably dressed and composed--a virtual spokesmodel for the Reclamation government. But something in the man's blue eyes told him that this was definitely not a social call.

He looks serious, for once.

"Fine, fine. Queue it up while I get some coffee. They do have coffee in your universe, don't they?"

"You'll sit and watch this, then we'll grab something on the go. And you should think about pants today; makes you look more professorial."

A harrumphing grunt marked Mordecai's full emergence from sleep. Paul's jokes were never funny unless he was awake enough to dislike them.

Paul slotted the cube into Mordecai's desk terminal, and then entered the sleep chamber to find him some clothes. As the sigil of the Harrison Institute for Applied Sciences coalesced above the desk, Mordecai called over his shoulder to his nephew.

"Don't mess around with my system. All the clothes are stored according to precise axioms, and a novice like you will just make a mess of things. Take whatever's on top, and come tell me what I'm supposed to be looking at."

Mordecai reached a shaking and spotted hand out to the image. The sigil dissolved in a shower of particles and reformed into an image from what looked like one of the topside securecams.

The angle looks right, but I don't recognize the ruins. Little wonder, I suppose, as I haven't been up there in years.

"Keep watching. And I know you own socks, so don't think you're getting away with wearing one of these outfits. You can't just wear robes all the time, even in your own universe."

Paul's use of a Russellism made him chuckle. Mordecai knew he wasn't a devotee, but Paul did try to "keep the old man happy" over and above what was required of his position. Unfortunately, Paul lived in the same universe as almost everyone else and was decades away from being able to embrace his own continuum.

Now then, what's all this fuss about an empty courtyard?

Mordecai kept watching, pointedly ignoring Paul's failed efforts to divine where the real clothes were kept. Sooner or later he would ask for help, and his universe would align with Mordecai's. But the holo existed in another continuum altogether, neither concealing nor revealing anything of interest.

Mordecai turned his hand over and pushed his palm into the image to collapse it. With only one eye, a holo never looked right, and he wanted to understand what was important enough that someone had convinced Paul to interrupt his sleep. Nothing seemed to be happening, so he expanded the image to make sure the timestamp was accurate.

He almost fell out of his chair when it shifted from showing him shadowed ruins of gray and green to a wide sheet of vivid orange.

"Three Passions, what is that!"

"Keep watching."

In all of his one-hundred and seven years, Mordecai Harrison had never wanted to do anything more. As he watched, the orange plain resolved into a pair of strange, close-set protuberances. He reduced the image, and noticed they were irregular, almost organic in nature.

Then the plain shifted, and two eyes blinked at the securecam, one above the other and in sequence. A broad red line started just above the eyes and moved up its huge forehead, and when it turned away Mordecai could see the stripe continued down the creature's back side.

He also noted the extra pair of both eyes and ears on the other side of the creature's face. His rational mind knew what he was looking at; if there were other creatures in the universe that looked like a Transgenic Type 30, the human race had yet to encounter them. But at the same time, Mordecai's universe located them in another part of the galaxy.

"But that's...They're..."

"Keep watching."

Paul's voice was right behind him now, and he tsked at Mordecai's choice of display modes. He set down a full—and depressingly respectable—set of clothing on the desk, then reached into the image to pull it back out to its original dimensions.

"You have to let the neural recorders do their job, Mordecai, or they'll never be able to fit you with a proper eye replacement. Plus, you're going to miss the most important part."

Paul placed a second hand in the holo, rotating it until Mordecai saw a side view of the Type 30 as it moved out of frame, only to return moments later leading a decidedly female form wearing some kind of black bodysuit, being half carried by a taller figure wearing an SDF hardsuit covered almost completely in pouches. Both figures had unfamiliar objects in their free hands, held in such a fashion as to scream "weapon." The hardsuited figure's helmet turned slowly to survey the ruined courtyard, aided by the Type 30's hand pointing out the precise location of the securecam.

Black Bodysuit Woman slipped off Hardsuit's shoulder and slithered to the ground rather than falling. She held her weapon in both hands now, pointing it in the opposite direction of where her companion's was aimed. From this angle, Mordecai couldn't make out a rank insignia on the red blaze across its shoulders, but whoever it was inside seemed to know what they were doing.

"How long ago was this taken?"

"Twenty minutes. They're still up there, waiting."

"Waiting? Waiting for what? And why isn't there any sound?"

More figures came into the frame now, conducted into full view and posed by the Type 30 so that they were all "looking" at the cam. Three more bodysuits came first: two male, one female. The second female was standing slightly in front of one of the males, while the other one pulled out a flat object and began tapping on it.

Then came a sight that confirmed everything for Mordecai, one he'd been waiting for all his life. A sixth black bodysuit, standing not quite as tall as the Type 30 but with an additional pair of muscular arms. Each of the creature's four hands was holding a weapon, one of which was an SDF heavy slugthrower.

A Type 6. They're here, they're really here!

Last to join the group was another Type 30, this one without a red stripe on its head. Mordecai noted that both Type 30s were wearing gray-brown jumpsuits, each of which had dozens of small holes on the chests and legs. Instead of a weapon, the one in back was carrying a small child of indeterminate gender, wearing an SDF duty blouse with the sleeves cut off.

The hardsuited figure approached the tapping male and collected whatever it was he had in his hands. Mordecai stabbed a finger at the volume controls, then looked away from the holo to check if they were working. According to the desk unit, it was registering full sound playback, exactly as recorded. Paul waved his hand away and reduced the volume to half without saying a word, then pointed back at the holo.

The figure was standing directly in front of the securecam now, raised its gauntlets to the suit's neck seals, and released them with a quick twist. Mordecai's eyes widened at the return of sound to his universe, the soft hiss of escaping air.

They did all that, without saying a word?

As soon as the thought resolved in his mind, he dismissed it. Of course the people in the image were communicating, he just didn't know how.

Probably some variation of comms that the sniffers can't track, that's all. Why, I'll bet the answer is as simple as...

The helmet came off, and Mordecai's worlds collided. Doctor Mordecai Harrison, head of the Harrison Institute and tired old man had no reason to know anything about the woman in the holo. But Councilor Harrison, of the North American Reclamation and Senior Arbitrator of the SDF Allocations and Oversight committee knew exactly who she was, even before she announced herself in a clear contralto.

"I am Lieutenant Commander Mira Harlan. Despite what you may have heard, I am a loyal officer of the System Defense Force, and I am escorting an embassy from the Outer Colonies seeking asylum in your institute."

The most wanted woman in the Home System, and she just walks up to my back door and says hello. She looks different from her pictures, but not that much.

"Who else has seen this?"

"No one but our people."

Our people. Like all things worth saying, the words had many meanings. Paul could have meant the Reclamation. He could have meant Institute staff. But the urgency in his voice when waking Mordecai, and his insistence that he view this holo as soon as possible, spoke to a third intersection of universes.

One that expanded even further as Mira Harlan reached into a pouch on her belt and pulled out a small object. She raised it up high enough so the cam could capture it without distortion.

"I also bear a message, from a mutual friend. *De eersten zullen, de laatsten zijn.*"

He'd been wanting to hear that message for many months.

Mordecai was out of his chair and halfway toward the door when Paul spoke up.

"Mordecai!"

"What? What, man? I have to go to them, you know that!"

Paul simply reached for the pile of clothes he'd placed on the table and selected a pair of pants.

"They'll wait. I have a squad ready, and from what you told me after the accident, you've been waiting for this all your life. Might as well make a good impression, yes?"

Mordecai looked down at his bare knees, one real, one not, and smiled. Then he looked back at Paul, his pants, and the holographic image of a black chess piece floating over his desk. He walked over and reached for his clothes, thinking about Aloysius Martin and the way they'd parted.

Allie, you must still be pretty angry with me, if this is who you chose as your messenger…

MIRA

Jantine's thoughts weren't impatient; at least, that wasn't the way Mira read them. The Beta was simply formulating plans, and needed more information. Mira appreciated that, just as she did the space Jantine had given her over the last few hours. It hadn't been an easy night, even with the Omegas carrying the wounded most of the way. But now that the sun was rising on yet another insane day, it made sense to work up contingency plans.

Mira had no ready answer, but she knew that as soon as she took off her helmet there would be no going back. At least one group of people on Earth knew she was helping the Colonials, and the Omegas were hard to explain away. Artemus could perhaps be a clever costume, and no one had seen his face or gray skin yet. But three-and-a-half meter, orange-skinned giants with tree trunks for arms were definitely going to attract attention.

What she did know was that their party was no longer alone, and she sent that information along through the telepathic link she'd established with the strange, transgenic girl from another star system.

≈*There's a group waiting a few meters below us. There must be a tunnel complex.*≈

Group was an approximate term. But "four people with weapons" would only alarm Jantine further, and so far Mira had detected no hostility from them. Just anticipation, something she and her friends had in abundance.

Friends. Is that what we are, or is it something more? I told Jantine that I had family spread out across North America, but other than the memory I shared with Jason, I haven't seen the boys in person since I graduated. That night was our last together as a family, and after what happened aboard Valiant, *they probably think I'm dead.*

Jantine helped JonB to the ground and moved closer to Mira. At first she thought the Beta was going to say something, but then Mira saw the sun burst into life on her visor.

≈*Is it always like this?*≈

≈*The sunrise? I think so. It wasn't for a long time, after the wars. There was just too much particulate in the air. But the Reclamation has done their best to clean the planet up, and I suppose for those who pay attention every day is different in some way.*≈

This morning was certainly different from their last. Mira and the mods had spent yesterday traveling on a hastily converted train across the heartland of North America, and although they'd made good use of frequent stops to repair sections of track, walking all night after destroying a quartet of pre-Reclamation death machines left them tired in mind and body. Mira's recently transformed muscles could process fatigue poisons with only a few minutes of rest per hour, but the ration bars in her kit weren't formulated for her new metabolism. Without high-nutrition food to replenish her body's energy supply, she wouldn't make it many more kilometers.

Besides, some of us got blown up last night. Makes the sunrise seem downright tame in comparison.

Katra had suffered massive injuries during her fall, and JonB…

JonB's memories of falling beneath the train and losing his hand when the Omegas shoved it forward are bad enough, but him getting to his feet afterward and continuing his work is just beyond belief.

Katra was right. Betas are just…different.

If she'd known the Gamma couldn't swim, Mira might have planned her final defense against the hunter-killers differently. Katra's encounter suit had kept her from drowning, but after the bridge blew she hit the river's surface at a speed that made it effectively as hard as concrete, and her suit was the only thing keeping her alive right now.

Both injured mods were surviving on a diet of stims and painkillers—two more things the group was running out of faster than she'd like.

Mira was still getting used to her empathic abilities, and although the emotions of the mods were relatively benign at the moment, the pain in Mira's head was making it hard to think. Katra and JonB were reflective and more than a little stoned, with the former operating at a heightened state of alertness. Carlton was trying not to be too excited about meeting humans who weren't trying to kill him, and Mira had to admit that would be a pleasant change.

On the other hand, Artemus was a blank slate. The Delta had a weapon pointed in every direction, and Mira got the distinct impression that if he could operate one with his feet, he'd have asked for another.

Serene was, well, serene. During the hunter-killer attack, her fear was uncontrolled and infectious, and the Alpha child's own empathic abilities had turned her into a terror transmitter strong enough to override even the most disciplined of minds. According to Jantine, even the Omegas had been affected, and Mira felt partly responsible for that fear; Serene's well-founded terror was based on Mira's own childhood memories of pre-Reclamation war stories.

That reality had proven far worse was another matter altogether. Serene didn't actually see the robots in action, just the explosions as Mira, Jason, and Katra fought them to a standstill, and Carlton's memories of their initial encounter. Every time Mira closed her eyes, the image of house-sized death machines coming at her down the length of the tunnel with lasers blazing was there to remind her why people just didn't visit North America if they could avoid it.

At least this side of the river is supposed to be safe. Mostly.

The only calm minds around her were the Omegas, but Jason's concern for her and O-6913's unshakable devotion to Serene were intense in their own ways. It felt as if her head was being squeezed, and sooner or later what was left of her mind would be pushed out and replaced with the thoughts and emotions of everyone around her.

Her eyes had stopped twitching, and she could, for the most part, hear clearly now. But using her abilities nonstop was almost as draining as the ten-hour overnight march they'd made to get here.

But I can't let them know how close I am to passing out. They're depending on me to get them through this.

Jantine was lost in the sunrise, mind refreshingly blank. But standing this close to the Beta reminded Mira of how tightly wound the girl was, and almost losing two more of her friends had to be taking its toll on her emotions. Sooner or later she'd slip again, and all that pain would come crashing down on Mira.

The sun was several degrees higher when Jantine's thoughts resumed, a delay felt keenly by both the rest of the mods and the guards beneath their feet.

≈What can we expect from these people?≈

≈Honestly, I have no idea. Everything the captain knew is locked up inside that chess piece, and JonB's in no shape to continue his analysis. The only thing I do know is that this is where he wanted to bring Serene, so that he—≈

At the mention of JonB, Jantine lost control of herself for just an instant, and everything Mira thought was going on in her head came rushing out. Jantine's memory of JonB's screams as they huddled together on the other side of the river was enough to send Mira to the ground with one of her own.

Alarm spiked in the mods, adding fresh lances of pain to her agony. Mira could feel all of them coming closer, and their well-intentioned concern was just too much to bear. She struggled up to a kneeling position, one gauntleted hand on her head and the other waving off Jantine's offer of help. When her left hand brushed casually against Jantine's body, JonB's memories came at her as well, and Mira pitched forward, no longer able to see or hear.

And still the thoughts came. Serene's fear was back, overflowing Mira's formidable mental defenses and putting everyone else on edge. Katra hit the water again and again, screaming her anger at Jarl's loss every time. Carlton's confusion as to what was going on with her was somehow worse than the others' unguarded thoughts, as it deepened Mira's own and robbed her of control.

The ground shook, bouncing Mira's head against the dirt. She almost welcomed the pain, as it was something of her own to focus on. Every bit of brain power she had left was occupied with maintaining her control, not wanting her agony to infect the others like Serene's fear.

Then the fear was gone, replaced by a feather light touch she recognized.

≈*Jason. Am I dying?*≈

The Omega sent her reassurance, and the emotional onslaught stopped. The pain was still there, though, and despite Jason's efforts Mira still worried for her sanity.

≈*How am I supposed to deal with this? The parts of myself I have left aren't enough to make a whole person, and the rest of you keep leaking in through all the holes!*≈

Jason drew her back to the white plain of thought, where he and O-6913 were standing with a wide-eyed Serene between them.

"I'm supposed to tell you they're sorry, and that they never meant for this to happen. You hid your difficulties from us, from me, and I understand why now. But the memories…I think I know how we can help."

Mira didn't know how to respond. Serene was talking about *her* memories, stolen from Mira by the well-meaning Alpha along with those of the Gammas that had trained their fallen comrade Doria. Serene probably knew more about Mira's life than she did herself right now, and having to be rescued by the Alpha child was the ultimate embarrassment. But all Mira could do was hold on to what was left of herself and whimper.

Jason came forward and held out one of his hands. Despite the pain, Mira formed a thought image of herself, reaching up from the ground for the help he offered. But instead of pulling her to her feet, he yanked back his hand so fast a misty outline of Mira came with it.

The pain in her head lessened, and her understanding of the Omega's capabilities grew.

Jason brought his other hand up, and started squeezing transparent Mira into a square shape. It solidified into a thick cube of stone, but Mira still recognized it as being a part of herself. Jason set the stone down, stood next to it, and held out his hand again.

Mira crawled forward and reached for the stone. It was smooth and cool to the touch, and just being near it made her feel stronger. She traced the edges with her fingers, breathing in the dusty smell of the playa that came into being around her. The desert sun beat down on her naked back, and she looked lazily into Tommy's eyes as he reached behind him for another beer. His toned body glistened with sweat from their exertions, and she took the bottle he offered gladly.

"They say this is who you are," he said. "You are strong, and independent, and no one can take that away from you. When the pain is too much, come back here to this place and set down another stone."

Mira wanted to change the past, to lie and tell Tommy that she loved him too. But she was due to ship out for the *Valiant* in a few hours and didn't want anything to spoil her last day on Earth. Instead she made the same mistake all over again and drew him to her for another kiss.

Mira felt Serene's embarrassment, Jason's interest, and O-6913's growing confusion. She wrapped them and Tommy and the playa all up and pressed them together, making a second stone to place alongside the first. The pain in her head went down a notch, and she could speak again, at least inside her mind.

"Thank you. All of you. Can you tell the others I'm all right? I just need a moment to myself."

Dream Serene and the Omegas faded from view, leaving her alone inside herself for the first time in days. The playa stretched out in all directions under a perfect blue sky, the ground cracked and dry under her feet. Her uniform was perfect, right down to the shiny new rank insignia on her collar. Only one thing could have made the memory better, and Mira was glad to find it there waiting for her in the beer cooler.

She reached in and pulled out a deep, rolling thunderclap, smiling as the hot wind of its passing blew through her close-cropped hair. The sky purpled, and a flash of lighting split it in half. Mira danced and jumped and left her clothes behind with her worries as the rain started to fall, laughing as the storm's power soaked into her bones and healed her soul.

When she opened her eyes, Serene was snuggled up against her while the Omegas stood guard. It would have been a touching moment were Mira not wearing full body armor, but Serene's aura of happiness chased away the worst of the pain.

And I wonder how all this looked to our friend on the other end of that video feed?

Jantine's relief was easy to pick out from the conflicting emotions on the other side of the Omegas, and Mira had the distinct impression she was being shielded from the more powerful thoughts aimed in her direction.

She kissed the top of Serene's head and helped her to stand up, resolving again to get the girl some real clothes at the earliest possible opportunity. It wasn't so much that she looked bad wearing cut-down uniforms, but her grass-stained knees and bare feet made her look like almost feral, and whoever was coming to meet them from underground would likely wonder why she wasn't armed and armored like the rest of the mods.

Once Serene was standing on her own, Mira rolled to her feet and sent another thank you to the Omegas. Jason was as happy as ever to feel the touch of her thoughts, but O-6913 surprised her by offering his own satisfaction.

Why, you old softy.

Mira smiled and pushed her way through to the others with Serene clinging to one of her gauntleted hands. She sent a wordless acknowledgement to Jantine, who then returned her attention to JonB.

Mira was about to say something when she detected a shift in the almost-forgotten emotions of the guards in the tunnels below. It was as if they were paying more attention to something, and although their minds had the same oily feel as Captain Martin's had before he died, she got a strong sense of respect from them, mixed with wary preparedness.

"Get ready, everyone. They're coming up."

Mira reclaimed her slugthrower, then realized she had no direction other than "down" to aim it at. As if sensing her need, Jason lent her his eyes, and a complex web of power lines drew itself across the ground. There was a glowing network of them forming around a section of faded tile work, and she relayed the location to Jantine, Katra and Artemus.

Then a new mind appeared on her mental landscape, one completely free of worry or distractions. It was the eye of the storm in the emotional hurricane surrounding her, and she felt vaguely guilty about the weapon in her hand.

The tiles split into a dozen triangular sections, each of which drew back slightly and fell away into darkness. From the hole they revealed came the sound of a whirring motor, and Jason's eyes supplied a power usage curve Mira recognized as a telescoping engineering platform. The top of a bright red safety cage emerged from the hole, followed by a shock of white hair framing one of the most striking male faces Mira had ever seen.

A wave of alarm ran through all of the mods save Serene, whose only reaction was to hold on tighter to Mira's free hand. Mira took a step in front of the child, and the girl shifted her hands around to the back of Mira's armored left leg.

The man in front of her was the source of the calm thoughts, and Mira borrowed as much of Jason's vision as she could to study his face. As if he'd orchestrated it, the rising sun was eclipsed by his wild halo of hair, making it hard to see him clearly.

The cream-colored eyepatch was easy enough to make out, as was the wide smile that formed as he took in the assembled mods. His skin was a shade darker than Tommy's, but that didn't mean all that much in the Reclamation. What was most interesting about him was that Mira detected no apprehension whatsoever about the weapons pointed in his direction, or even how many hands there were holding them.

Instead, she felt waves of pure joy radiating from his perfect awareness of the scene, which brought to mind Serene's initial moments of consciousness after emerging from suspended animation.

"Marvelous. Simply marvelous. You have no idea how glad I am you've come into my life."

The man stepped off the platform, and Mira noticed he was using a cane. One of his legs was alive with energy, and she was impressed by the sophisticated prosthetic. The skin on his right hand was mottled, and though she recognized the signs of healed burns, the fingers were strong and healthy.

"Lieutenant Harlan, how is Aloysius? I was expecting a message from him a few days ago, and I am very surprised to find you on my doorstep in his stead."

Lieutenant…He doesn't know! Why, I bet no one knows, and that's got to be good for us.

"Captain Martin sends his regrets. He wanted to be here, believe me, and…"

The lie felt wrong on her tongue, but Mira didn't know what else to do. She recognized the half-cape and brown and gold vestments of a senior Reclamation councilor, but she'd been away from Earth for a few years and honesty had no idea who the man was. The clothing had a complicated sensor web built into the rich fabric, and when Jason clued her into the transmission beaming its way into his ear Mira knew this was no one she could hope to deceive for long.

"…some kind of phased plasma weapons, but Harlan and the big one also have slugthrowers. I really wish you'd let me send the team up the accessway; I don't care who you think sent her, that woman is bad news."

Whoever the man was on the other end of the transmission, he wasn't one of the guards below her. Their emotions were more or less constant—anticipation, boredom, and a dash of concern for the man at the top of the scaffolding. They had none of the focused attention evident in the unknown speaker's voice, which made Mira both happy and apprehensive.

For his part, the old man just shook his head, waiting for her to continue. Then Jantine stepped forward, and Mira was surprised by the combined trepidation and...*loathing? Jantine, what's wrong?*

Mira realized she hadn't actually sent the question to her when the Beta began speaking. The Jantine she'd come to know in the last two days was gone, at least temporarily, replaced by the battle commander who had blasted her way out of one of the most advanced warships of the fleet as if it was just another day at the office.

"I am JTN-B34256-O, called Jantine. Who are you, and whom do you represent?"

This did get a reaction out of the old man, and not the one she was respecting. Instead of surprise, it was relief, and a deep sense of longing.

The voice on the other end of the transmission, though, was far from calm.

"Mordecai, did I hear that right? Get out of there, get out of there right now!"

Mira's hands tightened on her weapon, but neither Jantine nor the old man noticed. Much to the consternation of the younger man on the other side of the transmission, he reached up his right hand to his ear and disconnected his associate in mid-sentence.

"What are you doing? You can't just—"

The motion cemented for Mira what she'd suspected from the first moment she'd seen the man's face—he was someone who made his own rules, and answered to no one.

"I am Mordecai Harrison. Doctor Harrison, if it matters, but there are those who prefer to call me 'Mister,' 'Councilor,' or 'that crazy old fool' depending on who I've offended most of late. May I see your face, Jantine? I dislike anonymity, and given the company you keep I'm sure there's no need to hide, yes?"

Jantine turned her visored head to Mira, who nodded.

"It's all right. I think we can trust him."

Mira wasn't completely sure that was true, but since Harrison was the only person she'd met in the last two days who didn't make her head hurt, she was willing to take the chance.

Jantine unsealed her helmet, exposing her flawless alien features to

Harrison. Mira saw his eyes shift between the mod and herself, and she sensed a hint of surprise in his thoughts that he squelched almost immediately.

It took Mira a moment to figure out what it was, then she remembered that her own face had undergone changes when the Transgenic virus turned her world upside down. Gone were the freckles Tommy used to tease her about, and her eyes had a more almond shape to them than before.

And who am I now? What am I?

"Fascinating. All of you, such wonderful diversity. Welcome, welcome to our world. And who is this, peeking at me from behind her fingers?"

Harrison's voice rose sharply at the end of his question, in an annoying tone Mira had last heard from one of her grandfathers. His smile was about as fatuous, but Mordecai Harrison's thoughts contained none of the condescension Seamus Weston had for his daughter's offspring.

Too bad Serene doesn't realize what he's doing, or she'd probably teach Mordecai a few new tricks…

Mira hastily buried her thoughts, lest the barely trained empath clinging to her leg detect them and do something everyone would regret. Instead of introducing the girl, she tried steering the conversation in a different direction altogether.

"Doctor Harrison, two of our party are in serious need of medical attention. Are you here to grant our request for asylum, or should we make other arrangements?"

Harrison sighed, the deep exhalation of a man who'd known real disappointment. But his smile was still in place, and when he spoke it was without premeditation.

"I'm afraid that's somewhat of a loaded term at the moment, lieutenant. Jantine's broadcast upset quite a few powerful people, and my own status in the Reclamation government works against me in this instance. As Private Citizen Harrison I can offer you every resource at my disposal, and do so gladly.

"But Councilor Harrison cannot accept your request, especially not with so many guns pointed at him. Can we lower them for a while, or possibly put them away? I assure you, you have nothing to fear from an old man like me."

Mira sent a burst of confirmation to the mods, wincing slightly as her perceptions brushed against Katra's and Artemus's thoughts. The Delta had half his weapons aimed down into the hole, but Katra's pulser was pointed directly at the back of Harrison's head, and Mira knew she never missed.

"Is this really one of your leaders? How can you allow this to happen? Captain Martin was near the end of his usefulness, but at least he died a warrior. This...cripple...is there no one else we can talk to?"

It took a moment for Mira to understand what Jantine had said. The loathing she'd felt from the Beta was now flavored with a dash of contempt Mira remembered from their first encounter.

Mira was shocked by the intensity of Jantine's disgust. The open-minded, tolerant friend for whom she'd risked her life had an ugliness in her that, for the first time, made Mira think of her as truly alien.

Jason detected Mira's confusion, and without prompting sent her a series of images from his life in the colonies. Dozens, hundreds of smiling faces, going about their lives in well-ordered patterns and working toward the good of all. It seemed like a perfect society, and Mira wasn't sure she understood what the Omega was showing her.

Then Jason "introduced" her to another few hundred faces, who performed much the same tasks with similar smiles. Then there were hundreds more, and hundreds after that. As a pair of dim stars spun across a green sky, she had the impression that many years were passing. Decades, in fact, and all the while Jason worked building fantastic structures impossible to imagine in Earth's deep gravity well. The night sky's stars changed subtly, and Mira witnessed with him the birth of O-6913, and then many years later, that of Jantine.

Dear Lord. Jason, are you telling me that...

The Omega sent her a confirmation tinged with regret, one O-6913 echoed. She'd felt more maturity from Jason than any of the other mods, but she had no idea how to react to the fact that he'd lived so long that almost everyone he'd ever known was dead.

And not one of mod faces he showed me was any older than my father's...

Mira swallowed the beginnings of something that might have been anger, were she still capable of that emotion. She'd just learned yet another damning truth about Colonial society, but this time it was something she could change. Choosing her words carefully, she tried to explain the truth of life on Earth to her friend.

"Jantine, it is very common for people to live well past a century on Earth. Captain Martin was nearly sixty, with many more years ahead of him in the fleet. The fact that I was even considered for a command at my age is very unusual."

Jantine's response was incredulous, and immediate. She moved forward and grabbed Mira's arm, leaning in close to her ear to whisper her next question. Serene shifted to the other side of Mira's body but still clung tight to her legs.

"But why is he so selfish? A Gamma should have scanned his knowledge into the crèche long ago, instead of letting him linger on in this state. How can the next generation improve upon his works if they cannot experience them first-hand?"

"We have no Gammas, Jantine. We have respect for our elders, and the will to overcome adversity."

≈But...≈

Mira shook her head and pulled away. What she had to say was for all the mods, and her head hurt far too much to even attempt linking them all in at once.

"No buts. Not anymore. How do you think we survived the hunter-killers last night? Luck? I learned to fight them from a man almost as old as this one, who's still alive and could probably teach Artemus a thing or two about strength. You're not in the colonies anymore, and if you can't control your prejudices, you should let me do the talking from now on."

Jantine's jaw closed with an audible snap, and Mira felt the Beta's mental defenses go up. But not before a burst of annoyance smashed through her own, one strong enough to steal Mira's sight for several seconds until Jason could pull it away and add another stone to her wall.

When she could see again, Mira turned to face the man whose next words would decide the course of her future.

"Doctor Harrison, thank you for understanding, and for your offer of assistance. I think we can definitely arrive at a mutually acceptable diplomatic fiction. But if possible, can we discuss it in your medical facilities?"

Harrison gave the entire group another look.

"Of course," he said, "of course. But I'm afraid that the lift can't accommodate everyone at once, and your Type 6 and Type 30s may well be too much for it to handle. But I'm willing to—"

Jantine's anger boiled over, and this time she didn't bother to hide it.

"No, Earther. We go together, or not at all."

"Jantine, what are you doing! We can trust him."

"I will not let JonB and Katra out of my sight. Too many have been lost, and he cannot speak for all who dwell below." Jantine's features and mind were locked down hard, but Mira didn't need empathic abilities to recognize her stubborn streak.

Was I any different, at her age?

"Jantine, Katra is going to die soon. We both know it, and so does she. This is not a negotiating tactic, because there are no more options. She needs help, and he can give it to us."

"Not without an escort. You need to stay with the Omegas, and Serene is certainly not going anywhere without one of us. Do you propose to send Carlton in there? Alone? Even he cannot be spared."

Mira stared at Jantine, not bothering to hide her annoyance. The Beta was staring daggers at Harrison, whose face and mind were still blissfully calm. Serene sent a confused feeler in her direction, but Mira didn't want to involve the Alpha just yet. Besides, Jantine was not so hard-headed that she'd let Katra, or even JonB die. Sooner or later, she'd have to realize that...

Serene's next sending was not a request, and pushed through both the Omega's shields and Mira's own barely formed defenses with no difficulty. It wasn't a shout, but it chased the rest of Mira's thoughts away with a question she should have thought of herself.

≈*Mira, I don't understand. The machine he used to reach the surface is bigger than the hole, and he knows that. Where are the other entrances?*≈

A moment after the pain faded, Mira felt like kicking herself. Jantine hadn't let Harrison finish, and although Serene didn't understand everything that was happening, she was still at least as intelligent as the Betas, and with the Gamma memories she'd stolen from Mira, she had the insight of dozens of lifetimes to draw upon.

Bless you, child, for keeping a straight head. You've given her a way out.

"Doctor Harrison, I believe you were about to mention an alternative to the lift?"

Now Harrison smiled even wider, and there was definitely a grandfatherly twinkle in his eye.

"Yes, well, I meant to say that I was willing to offer myself as a guarantee of sorts, while my assistant arranges for a closed transport to ferry us all inside. I think we can come up with something fairly easily to fit Miss Jantine's needs."

Despite his pleasant tone, Harrison's words did nothing to settle Jantine's fears. If anything, they just made her angrier.

"*Commander* Jantine. And I accept your parole on one condition."

Harrison cocked an eyebrow, a gesture that might have completely disarmed his smile if it weren't for his eyepatch. But Jantine's emotions were near the boiling point, and Mira wasn't sure that the Beta would accept any further compromises.

"Yes, what is it then?"

Mira could feel satisfaction from both Jantine and Harrison, and she was relieved that he was willing to at least listen. His assistant, on the other hand, was shouting into the transmitter Harrison had clutched in his hand as if mere willpower could reactivate it.

"*Are you out of your mind? I'm sending up the team now! Hold on, Mordecai, I'm coming to get you!*"

Mira felt the guards below go from practiced disinterest to focused alert in a heartbeat. Still trying to defuse the situation, Mira shook herself loose from Serene and turned her face toward the securecam.

She was about to tell Harrison's assistant to stand down when Jantine dropped the proverbial other shoe.

"That you offer your unconditional surrender to my force, and place yourself under the dominion of The Outer Colonies. You and your institute are now prisoners of war, Councilor Harrison, and as such are bound by the terms of the Interstellar Compact and the Magellan Accords."

JANTINE

"No," said JonB.

Jantine turned to look at him, furious at his interruption. Mordecai Harrison remained where he was, neither accepting nor refusing her terms. The old man smiled his too-old smile and put more weight on the rod in his right hand, which Jantine still suspected was a new kind of weapon.

≈*Mira, relay. JonB, this is not the time.*≈

Mira did not comply, at least not in a way Jantine could detect. JonB was struggling to his feet with Carlton's help. At some point while she was taking to the ancient farther, he'd removed his faceplate, and in the morning light his face seemed even paler than it had been last night while screaming in pain at the full realization of his injury.

"No, Jantine. No terms. Not now. We're beaten, can't you see that?"

JonB took a tentative step toward Katra, then another. Carlton left him standing on unsteady legs, then bent and scooped up the unresisting Gamma. Katra's head rolled against the left side of his head, and their faceplates met with a clink. JonB took a third step toward the old human, then slowly drew his hand weapon and let it drop to the ground.

"Mira!"

"Listen to him, Jantine." Mira's words had the same tone of resignation as JonB's. "This is not the way."

Jantine had neither the words nor training to answer this betrayal. Of all people, JonB was supposed to support her decisions. Question them, yes, but open defiance was not in his character. It wasn't why he was here.

Once Carlton had Katra in his arms, JonB gestured toward the old man. Carlton adjusted her arm so that her pulser rested on her stomach, then moved toward the platform that presumably led down to the Harrison Institute.

Jantine found her voice, but the words that came out of her mouth were little more than a tight whisper.

"I will break you for this, JON-B34726-S."

"Why? What possible purpose would it serve? And to whom would you report me? Serene?"

"What does that mean?"

The urge to answer Serene's question was almost overpowering, but Jantine kept her eyes on JonB.

Mira started whispering to the Alpha, but to a Beta's ears she might as well have been shouting in the nearly silent courtyard. "It's a rhetorical question. He's trying to make a point to her, one she doesn't want to hear."

"But why?"

Janine took a step forward, hand tightening on the handle of her hand weapon. JonB just shook his head, and Jantine's anger finally boiled over. All her frustration at his constant questioning, his knowing smiles, and the basic unfairness of his survival when Malik was dead raised her arm for a blow. The weapon she held flashed in the sun as she swung, nearly reaching his head before his remaining hand caught her wrist.

"Go ahead. I can't stop you, not for long. Kill me if you want to; I'm half dead already. But Katra is dying faster than I am, and I won't let you kill her, too."

Jantine's eyes flared, and her face twisted into a snarl. She wrenched her wrist from JonB's grasp and smacked him across the face with the back of her hand. The civvie went down in a heap, fresh blood running down his face and onto his encounter suit.

Something broke in her hand when it impacted JonB's nose, but despite the pain, Jantine kept a firm grip on her weapon and set her aim right between his eyes. Her finger touched the first firing stud, and her thumb brushed the edge of the second.

≈*Jantine, STOP!*≈

At Mira's mental command, Jantine's anger drained out of her in a rush, and her body went rigid. A warm cloud enveloped her senses, and everything around her seemed very far away. She could still see JonB on the ground in front of her—still saw the old Earther with his inscrutable face staring at her. But she couldn't move, and after a few seconds, she was thinking clearly again.

And with clarity, came shame.

JonB. What have I done?

Mira was at her side, gently pulling the hand weapon from her clenched fingers. JonB wisely moved out of the line of fire, and Artemus helped him to his feet with one pair of hands while reaching out the other to collect her weapon and place it into his pack. Jantine felt Mira's gauntleted hands grab her arms, and when the Earth woman spoke, her breath was mere centimeters from the back of Jantine's neck.

"Just…just…Hell, I don't know anymore. Just don't."

JonB put his hand up to his face, and jerked. Jantine's senses and body came back under her control as his nose cracked audibly. JonB coughed, bowed his head for a moment, then turned his battered face back to Jantine.

"Son, let me look at that," Harrison said. "Broken noses can be tricky, believe me. And…oh, Love of Reason—put those weapons down, you fools. Now!"

Four Earthers wearing suits of armor like Mira's entered the clearing. Artemus raised all four of his weapons, aiming each one at a mirrored faceplate.

Mira's hands came away from Jantine's arms, and the Earther took an unsteady step around Jantine toward Artemus. It was a noble gesture, but all four of his arms were over Mira's head, and she did nothing to impede his line of fire. Whatever mental hold she had on Jantine disappeared though, and she was free to speak.

"JonB, I—"

"Don't say anything you don't mean, Jantine. Because you're right. In the Colonies I'd be stripped down and scanned for this, then conveniently shuffled away to run a mine somewhere."

"I'm... "

Jantine felt a wave of something warm and pleasant from Mira, but it cut off almost immediately as the Earther gave out a groaning sob, then fell limp. The unfamiliar words of an apology died on her lips as Serene charged past her just ahead of Jason's thundering footsteps.

"Mira? Mira? Please don't be dead." Serene's voice tugged at Jantine's heart as Jason took Mira in his arms.

Artemus's face plate rested in Jantine's direction for several long seconds before the Delta threw down his weapons and sat on a piece of collapsed wall.

Mordecai Harrison stepped up to Jason, and for a moment Jantine thought the Omega would stomp him into the ground for daring to touch the woman in his arms. But instead the Omega knelt down and laid Mira on the ground, and Harrison knelt beside her under the watchful eyes of his guards.

It took Jantine half a heartbeat to locate JonB again, and when she did she saw he'd almost reached the platform. Carlton was standing on it, supporting Katra with one arm and with his back against the orange-striped railing. The Gamma's pulser was on the ground, and JonB stepped over it as if it wasn't even there. Once he was on the platform as well, he grabbed for one of the rails and sagged against it.

"We're not in the Colonies, Jantine," he said. "Not anymore. Our mission is a failure, and it's time to start thinking for ourselves for a change. Come find me, when you're ready to talk. I really wish you would. But I'm going down there, and I don't care what you think about that."

The Beta hadn't bothered to wipe away any of his blood after adjusting his nose, and his face was already bruising where she'd struck him. But his gaze was fixed on Jantine's face, boring straight through her eyes and into her soul.

"Are you all right, Janbi?" Mordecai Harrison was standing now, and his voice was much stronger than his small frame seemed capable of generating.

"No, Doctor Harrison. I'm far from all right. But in time, I think I will be. And it's…"

JonB's battered face fell into his puzzle-solving expression for a moment, and when his smile returned, the intensity of his gaze dimmed. He was still looking at Jantine, but he seemed different somehow. And instead of the imperious correction Jantine expected to hear in his words, his voice was soft and thoughtful, containing more genuine emotion than she'd ever heard him express out loud.

"Actually, I take it back. Yes, why not? I am called *Janbi*. My name is Janbi, Mordecai, and I surrender myself into your care."

Jantine had no idea what she was supposed to do next. As the platform moved downward and out of sight, her failure was complete. Her choices had split the team apart, she'd lost the respect of her closest friends, and the worst part of it all was that JonB was right.

Again.

All she could do was wait, and hope that things resolved in her favor. Taking a cue from Artemus, Jantine sat down and let the world move according to its own schedule. Only Mordecai Harrison was looking at her, and his previous expression of practiced neutrality was replaced with one of concern.

Jantine looked to the sky. The Home Star's yellow-white radiance painted everything around her with the colors of morning, but it did nothing to help the pain in her heart.

Don't look to me for answers, Earther. I'm not their leader anymore. Mira is, and she's welcome to them. Assuming, that is, that I haven't killed her, too.

ANDREISON

Even though they were several hundred years older, Marya's new quarters were laid out exactly the same as those she'd left behind on *City of Lights*. Bunk, sanitary sink, shower alcove, hamper, desk—everything a young officer needed to get through her day.

Almost. I'm still not in charge of my own life, despite what the commodore said. And she made it abundantly clear that she and Captain DeMarco are the only things standing between me and another court martial; this time for desertion, with a side of treason to go.

Things were so much better when my own crew was trying to kill me. Should have quit while I was ahead.

Without any gear to stow, settling into her new berth was simple. She completed her onboarding inspection in record time, using the fresh comm bracelet she'd found on the desk to report her findings. She made sure to note a few micro-fractures around the out hatch that merely human eyes would never have found, and that her uniform hutch did not have inspection tags as per regulations.

The last time this ship saw any serious action was the Utopia rebellion, so sometime in the last 150 years I'll wager some clever entrepreneur stashed something in there for someone else with more money than brains.

Just my luck.

Also on the desk was a holo-editing package that could have come straight out of one of Deb's labs, and a control wand with a piece of blue ribbon tied around it.

Marya had to smile at that—she was used to just grabbing whatever tool was at hand to get her job done, and it was hardly her fault that Captain DeMarco kept leaving his command baton just lying around. She unwrapped the wand, noting the hidden presses and inset projectors—Deb's work for sure—that marked it as a superior version of the one she'd been borrowing.

Better for what I need to do, anyway. I won't be commanding a ship with this one.

At least, not from factory specs...

Marya sat down to check out her new workstation, and whistled in appreciation. She'd made it clear that she needed full access to *Clarke*'s central core to deconstruct the *Valiant* data, and that the work would go faster with some skilled help. The commodore had patiently listened to her list of requirements, then said, "Samuel will take care of all that."

The captain had done that, and more. Even though her workstation was right against a bulkhead, the holo-editor had a near-field package so sophisticated it could fool even her artificial eyes for a few seconds. The test sequence she pulled up extended deep into what should have been the next compartment, and far enough around her head to accommodate her expanded peripheral vision.

Marya twirled the wand through her fingers while she prepared her plan of attack. *Indomitable*'s comms officer had done the best she could in a limited time, and it apparently was a good enough forgery to fool people all the way up the chain of command. If Marya hadn't been in with the captain when it arrived, they might have pulled off the greatest hack in centuries, and it was up to her to unravel it all in time for dinner.

Okay, let's break some stuff. First off, we clear Mira, and then we ruin someone else's career for a change. Then, if they'll let me, I need to get a message to Deb letting her know where I am. Sooner or later they're going to tell her that Mira's dead, and she needs to know that's not true.

The desk was already loaded with all of *Valiant*'s footage, but for a complete report on what Captain Kołodziejski's faction was up to, the commodore would need Marya's data-recorder and subsequent analysis of the gennie transmission. She was loading it up when a message alert buzzed on her wrist.

>>Rpt to Flght Comm. Full Uni.

Marya's eyebrows shot up at both parts of the unusual request. First, although she'd initially accepted the offer to be Captain DeMarco's personal pilot, she'd assumed she'd be off the books as usual. Reporting to the head of flight operations on a Fleet vessel meant she was being officially logged for full duty as a pilot, something she never expected to happen.

And where the hell am I going to get a full kit on such short notice?

The answer to Marya's question hit her like a hammer blow, and she turned her head to look again at the slim compartment to the left of her bunk. As she'd noted in her report, the inspection tags were missing, but the hutch was properly sealed. The whole compartment had been cleaned before her arrival, and someone had certainly brought in the holo-editor.

Maybe they left something else behind as well.

Marya shut down the desk, and slipped the wand into a pocket of her mess tunic before getting up. It was only a few paces to the hutch, but her hand hovered over the release for what felt like hours until she was brave enough to open it.

With a press of a button, out came two racks of perfectly pressed uniforms, including a fresh jumpsuit and a new mess tunic. A compartment at her feet presented her with two shiny pairs of boots, but Marya's eyes, and still outstretched hand, were drawn to the ribbon bar on the tunic's breast, and the note pinned next to it in tight, quick script.

"This should be everything. Let me know if I missed one."

Marya took her new, and finally complete, dress uniform from the rack, and laid it on the bunk. Her fingers rubbed over commendations and awards she'd been told about, but never received, enough to double her current display.

Also, according to her collar, she was now a 1st Lieutenant, a step above the billet she should have received when transferring aboard *City of Lights*.

Deb teased her sometimes about not being able to cry, assuming Marya's light-hearted banter was her normal reaction to emotional situations. But although it was true that Marya's prosthetic eyes couldn't replicate proper tears, she still felt things just as strongly, and for the same reasons. She hugged her new tunic to her chest, careful not to disturb its perfect creases as she rocked gently back and forth.

Five minutes later, she was showered, dressed, and moving down the corridor towards Flight Ops. She hadn't worn a full dress uniform in years, and was still getting used to how it moved when she saw the first salute.

A couple of power techs had jumped to their feet with their eyes tipped up under their palms before she knew what was happening. She stopped for a second to acknowledge them, and then kept walking. Forty meters later a couple of jump-suited sub-lieutenants repeated the performance, and as she nodded them on her way she realized why.

I spent the last few years working with civvie astronomers, who thought of me more as a tech genius than as a bonafide hero. And I spend more time trying to forget my past than glorying in it.

A newer, shinier version of her Distinguished Service Medal bumped lightly against her chest as she walked, and thinking about it made her blush. Luckily, the rest of her path to Flight Ops was free of salutes, or she might have passed out from all the blood rushing to her face.

Walking into the pilots' ready room made her feel like a cadet again. There were a dozen jocks huddled around a table and cheering a holo, surrounded by half-eaten sandwiches and bulbs of coffee. Flight simulators, games, and holopods lined one long wall of the compartment, and a flat display of *Clarke*'s current position and the pilots' board dominated the other.

Her eyes registered her name at the top of the board at the same time she found the commander's office, an open cubicle with "LCDR Awola" marked on the wall. Marya used the distraction of the jocks shouting, "play it again, play it again!" to walk over and introduce herself.

Awola was a somewhat pudgy desk officer, but his flight wings were as shiny as Marya's own. She barely got out "Lieutenant Marya..." before he was out of his chair and continuing the embarrassment with a sloppy salute he probably hadn't had to use in years.

At least he's earned one in return, so I'm not completely without a response.

Marya lowered her hand as soon as Awola dropped his salute, just in time for him to come around his desk and shake her hand.

"Welcome aboard, Lieutenant. Welcome aboard! It's a pleasure to meet you. Please, have a seat." Awola released her hand and stepped back, waving at one of the two chairs in front of his desk. By the time she sat down he was already back on his side, as if he'd never got up in the first place.

"Thank you, sir. I'm happy to be here."

Awola's smile was wide and happy, and he leaned forward as he talked. His flight suit was as rumpled and well-loved as her old one had been, and she wondered how long it would take to get her new one that comfortable.

"Excellent, excellent. The captain commed down that you were to be put on the flight list, but in reserve status. When your name hit the board it caused quite a bit of commotion among the jocks, and I think you've got a few fans out there. Is there anything I need to know?"

I suppose I'd be asking the same thing if a mystery officer showed up under my command, short though it was.

"Not that I know of, sir. Captain DeMarco drafted me as his personal pilot, said that his previous jock was on loan."

Awola kept nodding as she talked, and his enthusiasm made

Marya think she was right in assuming he wasn't part of the commodore's cabal.

"Ah, yes, of course! Captain Martin took Marcus with him a few weeks back. Very hush hush."

Marcus? From the ship's compliment I reviewed, Commander Callaway outranked you by a lot. Probably as much as I do the jocks out there, now that I've got these pretty new pins.

Except all have you have been doing real flying for the last seven years, instead of manning the occasional tumbling sensor pod.

"I don't know about that, sir. I'm just here for a few weeks, administrative duty with the occasional shuttle flight. Though I'm of course available for whatever you need."

The alibi Commodore Maranova had drilled into her seemed to satisfy Awola, and his nodding stopped. But his eyes were drilling a hole though Marya's medal, and she was starting to blush again.

"Of course, of course. We don't really do much here, just some maintenance flights and corridor patrols. If you have time and want to go out with the team, I'm sure we can shuffle the squadron around for a run here and there."

You're goddamn right I want to fly out under the stars! Point me at a Shrike and let me...

"I'll keep that in mind, sir, thank you."

"Excellent, excellent. Well, let me know. It would be an honor to fly with you."

If he calls me Ma'am I'm going to lose it.

"I will sir, thank you. Is there anything else?"

"No, no, We're done for now. Have your on-board physical completed by 1000 shiptime tomorrow, and we'll get you booked for a rating check in the simulator. Other than your desk time," Marya smiled at his non-mention of her incarceration, "your records are good. In fact, they're more complete than most of the jocks out there had when they came aboard. Whatever they're grooming you for next must be pretty big."

Huh. My non-cover might actually be too good. A few years of complete obscurity must seem like a completely fictional career to a desk pilot, and even if he goes digging, he won't find anything to the contrary.

Might as well have some fun with it while I can.

"I really can't talk about that, sir. But it's good to know that my records have arrived. I've had problems with that in the past."

"Of course, of course. Happens to the best of us." Awola's eyes drifted down to her medal again, but he caught himself short of a full stare and stood up with an outstretched hand. "Well, if there's anything you need, please let me know."

Marya shook his hand, then returned his surprise second salute. Thankfully, it didn't go on too long, and she gave a sharp turn and left his cubicle when it was finished.

She'd almost made it out of the compartment when one of the jocks caught sight of her. He straightened up and saluted from ten meters away, using his free hand to smack the pilot next to him. The slim woman ignored him at first, consumed by the holo the other jocks were watching. Her reaction to the second hit was more intense, but as she rounded on him she also caught sight of Marya, and nearly fell over the bench as she came to attention.

"Lizzie, what the hell! Now we've got to start it ov..."

Oh shit, here it comes. I should never have put this thing on, and I'll have to think of a creative way to "thank" Captain DeMarco.

The rest of the jocks, some with crisp haircuts and uniforms marking them as fresh from the academy, came to attention as Marya changed course and walked toward them. She gave them a brief return salute, dropping her hand as fast as she could so they could breathe again.

"Relax, boys and girls. I'm just a pilot like the rest of you."

One of the last jocks to stand looked like he was about to throw up. But somehow he gulped it down and found his voice.

"With respect, ma'am, no, you're not."

Okay, that does it.

Marya was about to deliver clever verbal diversion #4 when she saw what the jocks had been watching. Then she glided over and sat down in front of their holo emitter, looking up into the stilled image from the reviewing stand as her trainer shot overhead at full power.

I've never seen it from this angle. When did this get declassified?

"How did you do it? All those people, you saved them, and then that other pilot."

Marya wasn't sure which one of the jocks was talking, as she only knew their names from the ship's registry. But if they had access to the holo, she was fairly sure she could talk about it, and the knowledge might save their lives someday.

Marya reached into the image, and twisted it on an axis she was sure the young pilots around her knew nothing about. She verified its metadata, smiling a bit when she saw her own name amongst the authors. It would do what she needed it to, and it was more than a little flattering that this was the thing they were focused on, instead of the rat bastard's just desserts.

Marya picked up the emitter and carried it over to the nearest simulator pod, as the jocks watched with a mix of admiration and fear.

"If you really want to know, this is the wrong way to look at it. You should know by now that the world looks different from up high. Different from anything you can see with your feet on the ground. So if you want your answers, you're going to have to sit where I sat."

Marya opened the simulator's access port, and entered its ID into the emitter. She then activated the unit, stepping back as the top of the simulator opened with a hiss.

A little more room than I had in the trainer, but these kids won't know the difference.

"Come on then, who wants a go?"

The jocks almost fell over themselves to get to the pod, but in the end it was Mr. Knowitall who won the footrace. Nelson, if his flight suit was to be believed, which made him Sub-lieutenant Franklin Nelson, from New Ontario Station.

"Okay, Nelson, you're up." Marya didn't see a helmet inside the pod, so she'd have to adjust for that as she ran the simulation.

Shit, am I really doing this? Again? These kids aren't a board of inquiry, but how many times do I have to run this through before it makes any sense?

Nelson climbed inside the simulator, and sat back with a start as the controls morphed into those of an Academy trainer. He looked up as if to ask her a question, but she dropped the lid on him instead.

"Some of you were on Flight Squad, so you've got an idea of what's coming next." Marya put the emitter down on a nearby game console, then used her wand to activate the simulation she'd prepared for the board as soon as she got out of the hospital. Her new eyes were still healing then, and she'd done most of the work through virtuals and the implants they'd stuck in her head to keep everything working.

Hell, I could probably run this thing with my headware, but a control wand is a lot easier to deal with than the headaches.

"Our final approach was a modified spin drop from the edge of atmo." Marya waved the wand, and the compartment was filled with black sky and too-bright Earth below. Her breath caught, remembering how beautiful it all was to her human eyes. Inside the pod, she heard Nelson say, "Wow," a reminder to give him a simulated helmet and not enough oxygen.

"Lieutenant Nelson, would you care to begin the maneuver? Your simulated wing is waiting."

"Yes, sir, I mean, ma'am! Sorry, ma'am."

"Apologize on the ground, if you make it."

The holo dipped, simulating the plunge the flight group made to cap off Mira's graduation exercises many kilometers below.

The rest of Flight Squad had been awarded their commissions a week earlier in a private ceremony, to give them more time to practice. But Marya had taken six months off to handle her parents' affairs, and was still catching up on her coursework. This exercise was supposed to count as both her final exam for Advanced Flight and her thesis project in Assisted Robotics, and there was no way she was going to screw it up.

Hopefully, Nelson won't either, but we all know how this story ends.

As the nose of the trainer heated up. Nelson started the spin, as did the others slaved to his—or rather, her—controls.

It was a perfect descent, with all five trainers dropping like hot rocks into a perfectly clear Colorado sky. In most official records, the crowd watching a satellite-assisted holo below were cheering as each member of the formation fired missiles that detonated just off the spinning wings of the following trainers. Marya raised the temperature inside the simulator with each explosion, and the assembled jocks were both cooing and flinching away from the impressive blasts.

"Now comes the fun part. Nelson, what happens next?"

"The holo shows you bottoming out at three kilometers, then executing a roll over the reviewing stand."

"Don't tell us, Lieutenant. Show us."

Marya usually narrated this part for the non-pilots common to flag ranks, but here there was no need. Nelson fired his wing jets to cancel the spin, then kicked in aft thrusters to bust through a couple more sound barriers with his squadron in tow.

The simulated reviewing stand rocked as they passed, but only Marya knew what Nelson was seeing. The rest of the jocks were scanning the surrounding hills for the surprise guest, instead of looking straight ahead like a good pilot should.

The official reports blamed an improper security sweep for what happened, but after thousands of hours of review, Marya knew it was dozens of satellite tracking lasers spinning off the squadron's super-heated hulls that had attracted the hunter-killer.

When Nelson released the squadron from his control to execute the final maneuver, his/her trainer was the first one to start back toward the airfield. The others tore off at maximum acceleration to meet Marya there, and simulated Mackenzie's wingtip thrusters blasted a seven-hundred meter strip of rock wall into nothingness, leaving a shining trail of exposed metal behind.

And here we go in 3...2...1...

"What the hell is that?"

Marya didn't answer, and didn't have to. Simulated Jarovic's trainer erupted in a fireball half a klick from the reviewing stand, and tumbling through the sky in its place was a building-sized death machine with a half-dozen legs and two wing thrusters in its forward "hands."

Marya and Nelson were rocketing straight for it, and her artificial eyes were already dilating to protect her. The monster stared her down from the past, there was a quick flash of light, and then she cut Nelson's visual feeds.

The rest of Nelson's forward sensors were scrambled too, but she remembered the blaring warning of a targeting lock, the pinging rangefinder, the spin of the autocannons she'd powered up as soon as she'd marked the threat, and the sound of her engine roaring to life as she pulled up and away from the rest of her squad, as if humanity's second worst nightmare hadn't just crashed the party. She threw them all in for good measure to see what he'd do.

He didn't.

The simulated trainer plowed straight through the hunter-killer, showering fire and hot metal down on the reviewing stand. Marya's heart fell through her feet, knowing simulated Deb had probably died first from the shrapnel, and simulated Mira at the podium delivering her honors speech would have fallen twenty meters to her death immediately afterward.

Every damn time, but the one that mattered. Six months of playing it back in my head, three months of reconstruction, then a year of review panels in front of every officer in the worlds who wanted someone to blame.

Someone besides themselves, that is.

Marya left the simulation frozen on the destruction, and then let Nelson out of the pitch dark pod. The junior pilot tumbled out onto the deck, visibly shaken and in no shape to fly. He'd clearly learned the lesson she'd prepared, but there were eleven other students to deal with.

Nope, thirteen, she thought, noticing Awola and Captain DeMarco looking on from the edge of the cubicle.

"Questions?"

The first comment came from Lieutenant Elizabeth Armbruster, whose file was full of commendations and admonitions for hotshot piloting.

"That wasn't fair! How is he supposed to fly if he can't see anything?"

Marya tried not to smile as the other jocks pulled slightly away from Armbruster. Keeping her eyes fixed on the hotshot, she reached behind her to take Nelson's hand, and pulled him up.

"You can't always trust your eyes, Lieutenant. Your cockpit is full of things that tell you where you are, how fast you're flying. And the more time you spend looking at them, the less time you're actually piloting. Nelson?"

"Yes ma'am?"

"What was that flash?"

To illustrate her point, Marya turned one of her eyes completely to the right to look at Nelson, while keeping the other on an amazed Armbruster.

"Uh, targeting laser, I guess."

"Close. Anyone else have a guess? And not you, Cadet DeMarco. Students who arrive late have to stay after class."

The captain smiled as he put his hand down, enjoying the shocked faces of the assembled pilots who spun around at attention.

"Sorry, ma'am. You were saying?"

DeMarco's booming voice carried all the way across the compartment, and did nothing at all to set the jocks at ease. The braver among them turned back to Marya right away, and the rest found something else to look at before finally joining them. But it was Nelson who puzzled it out, probably because he'd spent the most time in close proximity to the holo.

"Was it a microwave cannon?"

"Yeah. Fried every forward sensor I had, and cooked off half my cockpit before the flash got my eyes. All I could do was execute the climb as planned, and hope the squad could follow me to safety."

"But, how. You were...you were blind!" Armbruster came forward, staring into the simulator as if there was some secret readout only visible from inside.

"Mr, Nelson. What happened inside the cockpit after you lost visual?"

"Uh, Everything. It was loud and confusing and I just lost control."

Marya stepped around Nelson and Armbruster to the simulator, waving her control wand. The darkness within went away, and a much younger, helmeted Marya appeared in the air above it, staring right into an oncoming relic of the Transgenic wars.

"How about now? Ms. Armbruster, your thoughts."

Simulated Marya's head flew back and to the side, and Marya winced at the memory of previously unimaginable pain. But then the view of the hunter-killer disappeared, replaced quickly by a cloud of smoke and a deep blue sky. Armbruster found her voice as the trainer cut thrust, spun on wing jets and came back down on virtually the same trajectory.

"You, you completed the maneuver! But how?"

Marya paused the holo, and looked over to Nelson, whose lips were pressed together in a tight smile. She arched an eyebrow at him, and gestured up at the image.

"Because that's what a squadron commander is supposed to do, Lizzie. She got her team out of harm's way, then went after the threat."

"But blind? Without instruments?" Armbruster looked like she was about to pop a blood vessel, so Marya let her off the hook.

For now. And I can't really blame her, most of the senior officers who've viewed this footage had the same reaction.

"I never said I didn't have instruments. I said my forward sensors were fried. Mr. Nelson, what's still working?"

Nelson leaned inside the simulator and pulled up some control surfaces.

"It looks like your targeting and satellite links are down, but I remember hearing screams from somewhere, and...Yes! Collision alarms and the radio are still intact, and..."

Armbruster figured—then blurted—it out.

"You overrode the flight computers on the other trainers, and slaved them again."

Marya nodded at her, and said, "What else?"

Armbruster scanned the faces of the other pilots for help, and Marya put her palm down to forestall Nelson's own revelation. Marya let the holo run so she could get a better look, and it took Armbruster a few more seconds of mental gymnastics to come up with the right answer, but when she did, it was in an awed whisper.

"You came back, and drew the robot away."

"In essence, yes. Its momentum carried it well over the stands, so I had to guess as to where it was until the other trainers could pick it up with targeting scanners from on high. Then I fired everything I had at it to get it to chase me."

The holo caught up with her account, and simulated Marya flew straight at the cliffside Mackenzie had torn up on his approach.

"I could hear the 'bot pinging me from behind, and the collision alarm counting down to my closest obstacle. I knew I was faster and more maneuverable than the 'bot, so I scraped the paint a little and let the laws of physics do the rest."

Simulated Marya pulled up at the last second, with the killer robot hot on the trail of her exhaust plumes. It smashed into the cliffside, exploding in a much more civilian-safe fashion as the holo ended. In real life, Marya had rejoined the other pilots in the sky, and circled the airfield until one of them got instructions from the tower.

"The tower got everyone but me and Mac down safe on remote, but I had to fly him in off my wing. His hull was fragged by what was left of Jarovic's trainer, and he could neither burn for orbit nor deploy his landing gear. They wanted us both to ditch in the desert, but with a little luck and a lot of effort we were able to make it in soft."

And then I fucking lost it, but the holo never shows me crying for the very last time inside my helmet, itching all over from the radiation, and bleeding out from a piece of Jarovic that made it through the trainer's hull.

From what I'm told, it wasn't a pretty sight.

Marya shut down the holo, and a chorus of questions started before the emitter fully powered down. But Captain DeMarco raised his wrist from the other side of the compartment, tapping his comm with a knowing look.

Marya checked her own bracelet, and saw an unread message she'd missed while flying down memory lane.

>>Grb gr. Launch in 30.

Well, shit. Here I am grandstanding in front of the boss on my first day when there's work to be done.

Guess my luck hasn't changed much after all.

Marya raised both hands to chest height, and the questions stopped.

"Everything you need to know is in that holo, if you know how to look for it. They tell me I took out a factory nest inside the cliff face, but I never saw it." Marya tapped a finger against one of her artificial eyes for emphasis, then lowered it to her right breast.

"The thing you have to remember is, this isn't the important part about that day." The jocks followed her hand to the medal, and as she raised it slightly to her wings. "These are, because without the work that went into them, I never could have pulled off any of it. But it was my squad that really saved the day. Working together, we took out that mechanical monster, and that's what matters. And although I'd love to stay and talk some more, it looks like I've got somewhere to be."

Marya's name at the top of the board was flashing red, displaying just enough time for her to get back to her quarters and change before she'd be late for her first official mission. She moved through the crowd of pilots congratulating her for living through the second-worst day of her life, and drew abreast with Captain DeMarco, who also offered her a quick salute before leading her out of the ready room.

"Well done, Lieutenant. I don't think they'll forget that anytime soon."

"Yes sir. Thank you, sir. It wasn't my intention to cause a scene, and I'm sorry if I was out of line."

"Never apologize, Andreison. Just don't make a habit of it."

Marya had to take an extra step now and then to keep up with the captain, who thankfully was heading in the same general direction as her quarters.

"Where are we off to, sir?"

"Earth. Apparently the commodore and I have been summoned to a meeting, which should give you enough time to finish that analysis you owe her. Unless, of course, you'd rather stay here and continue teaching Advanced Flight to the rest of the jocks. I'm sure Mr. Awola can make them available for another class."

The captain stopped outside her quarters, and for a second she thought he was waiting for her to invite him in. Then she realized that there was a question in amongst their banter, and blushed again.

"No, sir, I think a nice, easy flight to the surface will suit me just fine."

"Excellent news, Ms. Andreison. So glad you can join us. Wheels up in 20, don't be late!"

Marya smiled at his back as he continued down the corridor, knowing that Captain DeMarco was probably the one who'd loaded the holo into general access in the first place. There was no need to get him back for embarrassing her—if anything she was even deeper in his debt than before.

As she entered her quarters and hurriedly donned her new flight suit for the trip planetside, she reflected on this new Marya, and where she might have come from. When faced with people who didn't care about Tommy Watson—or rather, what she'd done to him—she found not lashing out against their expectations wasn't so bad after all.

And here I am enjoying being an officer again, when a few hours ago I was ready to quit. Now, if I can just avoid any more life or death situations, and possibly get some real sleep, today might turn out just fine.

OLVRSDÓTTIR

1000 SHIP TIME, **SDF** *VALIANT*

Lieutenant Astrid Olvrsdóttir pulled Alonso Ramirez into a tight embrace at the base of the shuttle's ramp, not exactly sure of her feelings, but at the same time not wanting to say goodbye.

"You'd better come back safe, Sub-lieutenant. I've already become used to your Earther face." It wasn't exactly a declaration of love, but whispering it into Alonso's ear had the desired effect. Alonso hugged her back, and whispered his own *bon mot* at her.

"I will. But you have to promise to stay alive as well. I don't commit mutiny with just anybody, you know."

For his part, Alonso did cut a somewhat dashing figure in his flight suit, though the dark circles under his eyes and sunken cheeks betrayed an unhealthy level of exhaustion.

He's already seen too much death for a man his age. For that matter, so have I, but at least I'm used to hiding my pain.

And what does that say about our future, I wonder?

"Are you two about done? Or should I go save the worlds by myself?"

Commander Marcus Callaway looked slightly better rested than

Alonso, but the dwindling oxygen supply in the Hull had paled his skin to an ashen tone in the last few hours, and despite his jocularity, his eyes were focused a million kilometers away.

Neither of them should be anybody's first choice of savior, but since they keep saving us all anyway, they're the only ones we can trust to do the job right.

"We are done, Commander. Consider the mood officially killed. But now that I am lacking in hugs, I hold you responsible for his return as well. Do not disappoint me—after all, I saved your life too."

Their banter was a necessary fiction to disguise their true motives from the crowd of onlookers that had gathered to see them off, though she did like Callaway, and Alonso she liked...very much. The three officers had been through a lot in the last several shipdays, from *Valiant*'s unexpected encounter with both a giant space rock and a gennie invasion force, to Astrid's own arrival on the ship to arrest its captain—and Marcus Callaway—for treason, and capped off by desperate hours keeping sixty-odd souls alive in the literal middle of nowhere while Alonso and his engineers stabilized the ship's life support systems.

Another glorious day in the Fleet...

The two men were preparing to fly the only working shuttle in many millions of kilometers out to scavenge materials from destroyed missile tenders at the edge of the debris field, but that was only part of their mission.

Their true goal—unbeknownst to the crew who had volunteered most of their remaining oxygen to the cause—was that they were leaving on what would normally be called a suicide mission, were suicide not so readily available on a dying starship. Her lover and her friend were actually taking the shuttle—which contained every spare milliliter of oxygen and all the power cells they'd been able to scavenge—much, much farther, in the vain hope that they could reach, retrieve, and reactivate an untested piece of gennie tech currently spinning out of the solar system slightly faster than the shuttle could reach it.

A hyperspace device, which, if salvaged, may kill us anyway.

It should be me in the shuttle, not you, Earth boy. You've done enough already.

"No promises, Lieutenant," said Callaway, loud enough for the members of the crew milling about in the transfer bay to hear, "but since I'm trusting you with the safety of our people until we get back, you've got some work to do yourself."

"Yes, sir, Commander, sir. I promise not to kill or endanger any more of them than necessary while you're gone." Astrid smiled, and so did Callaway. Tired, worlds-weary smiles that said both officers would rather crawl back into bed and sleep through the hours they had left, rather than fight tooth and nail for survival until the very last second of their lives.

But fighting is who we are. Survival is what we do. And if the Earthers don't want me to save them, well, they're free to explore the alternative.

Astrid released Alonso from their embrace, but only after biting down hard on his earlobe to give him something to remember her by. She then planted a quick kiss on his cheek and shoved him stumbling into Callaway's arms. For her erstwhile commander, she offered a quick, professional salute, holding his eyes as he passed Alonso back up the ramp.

Callaway took his time raising his hand to his brow, and after releasing his salute a few seconds later, turned and walked up the ramp without another word.

Godspeed, Marcus Callaway. And good luck.

Astrid turned and shooed the crowd from the transfer bay, clearing it just before the amber warning lights turned green, signaling depressurization in progress. She stood at the observation window as the shuttle's grav drive spun up, the bay doors opened, and the shuttle rose gracefully from the deck and floated out into space.

She stayed there for some time, ignoring her buzzing wristcomm and staring at the bay doors, willing them to reopen and bring her lover back.

After the messages stopped coming, she searched through them for the one she wanted, and activated a private channel.

"Is it all set up?" Astrid said as soon as the conversation was live, neither waiting for, nor offering a greeting.

"Yes, Lieutenant. They're assembled in the wardroom. It took some doing, but…"

"Good. I'll be there directly." Astrid terminated the call and started walking, unconcerned with the exacting operational details Specialist Carson was fond of sharing. If he said it was done, it was done, and that was good enough for her.

When she reached the stairs leading up to the wardroom's level, she couldn't help but think of how she and Commander Callaway had first met Carson in this very junction as they journeyed to *Valiant*'s command center. He was attempting to remotely seal a hull breach in Main Medical two decks away, using a drone that could easily have freed him—were he willing to sacrifice six other lives.

Since she'd come aboard from SDF *Indomitable*, Astrid had witnessed many such acts of bravery and courage from *Valiant*'s crew, while the troopers under her command were indifferent at best to their continued survival. Having already been abandoned and left for dead by Captain Kołodziejski, most of them were now resigned to actual death, and saw no reason to exert themselves for what they considered a lost cause.

Our planet has been dead for billions of years, yet at home we fight every day to build a better future.

Why choose now to give up?

About a dozen of *Valiant*'s crew had chosen a quicker exit in the last few hours, voluntarily stepping into an airlock while the next person in line suffocated them. The last two to go were the hardest to lose; Lieutenant Katrinka Petrovina and Specialist Henry Powell, Marsborn Loyalists she'd served with for just over a T-year. They went together, locked in a passionate embrace and staring into one another's eyes while they floated out into space, together for all eternity. Astrid had fought bitterly with Marcus Callaway for permission to retrieve their bodies, not wanting to leave any more crew behind than necessary.

No one needs to know it was suicide, and at least their families will have something to bury when we get home.

Now that her lover Alonso was fully committed to retrieving the gennie hyperdrive, she too had to believe she really would be going home, even if it was only to resign her commission and say goodbye to her foster parents.

Max Olafsson and Isobella Ivanova were the only people in her life who had ever shown Astrid real love, explaining to her who her parents were when she was old enough to understand, and when the time came, helping her pick her real name.

These are the people we leave behind when we choose the Fleet, and who should never have to understand the things we do to protect them.

The sound of angry voices echoed down the corridor as Astrid climbed the last few steps, and she heard more than a few Martian accents in the chorus. By the time she arrived at the wardroom, Carson and several armored troopers were backed up against a wall of supplies she'd had them collect from around the ship. She'd instructed her teams to gather all the remaining food from the Hull's skeleton crew, knowing that it would be an unpopular decision.

Astrid's piercing whistle—another useful lesson from Max— focused all eyes on her, and the crowd parted as she walked straight up to Carson.

"Ma'am, I'm sorry, I tried to tell them, but..."

"It's all right, Roger. You've done well," she said, gesturing to the supplies. Astrid turned to regard the crowd, then pulled over a crate to use as a podium so she could see all their faces at once.

The murmuring started as soon as she climbed onto the crate, and she let them stew a bit longer before she spoke.

"Shut up. All of you. You are not here to fight, although if that is what you truly want, I will allow it. Commander Callaway told me to take care of you all, and that is exactly what I am going to do. Whether you like it or not."

The assembled crew went from silence to shouting in less than a second, which was Astrid's cue to start the next phase of her plan. She tapped her wristcomm, and six armored Marsborn troopers came marching in, each carrying a double armful of folding chairs.

The crowd reacted with a mixture of curiosity and panic—especially the Marsborn who'd decided never to wear armor again. The troopers began setting up the chairs in rough circles of six, moving into the crowd when they ran out of space at the back of the wardroom.

"The last time I addressed you from this room, I showed you the face of our enemies, the gennie invasion force who crippled your ship. But now look at you. Hoarding fresh food, while those around you eat ration bars. Hiding luxury items from the collective, when you should be sharing them with open hearts."

Astrid looked behind her for one of the crates Carson had mentioned earlier, and popped it open with a prybar he'd left for her. She threw the lid into the crowd, scattering a group of engineers who were refusing to make way for the troopers setting up the last circle of chairs. Not caring if they moved or not, Astrid took a dusty bottle from the crate, and an equally dusty embossed card.

"One of you even raided the Captain's mess, and stole this wine, a gift from Commodore Maranova herself. Would you like to know what she wrote on this card? Hmm?" Shocked stares and wide eyes—especially those of the engineers—were the crew's only reply. Astrid smiled as she "read" from the card, substituting her own legend for the information about the wine written there.

"It is a message of friendship. It says 'Aloysius. Don't forget to entertain your troops, and for Dod's sake, do not forget where you came from.'"

Astrid had them now, all eyes either trying to guess her next words or hoping to catch a peek at the card in her hand. She smiled for both groups, tucking it inside her borrowed Earther jumpsuit and continuing her speech as planned.

"You may be thinking to yourselves, 'Captain Martin came from Earth, you Duster bitch.' Don't deny it, I have heard how you speak when you think no one is around. But once upon a time, my family was also from Earth, just like the families of every Marsborn in this room— even though some of them talk about 'Earthers' exactly the same way."

Astrid hopped down off the crate, still carrying the bottle of wine. She walked into the crowd, and it melted away from her she stepped inside the final circle of chairs.

"But all that ends now. What the commodore wanted your captain to remember is that he came from a large family, with many brothers and sisters. And as the captain of this ship, he was your father, and I think he would be ashamed of what you've become.

"So here is where we are. None of us can survive on stolen wine and secrets. We must come together as one people if any of us want to go home. No more secrets, as promised by Commander Callaway. We are all family now, and you are going to sit, and eat, and drink, until you remember how to share."

Astrid unwrapped the foil on the bottle's neck, and teased it open with a loud pop. She palmed the cork, then took a long swig straight from the bottle, savoring the sensation of the bubbles rising at the back of her nose. She then took a deep breath and belched loud enough to startle the nearest members of the crew.

"Because he is out there now," she said, waving the bottle at the wardroom's ceiling hard enough to make it foam, "trying to save all our lives. Trying to make them mean something more than numbers on a page, or remaining hours of heat and light. And when he comes back, we will all be one crew. So sit down, make some new friends, and enjoy yourselves.

"For tomorrow, we live!"

The crew's voices rose as one, and Astrid gave Carson the signal to start distributing the food. No one would go hungry tonight, and she hoped the crew would stay sober long enough to remember which bunks they'd chosen.

And if not, it's a good thing we commandeered some blankets as well.

Once the room was full of laughter and conversation, Carson approached her with a handheld and a worried look. Grabbing another bottle from the stash at her feet, Astrid unfolded herself from her chair and pulled him aside, making a show of smiling as they walked.

"What is it, Roger? Do you not like cheap wine from Ganymede station, magically transformed by the power of bullshit?"

Carson's eyes smiled, but his mouth did not.

"No, ma'am. I appreciate the story, but I don't drink. The Prophet forbids it."

"You are upset at the rest of us who do, then?"

"Umm, not really, but there's something you need to see."

Astrid sighed, handing off her half-empty bottle to a passing woman, then dragging two chairs to the side of the wardroom. She waved Carson into one of them, then sat down beside him, legs and arms crossed.

"Tell me. But keep in mind that I have at least three weapons hidden around my body, and I do not like surprises."

Carson gulped, eyes widening until he saw her smile. He relaxed somewhat, trusting that she was telling a joke and offering her his handheld.

Silly boy. I have six.

"So, what is this then?"

Carson leaned closer and tapped the handheld, bringing up a still image of a shuttlecraft, grav drive lit up and thrusters firing.

"I tasked a drone to follow Commander Callaway's shuttle, ma'am, just in case something went wrong within the debris field and there was still a chance we could help him. When he didn't alter course for the *Cessnock*, I tried to relay a message through the drone, but I kept getting interference. The same interference, in fact, that we've seen out on the Hull, whenever we get near a cluster of that black rock."

Astrid brought the handheld closer to her face, trying to imaging Alonso looking back at her from the other side of the screen.

"And? There are rocks all around us. What does this mean?"

"That's just the thing, ma'am. There aren't. Not any more, that is. I got one of the exterior cams working, and it relayed this image," he said, swiping away the shuttle for a still image of the Hull.

An image showing a long, thin line of black rocks floating away, leaving *Valiant*'s surface scarred and pitted, but free of all fragments. Carson swiped through several more, all showing black rocks moving away from the Hull, in a decidedly unnatural way.

"The last images the drone captured were of the shuttle, just as it moved out of the debris field. The only problem is, it didn't."

Carson tapped the screen, and the stills ran on a continuous loop, showing clusters of rocks near the shuttle come together in ring formations, then move into alignment directly along the shuttle's path.

"I tracked them all the way out, ma'am. The rocks are definitely following the shuttle, maybe even moving to intercept it, and I have no idea as to why. Nor can I tell you why the shuttle didn't make its rendezvous as scheduled."

I know that one, but I also know more about the rock than you do.

Or at least, Alonso did, and it looks like he's about to know a whole lot more whether he wants to or not.

She pressed the handheld back into Carson's hands, and turned her head until she could see his whole face at once.

"So, the rocks are gone?" Astrid stared straight into Carson's eyes, and he flinched. She waited for his reply, and when he stayed silent, she snapped her fingers in front of his nose.

"Focus, Roger. The rocks are gone, yes?"

"Yes, ma'am, but that's not…"

"Rocks are gone. Rocks are gone, which means interference is gone, and you can use external sensors." Astrid stood up, still fixing all her attention on Carson's eyes, this time using one of Isobella's lessons on how to make men do what you want.

Carson stood up in self defense, not knowing exactly what she was doing, but unwilling to let her do it sitting down.

"Yes, but…"

"Interference is gone, three problems just got solved at once. Go turn on *Valiant*'s transponder, Roger. Redirect whatever power you need to, but turn it on, and keep it on, until I tell you otherwise."

Astrid quickly surveyed the room, looking for people as sober as Carson, or at the very least only half as drunk as she was.

"I'll find you some people to finish Alonso's repairs to the command center, but I want us battle ready within the hour."

"Battle ready? But why? We're all alone out here, no one's even looking for—" Realization dawned on Carson's face, and he nearly dropped the handheld as he drew himself up to full attention.

"Yes, ma'am!" Several partygoers started at his shout, but returned quickly to whatever conversation they'd been having. Carson picked up his handheld and nearly ran from the room, leaving Astrid standing alone by the bulkhead and missing Alonso so much it hurt.

I hope you find what you're looking for out there, my darling Earth boy. Because I have a feeling the fun's just about to start back here.

JANBI

JANBI LOOKED UP FROM HIS BORROWED DESK WHEN JANTINE ENTERED THE room, but he almost didn't recognize her without her encounter suit or coveralls. Dressed in soft white garments bearing the logo of the Institute, she had none of her habitual swagger, nor the air of command he'd come to associate with her every move.

The mod standing in front of him just looked tired, almost as tired as he felt himself. He knew what he was feeling was the combined after-effects of the stims and whatever Mordecai had given him to sleep, a state the old doctor had predicted would be "one monster of a hangover." But Jantine's face had changed since he last saw her, and despite the pain in her eyes Janbi had to admit he liked it.

She's finally accepted it. We failed in our mission, and as such no longer have purpose. And it terrifies her, almost as much as it does me.

Janbi set his handheld aside and dimmed the panel, letting the search routines he'd worked out do their job. He leaned back in his chair and smiled, hoping his new face wasn't too hideous to look at.

"JonB...Janbi, I'm sorry. I shouldn't have struck you. You were right."

He hadn't expected a full apology; it would take the Beta more than just a few hours to come to terms with the mistakes she'd made.

But although he expected her to have more to say than that, he decided not to punish her for being who and what she was.

It's not her fault they made us this way.

"Yes, I usually am," he said. "But I didn't ask you to come to me to make you feel bad. I just wanted to talk to you. Really talk, for once, without any expectations or demands on either of us. Do you think that's possible?"

Jantine was silent for fourteen and a half seconds, and then nodded. Janbi got up from the desk and moved over to a pair of over-stuffed chairs, easing himself down into one as best he could with only one hand.

When Jantine realized what he was doing, she started to help him, but then stopped when her eyes registered his bandage-wrapped stump. As if in sympathy, she raised her own injured hand to her chest, then quickly moved it behind her body as if the sight of it might offend him.

When she sat down in the chair opposite him, Janbi saw a hint of her former self. Jantine was careful not to touch the sides of the chair, and she selected the exact center of the cushion to perch on instead of sinking into its comfort as he'd done. Her left hand brushed away invisible specks of dirt, and she kept her back perfectly straight.

Janbi smiled again, a bit wider this time. It was enough to make his nose sting, but Mordecai assured him it would heal straight and he'd have no problems breathing. Janbi hadn't mentioned to him how little time the process would take, and he wondered how the human doctor was reacting to Katra's much faster recuperative properties.

Janbi and Jantine sat silently for a while, each content to watch the other for signs as to what to do. In the end, it was Jantine who spoke first.

"I don't know what I'm supposed to say," she said.

"You don't have to say anything, if you don't want to. There aren't any rules now, not for us."

"But I'm supposed to know. Or if I don't, you're supposed to help me find the answers. None of this was covered in our education!"

It seemed to Janbi that Jantine was about to lose control. Given that the last time she'd acted impulsively she'd broken both his nose and her hand, he decided that perhaps they still needed some rules after all.

"Jantine, you know as well as I do that our mission was expected to fail. Just making it down to the surface put us far ahead of the projections, despite what it cost us."

Jantine rolled her lips inward, her jaw was trembling, and her left hand had a white-knuckled grip on her knee.

"But that's the problem with the Colonies," he said. "The Alphas, the Builders, even the older Betas think too big. The details are left for us to work out, and if I've learned anything from our time on Earth, it's that the little things add up over time."

Without thinking about it, Janbi was using his hands to emphasize his words. Or more accurately, one hand and one stump, and despite her best efforts Jantine couldn't stop looking at his left arm.

"This? This is exactly what I'm talking about. On Earth, they can make me a new one. I talked about it with Mordecai, and for something like a hand, the calibration time is just over a month. But back home, they'd push me aside for the next in line. And given how poorly you and I got along when we first met, JRD-B34721-S probably wouldn't last very long either."

Jantine's voice was almost a whisper, and her face was pale and drawn.

"I would never...I never asked for this. Any of this. I never wanted you to be hurt, I just..."

Janbi leaned forward, moving his right arm in front of the stump.

"That's right. No one ever asked us. In fact, I'll bet that until we decanted Serene, you'd never even met an Alpha in the flesh. But I have. There were four assigned to watch my crèche. And despite my early reservations, I'd rather be with her than any of them.

"Do you know what it was like, Jantine? Do you have any idea how they trained us?"

Jantine shook her head.

"Your picture was the first thing I saw every day when we woke from the rest cycle. I heard your voice during every meal. I knew everything about you before we even met, and when they told me why I'd been born, I was so proud.

"What does that make me, Jantine? Who am I supposed to be? Our genomes are perfectly compatible, but as people we couldn't be more different. They picked everyone else for this mission based on their merits, but I was *designed* for it."

Jantine sank back in her chair, making no attempt to hide her tears. Janbi didn't want to hurt her like this, but she needed to hear his story. Needed to hear all of it, no matter what it meant for their future.

"When you took a test, our crèche had half a cycle to study the same topic and get a higher score. Anyone who didn't was taken away. Even when there were only a few of us left, we had to be smarter than any Beta who'd come before us.

"You all think I'm arrogant, but what choice did I have? My entire life only has meaning based on how useful I can be to you, on a mission the Alphas knew might well fail. And for it to succeed, I had to challenge you at every turn, knowing how it made you feel. What does that say about me, about us?"

Jantine's muted sobs were like blows to his chest, and Janbi couldn't stand another second of it. He rolled out of his chair and stood in front of her, holding out his right hand.

When she reached for it, all he could think of was how right it had felt when the two of them comforted one another that first night after landing. He leaned back, pulling gently until she rose to meet him. Jantine flowed into his arms, and he held her as tightly as he could with only one hand. But she had more than enough strength for both of them, and they stood like that until she stopped crying, and a good while longer.

"I'm not telling you this because I want to hurt you, Jantine. But I've had a lot of time to think over the last few days, and I've made my decision. I'm not taking any more orders, not from the Alphas. Whatever happens to me from now on, I'm the one responsible for my actions."

Jantine inhaled through her nose, a long, sniffling sound that preceded a small gasp as she opened her mouth to speak. Her voice was muffled against the fabric of his soft garment, but he knew the sound of it so well he could have made out the words from across the room.

"What are you saying? Why are you telling me these things?"

Janbi rested his forehead on her hair, careful not to jostle his nose any more than he had to. Her smell was his entire world, and part of him wondered why he'd ever considered Mira Harlan as an acceptable partner.

"Our old lives are over. We don't have to follow their rules any more. No more plans, no more compatibility matrix. I want a real life, a human life. I want to be old, and weak, and read books that have nothing to do with science, or logic, or societal planning."

Jantine stiffened in his arms, and she pushed away slightly. Janbi took a step back, but when he saw the pain on her face, he almost rushed to hug her again.

"I don't understand. Janbi, I don't know what you're saying to me, or what I'm supposed to do. That's why I came here. I don't know anything anymore, but I didn't want you…"

Jantine's eyes brimmed with a fresh round of tears, and before Janbi knew what he was doing his left hand came up to wipe them away. But instead of recoiling from his stump, Jantine took his arm in her hand and pressed it against her face. She closed her eyes, and let out another shuddering breath.

"I didn't want you to hate me."

It was Janbi's turn to fumble for words, but instead of letting his mouth run free, he stayed silent. He knew it was the wrong thing to do, but he was as trapped by his programming as she was.

Perhaps that's why we're so drawn to Mira. She never hides her reactions, even when we don't like what she has to say.

"Jantine, I'm saying you don't owe me anything. You are free to choose whatever partner you want. I don't know what life will be like here on Earth, but I want to. I want to know all of it, and I hope someday, when you're ready, you will too."

Jantine opened her eyes, and Janbi took her smile to mean that she would at least consider what he'd said.

Janbi pulled away when his handheld chimed an alert, stumbling toward the desk with unexpectedly weak knees. Jantine opened her mouth at his abrupt dismissal, but the flashing panel was something he couldn't ignore.

When she did speak, it was with her old voice, and Janbi couldn't help but feel sorry for yet another missed opportunity.

"What is it?"

Janbi didn't answer at first, working his way around the desk until he could set the handheld down and tap out a few commands. Luckily, the desk's holo display responded to his gesturing stump, and equations formed in letters of light above its polished surface.

"I think I might have found them. The sleepers."

"What?"

Jantine's face was just on the other side of the holo, and her hands must have strayed into the projection. The equations spread out around them, and Janbi had to crane his neck to find the ones he needed to verify.

When he did, he shook the handheld very delicately, not wanting to disturb the image any more than it already was.

"I've been running a decryption program on the Earther communications network. Doctor Harrison gave me his access codes for the Institute's library, from which I was able to decipher his clearance codes for the Reclamation Council."

Jantine nodded, and Janbi knew she was extrapolating from his words the kinds of networks they could now access. It seemed that she too needed a challenge to pit herself against, which wasn't all that surprising given how he'd developed the same personality trait.

"Ever since we exited the debris field, I've been trying to figure out what happened to the other container. After the crash, the shuttle's core was too compromised to run this kind of search, but the ones they have here are a lot more powerful and we now have access to a very sophisticated microwave communications grid.

"This program," he said, indicating the equations with his stump, "has analyzed all encrypted transmissions moving through the Earther's network for the last seven hours. And I'm fairly sure I know where they are."

"JonB, are you telling me you know where the sleepers landed?"

Janbi didn't take offense when Jantine used the mocking designation she and the other mods had given him before he'd chosen a name, taking it for an excited utterance.

"No. As far as I can tell, they haven't landed at all. I think one of the ships that fired missiles at us recovered it, and has been trying to find a way inside ever since. There are multiple transmissions referencing 'modules,' and quite a few of them contain the word 'Chimera.' If we can find that ship, we can find our people. Jantine, we don't have to be alone!"

Janbi put the handheld down, raised his hand into the holo and made a fist. The holo obediently disappeared, giving him an unobstructed view of Jantine's face.

Her eyes were alive, and a tight smile teased the edges of her mouth. And the same eagerness she was feeling was alive in him as well. But he was completely unprepared when she leaned across the table, grabbed his head, and kissed him.

Janbi had to keep his hand on the desk to avoid falling, but he found it very pleasant to let Jantine maneuver herself around the side of the desk while maintaining contact with his mouth. Once they were next to one another, she drew him into an even tighter embrace than before, this time kissing him so forcefully that despite Mordecai Harrison's assurances, he couldn't breathe at all.

MARANOVA

-5.8, +0:50. Old Chicago.
The Harrison Institute for Applied Sciences

YKATERINA ILLYANA MARANOVA WAS NOT HAPPY. IT WAS NOT LIKE Mordecai Harrison to just summon her out of the blue, and spending five hours navigating the spacelanes around Earth was never on her happy list. But his coded communiqué said it was urgent, and they only used the Kasparov ciphers for cabal business.

If he really has called me down for a game of chess, there's gonna be hell to pay. What in the worlds could he have discovered that I don't already know? Andreison is as good as her word, and laid it all out for me like a holo-novel, complete with side sections and citations to explore.

Might be worth keeping her around, after this is all over. Maybe she can surprise us again somehow.

The shuttle switched to Earth gravity as soon as Andreison opened the loading ramp, and she and Samuel tottered down on space legs to put their feet on actual soil for the first time in forever.

The Harrison Institute was hidden away beneath the rubble of Old Chicago, a silent monument to human excess. The old-world governments had flattened the city in an attempt to drive out the hunter-killers, and were mostly successful. How the Harrison clan had survived the occasional raids and plagues was the story of the Reclamation wrapped up in a neat package, and more or less how Mordecai had laid it out when arguing with Horace.

I sure hope the Institute's patrol protocols are up to date. The shuttle is an awful tempting target for a self-repairing technovore, and I'd hate to have to walk out of here.

The indignity of the gravity well after so long in space offended her, but in truth it was anger at herself for not keeping up on her full-g training that upset her the most. There was always a meeting to attend, or a captain to counsel, or some other crisis to distract her, and over the last two weeks she'd been on high alert for any news of Aloysius Martin.

Now him, I'd play chess against. Maybe...

Ykaterina's foul mood deepened as Marya skipped down the ramp and began her pre-flight for the return trip. Andreison was just a few weeks removed from the surface, and clearly hadn't been skipping any workouts. But for a comms officer, the girl had taken to being a pilot again like she'd never stopped flying, and Ykaterina had to admit the trip down was one of the smoothest insertions she'd had in a long time.

Didn't even rattle my teacup! We're going to have to loosen our restrictions on prosthetics, if she's any indication. Not only is she virus-free, but a pilot of her skill is wasted in a sensor pod, or behind a desk. She needs the sky, and we took it from her for saving our lives.

"So, what did you break this time?" Samuel's question had a laugh hidden inside, but Andreison's dour expression was having none of it.

"There's some more micro fractures on that strut I warned you about before we left. I can do some welding while we're down here, but your best bet is to replace the assembly altogether. And I wasn't at all happy with the ventral thruster output on approach. Who did you say was your last pilot? They've got some explaining to do if I catch up to them."

Ykaterina's laugh caught in her throat as she remembered that

Marcus Callaway had been on *Valiant*, just like Allie and Andreison's wife Mira Harlan. Rather than pour more salt into an open wound, she let Samuel handle the news.

It's what he's here for, after all.

"A conversation for another time, Lieutenant. As long as she'll fly, lock her up and come with me. I may need your expert testimony again."

"Yes sir." Andreison took one more turn around the shuttle's undercarriage, then waved a hand at the ramp. To Ykaterina's surprise and delight, it folded up snug and locked into place. Ykaterina turned to Samuel to ask how she'd done it, and noticed he had his captain face on, and was holding his hand out to Andreison.

Andreison stopped a pace away, with the best "who me?" expression Ykaterina had ever seen on a junior officer. As if she was immune to Samuel's withering gaze, she cocked her chin up to look him in the eyes, something Ykaterina was rarely able to do when standing this close to him.

"What? I used my own this time. That's why you gave it to me, isn't it?" Andreison ended her statement by pointing at his belt, where *Clarke's* command baton rested in all its jeweled splendor.

Oh ho! She's got you there, Samuel!

Samuel rested his hand on the baton, shoving it deeper into its loop. He was fighting hard to keep his smile in check, and Ykaterina couldn't blame him.

There's just something about that girl. She may never get another promotion, but letting her leave the fleet is a definite mistake.

But as much fun as this is, we've still got work to do.

All of us.

"I don't know about you two, but these bugs are going to eat me alive. Someone's advertised a special on spacer blood today, and I'd like to get off the menu as soon as possible."

Remembering all the hidden staircases and entrances Mordecai's family had build up over the centuries, Ykaterina started walking to the middle of the clearing. There were bound to be cams on them right now, and someone would come to escort them inside before too long.

"Watch your step, ma'am. There's a lift right under your feet, and I'm about to call it up."

Andreison's warning shouldn't have been a surprise, but Ykaterina nearly jumped away from the clear patch of ground she was standing on. In the noonday sun she couldn't make out anything but dirt and rocks, but Andreison's eyes worked on another level.

The junior officer waved her hand again, and the ground split apart into a dozen triangular sections, each of which drew back into a wall Ykaterina could just make out in the hole they defined. There was a whirring noise from somewhere below, and she thought she could hear shouting in the distance.

A platform with a bright red safety cage rose up even with the ground, and Samuel opened the gate for her to step inside. He then waved Andreison onto the platform, and secured the gate.

"I'll catch the next one," he said, holding out his arms wider than the cage itself. Staring up at him from inside, part of his head was cut off by the cage, and she understood.

"All right then. Take us down, Ms. Andreison."

The cage took a few seconds to descend, after which they were greeted by a quartet of slugthrower-toting guards wearing jumpsuits bearing the Harrison Institute logo.

"Their weapons discipline could use some work, wouldn't you say, Andreison?"

The guards shuffled nervously, not sure who to point their weapons at.

"Yes, ma'am. They'll never pass muster. Especially not after I make them eat the ammo cans." The guards immediately shifted their aim to Andreison, who only smiled in response. It was enough of a distraction for Ykaterina to slip out of the cage, pull an induction pistol out of her tunic, and plant it in the nearest guard's crotch.

"Settle down, boys. We were invited. And my escort here has had a really bad couple of days, so I'd watch my step if I were you."

"Is everything all right down there?" Samuel's booming voice echoed around the chamber, and in the second it took Ykaterina to look up at him, two of the slugthrowers were at her feet, and a third appeared in Andreison's hands, aimed right between the eyes of the man in front of her.

"Drop it. I just got this uniform, and I don't want to get it dirty." The guard went white at Andreison's words, and slowly bent to place his weapon on the ground. The action brought his head in front of Ykaterina's pistol, which she waggled as she talked.

"Now, one of you boys should run along and fetch Doctor Harrison, and the others should go and make me a cup of tea. Old ladies like me get cranky when we're not properly greeted. Marya?"

"Yes ma'am."

"Be a dear and send the lift up for Samuel. He must be getting hot up there in the sun."

"Yes, ma'am."

Oh yes. She'll do nicely.

"Uh, ma'am?" The guard's eyes were crossing trying to keep track of both the induction pistol in his face and the rising lift with three slugthrowers on it.

"It's Madame Commodore to you, but go on."

"It's…It's just that…"

"Spit it out, sonny. I haven't got all day."

A bead of sweat rolled down his forehead and into his eyes.

"Madame Commodore, Doctor Harrison is in Main Medical, and gave orders that he and the new patients were not to be disturbed."

Well that is interesting. Especially since this place has only one kind of patient, and they always involve paperwork.

"Then I guess you'd better take me to him. Marya, you wait here for Samuel, and then the two of you should go have a word with whomever's in charge of this lot."

"Yes, ma'am. Happy to comply."

Ykaterina holstered her pistol inside her tunic, where it disappeared into a fake stomach pouch invisible to every sensor Fleet Appropriations had tried on it. It was the first time she'd had to draw one of the new McCallister holdouts, and she made a mental note to have them issued to all Flag officers as soon as possible.

Except for Horace, of course. Little pissant can requisition his own weapons.

Marya stepped away from the lift as it arrived, with Samuel holding one of the captured slugthrowers on the guards. He unfolded himself from the cage, then sent it back up to the surface with two now ammo-less weapons as passengers.

"Making new friends already, Andreison?"

"Not me, sir. Just following Madame Commodore's lead."

Ykaterina smiled, and pulled the kneeling guard to his feet.

"Just another day in the Fleet, Samuel. This fine young man here is going to take me to Doctor Harrison, while the two of you tighten up security. Come find me in Main Medical when you're finished, if I haven't sent for you by then."

Ykaterina gave the guard a push, and followed him down the hallway.

Samuel will set things right. He always does.

It wasn't a long walk, but the empty hallways and their sterile overhead lights bothered her even more than having weapons shoved in her face on arrival. Something had happened here recently, something big.

And it's sure as hell going to mean trouble for me, I can feel it.

MIRA

"WELL, MY DEAR," MORDECAI HARRISON SAID, "YOU HAVE SOME VERY interesting readings here. I'd like to talk to you about them, if you're feeling up to it."

Hearing Mordecai's Harrison's voice made Mira think of every time her grandfathers had come to visit. But unlike the Pappys Harlan, Mordecai wasn't here to hug her or slip her candy when her mother wasn't looking. He was a scientist, and if Captain Martin was correct, he was the foremost expert on the Transgenic virus in a thousand light years.

But from where she was lying on her bed, watching him absently tug on his wild white hair while his staff moved around the Institute's infirmary, he looked more like a character from a fairy tale than a preeminent scientist and statesman.

"I'm a lot better now that I've had some rest. My head's a bit fuzzy, but it doesn't feel like it's going to explode anymore. After the last few days, that's one heck of an improvement."

Mordecai's smile was as devastating as his voice, and Mira was having problems reconciling the avuncular professor with a High Councilor of the Reclamation. She didn't remember his selection to the council, or even if she'd voted for him. But it was easy enough to see how he'd earned the total respect of all the Institute's staff.

I just wish the captain had told me more about you before everything got turned upside-down.

To be perfectly honest, Mira felt great. Part of it was being out of her hardsuit, but another factor was the incredibly soft and decidedly non-regulation hospital clothes she had on. They were some kind of cotton blend, with an almost invisible set of seams on each side so the attendants could "open her up" if necessary to attach more ice-cold probes. They'd removed most of those before she went to sleep, but Mira could still feel a couple of them in uncomfortable places on her chest and back.

"Well, that's the thing. You were dangerously dehydrated, and even though we pumped you full of fluids, you burned through every kind of sedative we tried to keep you asleep. So Paul had the bright idea to get you drunk instead. Apologies if you're not a bourbon fan, but since we had some on hand it was easy to synthesize and introduce into your bloodstream."

"Umm, thanks?"

The last time she'd done any serious drinking was with Tommy, and she only remembered that because of the ribbing her fellow cadets gave her when she came back on duty with a very distinctive body odor. Mira offered up a silent prayer that she wouldn't have the same reaction this time.

"Paul's a fairly intuitive fellow. In another forty years or so, he might even be ready to take over this place from me. If I'm tired of it by then, that is."

A tall man snorted from several meters away, where he was examining a bank of monitors attached to Katra's biobed. The Gamma's injuries were far more extensive than anyone but Janbi and Carlton knew, but apparently she'd threatened them in some pretty inventive ways not to tell Jantine during their starlight run.

"He's just jealous because I'm so much better looking than he is. Hello, Lieutenant Harlan. I'm Paul Czgeny, but apparently you know that already."

Mira smiled. He was good-looking, if a bit skinny for her taste. But compared to the faces she'd been looking at for the last three days, he was a duck among swans.

"Not your last name, but I do recognize your voice. It's…complicated."

Paul shrugged in a very Harrison-like manner, and she wondered how long the two men had been working together. Mordecai held out a medicomp to Paul, leaning against her bed for support as he put his cane aside. The younger man swiveled his head between the monitors and the smaller device, then gave another shrug. His expression wasn't quite a frown, but it conveyed a similar message.

They don't know what to make of me. And as long as I'm sidelined by Paul's whiskey derivative, I can't use my abilities to figure out why. I can almost feel them, but after my emotional overload up on the surface, I'm okay with that for now.

Mira took a few seconds to consider this new development. It seemed foolish for her abilities to be counteracted by such a common substance, but she didn't have any referents for intoxicants in the Colonies. She'd have to ask Carlton the next time he stopped by to check on Katra. Bringing the matter up to Serene didn't seem right, especially if her current state gave her any advantages she didn't know about yet.

Paul stepped forward and took the medicomp from Mordecai, but he didn't seem pleased with what he saw.

"So as near as I can figure, Miss Harlan, you have two active strains of the T-Virus in your system. Neither matches the one your friend the Type 13 has, and—"

"Katra, Paul. And she's a Gamma, not a Type 13. Whatever information you have on the Colonials needs to be updated."

If Paul was chagrined by her words, he gave no sign of it. "Your friend Katra the Gamma, then. But you and she share some remarkable healing abilities that…that the young man who is so insistent on being called Janbi doesn't. Does she have…"

Paul waved the medicomp in a small circle near his head, and Mira smiled and shook her head.

"Okay, then. I can't explain either of you. But one of the active strains in your body matches the one in that little girl—Serene, is it? And unlike you, her readings are stable. Is she a Gamma too?

Interesting. Now I definitely need to talk to Carlton.

Mira wasn't sure whether or not to tell Paul the truth about Serene, but as she'd been prepared to hand the girl off to Mordecai sight unseen several days ago, she reasoned that there was nothing to be gained by silence.

"No. She's something else. An Alpha, but she does share my empathic abilities. More complicated stuff—I really don't understand it myself. Jantine, Janbi and Carlton are Betas; Artemus is a Delta. Jason and...well, the big fellas are Omegas, but don't expect a lot of conversation out of them. In fact, they're the reason I ended up like this, so if they ever decide to tell me why, I'll be sure to pass it along."

Paul nodded, entering data into the medicomp. She thought she detected a hint of curiosity from him, but it was nothing compared to the flood of it she felt from Mordecai. It was strong enough to bring back a bit of her headache, but when she tried to "feel" more, nothing happened.

Good stuff, that bourbon.

"Are you sure about that, Mira?"

Huh?

"Sure about what?

"You said Serene was an Alpha. Is that true?"

Mira nodded. Jantine would be furious, but after what she pulled in the courtyard, the Beta could lump it. Mira wasn't quite ready to forgive her yet, but if they couldn't trust Mordecai's people there wasn't really anything they could do about it.

"Yes, sir, I am. Captain Martin had more information, but he was sure this was the place to bring her. As for the virus, well, he told me 'she wasn't done cooking.' Something about how she'd spent so long in suspended animation that the rest of the human race just moved on, and so did the virus. I'll admit, the distinction is a bit beyond me, but that's what he said. If we can get at the data he left for us, we'll know more."

"I've asked a friend to come to the Institute to help with that,"

Mordecai said. "But I think I can explain what he meant, even if I can't explain how you ended up like this."

"I'm all ears, Mordecai. But my head's starting to hurt again, could I have some more of whatever it was you gave me? I don't recall dreaming about a glass and ice, so I'm assuming I didn't drink it."

Paul leaned forward and pushed a button on the side of her bed, and a few seconds later she was feeling no pain. It was just enough to knock the edges off the hurricane in her head, but not so much that she couldn't follow what Mordecai was saying.

"So it's like this: that girl, that marvelously strange girl, is from another world and another time. I can't say definitively where and when, but Paul, myself, and everyone here on Earth has a very stable strain of the T-virus. We see maybe a handful of minor expressions each year on Earth, and a few more in orbit. It's just enough to keep the grants coming in and rules in place about athletics and military service. I'm amazed that you have had such a complete transformation, but even more so that you've been infected twice."

"That's the part I don't understand, doctor. I'm not going to say that's impossible, since you're telling me it's true. But what they told us in school was that once you went active, you couldn't be infected again."

Mordecai's head was like a child's bobbing toy, and he started waving his hands around in the air as he spoke.

"I know! That's the best part. Serene's strain isn't causing your abilities, it's magnifying them. And none of the others are showing the same effects. You two are a couple of fascinating case studies, and I think we should keep you both under observation for a while just to make sure nothing happens to you."

Mira pushed herself up on the bed, feeling the sensors attached to her skin shifting. Then a spike of pain forced its way through the pleasant bourbon haze and past her strong desire not to be poked and prodded for the rest of her life. She closed her eyes and gasped, and she felt strong hands catch her before she could fall off the side of the bed.

Mira, what do you know about Chimera?

Mira was surprised by Janbi's sudden intrusion into her thoughts —and the very vivid mental image of his immediate surroundings that accompanied it. When she opened her eyes, Mordecai was shining some kind of small light on her face.

"Chimera? But that's a myth!" Her voice was much louder than she'd intended.

"Hmm? What's that, Mira?"

Harrison's upturned eyebrow was almost comical, but Mira was too confused by both Janbi's question and why he'd be asking it at this exact moment to answer him.

"Something above your pay grade, Mordecai," said a reedy voice from Mira's Academy days, and all activity in the room came to a halt. "And yours too, Harlan, but we'll get to that in a moment. Now, does one of you young people have an explanation as to why I had to come down the gravity well in the middle of the afternoon, instead of having a nice cup of tea in my wardroom?"

Mira was off the bed and standing at attention before she fully processed the appearance of Commodore Ykaterina Maranova in the room, resplendent in her dress blacks with the left half of her tunic almost completely covered in service ribbons.

In contrast, Mira's shapeless cotton outfit was woefully inadequate to receive a senior flag officer, but that didn't stop her from saluting. Or trying to, anyway. Between the fading pain of Janbi's unexpected message and the bourbon, she was having trouble standing up straight.

When Maranova stalked over and glared up at her, Mira felt just as awkward as she had on their first meeting, when, as a very junior midshipman, she arrived late and hung over for a fleet tactics symposium and had been called on to answer questions about the final days of the Tranquility uprising for the rest of a very long afternoon.

"What happened to your face, girl? It looks like someone took a brush and scoured off all your character."

Mira hadn't fully seen her own face for several days, save for chance glances at herself in the mods' faceplates. But she knew what the commodore meant.

"Well? How about it?"

"Ma'am, at 1245 ship time on July 17th, a then unidentified object made an unauthorized hyperspace emergence..."

MARANOVA

THE DOOR TO MAIN MEDICAL HAD TWO MORE JUMPSUITED GUARDS IN front of it, but Ykaterina's escort waved them away. She arched an eyebrow at that, but was too committed to seeing Mordecai to add another mystery to her list.

Inside the doors was another world, full of beds and monitors and noise. There were white-coated doctors everywhere, and directly ahead she saw the wild white hair of Mordecai Harrison, talking with another dark-skinned man and a young woman sitting on the edge of a bed.

The woman wobbled a bit, then closed her eyes and nearly collapsed into Mordecai's arms. She came to a second later, with Mordecai shining a light in her face.

Then she spoke, and Ykaterina knew exactly what was bothering her about the scene.

"Chimera? But that's a myth!"

Well I'll be. Mira Harlan. Marya was right after all. And the unofficial name for Horace's secret weapons laboratory isn't something a junior officer should be asking about, especially one who's been accused of gennie collab-oration.

"Hmm? What's that, Mira?" Mordecai continued his examination, intent on poking Harlan's arms and neck despite the hospital jumper she was wearing. The man standing next to him, though, was a bit more attentive, and spotted Ykaterina closing on them.

"Something above your pay grade, Mordecai. And yours too, Harlan, but we'll get to that in a moment. Now, does one of you young people have an explanation as to why I had to come down the gravity well in the middle of the afternoon, instead of having a nice cup of tea in my wardroom?"

Harlan was off the bed in a shot, trying and failing to come to attention. Her right hand was still connected to an i.v. unit, and she nearly fell over trying to correct for it.

From this distance, Ykaterina had a much better view of Harlan's face, and didn't like what she saw one bit.

"What happened to your face, girl? It looks like someone took a brush and scoured off all that character you had. Well? How about it?"

The freckles she'd seen in all the holos accompanying Kołodziejski's rantings were gone, and her eyes were a bit flatter than before. To complicate matters, Harlan's skin looked ten years younger, and was now almost the same shade as the gennie girl who'd blown up the *Valiant*.

Shit. She's infected. And there's no sign of Aloysius, which also can't be good.

"Ma'am, at 1245 ship time on July 17th, a then unidentified object made an unauthorized hyperspace emergence in the immediate vicinity of our battlegroup..."

At first, Ykaterina was impressed by Mira's version of events aboard *Valiant*. She'd performed her duty admirably, and even though she confessed to having killed Ykaterina's great-nephew in the transfer bay—*which stings more than a little, I have to admit*—Ykaterina could find no fault with her actions.

However, Harlan's account of their escape absolutely terrified her. Her time since blasting out of the transfer bay had been filled with one nightmare scenario after another, be it outrunning *Indomitable*'s missiles, having a telepathic space alien infect her with the Transgenic virus, or watching her captain fly off to certain death in a ruined shuttle while she watched over the uncorked Alpha Allie had tried so hard to hide away.

By the time she started talking about facing down a quartet of hunter-killers with a couple of gennies and some heat lamps, Ykaterina was sure Harlan was having her on. But her cadence never changed, and Mordecai was nodding along with everything she said.

Fucking nightmare, and I still only know half of it.

Shit.

"Okay, Harlan, slow down and run it for me again. And sit down while you're at it, I keep feeling you're going to fall over on me."

Harlan eased herself back into the bed, then grabbed her head and started whimpering. Mordecai put one hand on her chest, and did something to the side of the bed with the other that had her smiling big and wide within seconds.

Harrison's Doctor demeanor told Ykaterina she probably wasn't going to get another recitation of facts, and most likely would have some more bad news to deliver. But the securecams monitoring the room probably had captured her testimony, so whatever it was he had to say was...

Securecams... Security, Shitshitshit!

"She's had a rough go of it, commodore. I still don't know everything the virus has done to her, or even if she'll survive it. I'd like to keep her here until she's completely recovered, but if you really need to talk to her I can..."

No. Damnitall. I need more time!

Ykaterina made a snap call that she was sure Samuel would not like, but every second counted if she had any chance of getting out in front of this thing. She pulled Mordecai a fair distance away from Mira's bed, then waved over his younger companion for good measure before whispering to him in her best in-charge monotones.

"That can wait, Mordecai. Right now I need someone—you'll do, young man—to get down to your security station and sequester my pilot for a while. She's about Harlan's height, talks a lot, has funny eyes—you can't miss her. I need her kept away from gennies right now, and in particular far away from this room, and Mira Harlan. Can you handle that?"

The younger doctor looked to Mordecai, who just shrugged.

"Sounds okay to me, Paul. But stay on our frequency—I promise not to shut you out again."

"All right, Uncle. Let me know if Mira or Katra's conditions change, and I'll be back."

With that, the younger man walked away, stopping at the foot of another bed to make some notes on a medicomp. Ykaterina took a half step to the right, and saw him talking to another patient, a gennie by the look of her. What struck her most about the blonde girl in the bed was that being hooked up to a dozen machines didn't seem to bother her, nor did it stop her from checking the exits every three seconds.

When her eyes met Ykaterina's, the gennie smiled, and something Marya said during their first shuttle trip came to mind.

"We can't defend against the gennies unless we're prepared to use tactical nukes," she said. And that gennie over there is a living weapon if I've ever seen one.

Ykaterina turned her attention back to Mordecai, who was starting to look at her more like a Councilor than a Doctor.

She took Mordecai by the arm, and led him even further away from Mira Harlan and her strange new abilities. But despite the distance, she couldn't shake the feeling that even with a room full of doctors and several million credits worth of diagnostic equipment between them, the blonde gennie was still paying attention to her every move.

Let's hope her hearing isn't as good as her tradecraft, or we're all in trouble.

"Mordecai, everything I've put together in the last few hours about Horace and his people pales in comparison to what's happened to Harlan. So tell me before we go any further, is this something you can fix?"

Mordecai's remaining eye looked older than the rest of him, and he gave a deep sigh before responding.

"That's the thing, commodore. There's nothing actually wrong with her, at least not physically. This is who she is now, this is what the virus does. She's become the perfect version of herself for what she has to do, and there's no magic cure for that.

"I can keep her coherent and functioning for a few hours, maybe even a couple days. But the pain she's experiencing is caused by our thoughts intruding into her consciousness. Eventually, she's going to give in to the literal voices in her head, and then there won't be a Mira Harlan you recognize anymore. She'll be one of them, and fighting against it is probably going to kill her."

ShitShitShitShit

Ykaterina scowled at her feet, daring them to come up with a better plan than the ones in her head. Harlan's new abilities were an untapped asset, and from what she'd said, the gennies trusted her. But she was also a massive liability, and the most damning evidence in the worlds that Kołodziejski's Loyalists had been right all along.

And I can't have that at all.

"What about the other gennies? Like that one over there. Can they read minds too?"

Mordecai looked puzzled for a few seconds, then brightened up like he'd just been given a new puppy.

"Oh, You mean Katra! No, no sign of any extra-sensory abilities, but as I understand it not all Gammas are built alike. It's certainly true of the Betas that came in with Harlan. We haven't done a full workups on them yet but when we do, I'm wagering that their leader Jantine's cognitive abilities will be off the charts. If we only had more time to study them..."

Mordecai was still talking, something about plasmids and transmission vectors. But Ykaterina had stopped listening when he named the gennies' leader.

Jantine. He said Jantine, and now we're well and truly fucked. I have to get control of this situation before word gets out, and I can't have Harlan and her new friends snooping around in my head while I do so.

"Okay, Mordecai. How about we take a different tack on this. You say you can't cure Harlan, but can you make me immune? Maybe keep her out of my head for a while?"

Mordecai pursed his lips. "Do you have any allergies I should know about?"

Ykaterina's eyebrows shot up, and she stared Mordecai straight in the eye.

"What the hell does that have to do with anything?"

Well," said Mordecai, "that happy juice Paul cooked up for miss Harlan helps control her seizures, and suppresses her alpha wave activity. We could work up something similar for you, as long as you can handle the hangovers."

At this Maranova smiled, and draped an arm over Mordecai's shoulders. He shuffled away slightly as she leaned into whisper in his ear, but then relaxed with a smile of his own.

"Mordecai, you haven't been paying that close attention to my teacups these past few months, have you? Hit me with your best shot, I can take it. And if Harlan's face is any indication, I could really use a cuppa right about now."

ANDREISON

Marya didn't quite know what to do with herself, so she sat in an abandoned hallway outside the institute's security office on an old, rolled-up carpet and stared at the wall, daring it to make any kind of sense. As near as she could tell, all the hallways in this compound were built to do double duty as auxiliary infirmaries, although this one was currently serving as a chaotic storage unit.

The ridiculous misuse of space was maddening, but it did allow her enough privacy to reflect on her day so far. In the last twenty minutes she'd nearly been shot, had nearly shot someone, and was now left inexplicably on her own until either Captain DeMarco or Commodore Maranova needed her.

It's like I'm straight back in my old life again. I want to be doing something, anything, but everyone keeps telling me to be patient.

So, here I am. Patient, patient, patient.

The captain was inside tearing a strip off the Institute's security forces. All of them he could find, anyway, with whatever jumpsuited functionaries he could corral thrown in for good measure.

It seemed that no-one was really in charge of anything at the Harrison Institute, they just did whatever job came along when it needed doing—two of the guards she'd disarmed at the lift were actually molecular biologists, another was an accountant. All had received some combat training, sure, but not at Marya's level, and nowhere near enough to escort a couple of flag officers around a potentially hostile site.

Yep, that's me. Agent of Chaos. And the one time it actually came in handy, I'm the one who suffers for it.

She let her eyes relax a bit, taking in the warp and weave of the rolled rug. Her father had collected pieces like this while he was alive —extravagant, wonderful pieces of art with tiny, intentional flaws woven in by old-Earth crafters. She didn't have time to unroll this one and look for one, but the last time she'd found comfort in such a search, she had human eyes.

Besides, without my father to come yell at me for getting the rugs dirty, would it even be any fun?

She didn't miss Hugo. Not exactly. Her father was a bastard of galactic proportions, and long before she'd given Tommy the beating of his life she was regularly intervening in domestic disputes between Hugo and Samantha, and learned quickly to defend herself from both of them. Her parents had bonded over derivatives and vegetable futures, and Marya had often thought the only reason they chose to have a child was to save money when it came time to buy out the Proctor shares in the agri-station and put them in a blind trust for her.

They'd died together in an aircar crash, but Marya liked to imagine they'd gone out strangling each other. And even though she'd emancipated herself years before, Marya inherited everything anyway.

And what a happy time untangling that mess was.

Something moved at the edge of her sphere of vision, and both eyes tracked in on a little girl just a few years older than Deb's twins. She was crawling around the corner of a large box, wearing a shapeless white garment with an Institute logo on the back. Her skin was a strange shade of almost-tan, her head recently shaved and too large for her shoulders.

Something about the way she moved was tantalizingly familiar—even more so when the girl turned to give Marya a wide smile before holding a finger up to her lips.

Then a second form crept into the room from the opposite side, a long-haired cat almost too large to be believed. It was nearly a meter long from nose to tail, and probably outmassed the girl by a dozen kilos or more. But despite its bulk, the cat immediately went into a wiggling crouch, then launched itself across the room onto the girl's back.

The two went down snarling and giggling, and Marya wasn't sure which, or even if, one of them needed protection. When the girl's clothing wasn't completely shredded by the cat's powerful kicks, she decided to just watch them play.

"He's really something, isn't he?" The words were spoken by a soft, male voice, pitched low enough to startle neither cat nor child. Marya, on the other hand, nearly jumped out of her skin, and with the playful pair at her back, she turned to regard her fellow witness.

He was a tall man, a hair under two meters with dark skin and a white lab coat over the same green jumpsuit everyone else but the little girl seemed to be wearing.

"Pardon me?" Marya was still taking in the sudden appearance of this stranger, who must have practiced moving even quieter than the overstuffed cat.

"Edwin there. He usually doesn't like kids, but these two have been stalking each other almost since she got here."

Marya turned her head a bit to the right, to put the cat/kid combo back in her line of sight. The girl now had Edwin on his back, rubbing his white belly fur fast enough to make it stick straight up from static.

"Do you mind if I ask you a question?"

Oh hell, here it comes. Everywhere I go, there's always some guy with a question.

"Look, mister, I'm only here for a few hours, and you've probably got better things to do in that time than play 'where are my teeth?' I'm married, I'm not interested, and not looking for new friends." Marya punctuated her statement with an outstretched fist, placing her rings firmly in view.

But instead of apologizing or pressing suit, the man just laughed, and held up his own be-ringed hand.

"Relax, Lieutenant. It's not like that, and besides, you're not my type. My wife, though, is another matter. She might love it if I brought you home for dinner, but I'm afraid I'd end up sleeping here at the Institute for a few weeks while the two of you figure out where all your stuff will fit. I'm Paul, by the way, and I'm actually interested in your eyes."

Marya felt the beginnings of a blush, and let her fist fall into an open hand. Paul took it in his own, and the two shook hands briefly.

"Marya. And I really don't have that much time to talk. It was an accident, years ago. I…good Lord, is that safe?"

The strange child was now giving the cat a piggyback ride, climbing up stacks of crates and jumping off to land in a perfect ready crouch. Even this movement was familiar somehow, but between Paul and the cat, Marya was having a hard time making sense of the scene.

"Probably not, but that's the point of kids, isn't it? I'm sure Serene will be fine. Edwin's been around for a long, long time, and at this point, we're really not sure if he can die."

This did capture Marya's full attention, and she started examining Paul's face for micro-expressions that would indicate he was joking. But not only did he seem to genuinely believe what he was saying, he had a kind of openness she rarely found in men.

Or women, for that matter. But we're usually a lot more emotionally honest.

"Now I have questions. Starting with what in the worlds you mean by that?"

Paul gestured to the rolled rug, and Marya sat down far enough away from him to avoid any complications if their conversation went sour. Paul shrugged, and sat down at the other edge of the roll.

"As near as we can figure, Edwin's a triple miracle. Not only is he transgenic, which is next to impossible with lower orders of animal life, but he's drawn to anyone with an active expression, especially ones we've never seen before.

"And, also as near as we can figure, he's well over a hundred years old. Dr. Harrison remembers playing with him as a child, and Edwin was his father's cat before him."

Marya tasked an eye to get a more complete picture of the girl, while she continued talking to Paul.

Mostly to make sure she's safe from the mutant cat. Not because she creeps me out or anything.

Mostly.

"I'm still not following you. Aren't you a Harrison, like the rest of the doctors around here?"

"In a sense. I married into it, but like Edwin there, and Doctor Harrison himself, I like a challenge. You see, Edwin's a collector, carrying several dozen active expressions without ever exhibiting transgenic traits of his own. He gets a little larger every once in a while, but other than that he's fine.

"We don't know how he does it, but whenever we get a bad case in, Edwin knows, and finds his way into the room to plop himself down at the patient's feet. They usually stabilize within an hour, and he never minds the blood draws afterward."

Marya shook her head, refusing to believe another impossible thing until at least one of them started making sense.

"So right now, with that girl… "

Paul smiled, but his face and posture indicated that he was holding something back.

"Yeah, Serene is virus positive. A fairly unique strain, in fact, and incredibly stable. Neither of them is contagious, by the way, that's not how the virus works."

Marya nodded, still watching the child—the first gennie she'd ever seen in person, really—lost in play.

She's just like my girls. That could happen to my girls. How can I hate her, just because she had the bad luck to catch an alien virus? It's not like she asked for this to happen to her or anything.

"So about your eyes…"

Marya laughed, and kept on laughing.

"You're just not going to give up, are you?"

"Nope. I just need some data, that's all. My uncle—great uncle, to be specific—isn't keeping up with his neural training, and I'm beginning to worry we'll never be able to fit him with a decent replacement eye. I was wondering, how long did it take you to adapt? I won't insult you by saying normal, but how long until your new eyes were fully functional?"

Marya didn't have a ready answer for him, but she did have a practical one.

"I didn't have any neural training to speak of, and I think what they're doing now would have really helped me. Every case is different, I know, but my eyes were completely destroyed in the accident, right down to the optic nerves. They had to rebuild everything from the brain on out, including parts of my skull and spinal column.

"Once they were done, it all just sort of worked. But I had to spend three months recuperating from my other injuries, so I had a lot of time to get used to the implants. I also did tons of virtual work that let me visualize a lot of things before I ever had to look at anything but hospital walls and my friends' faces."

My wives, technically, and this is the now officially the weirdest fucking day ever. Years of taking shit for what I did to Tommy, and now everyone I meet wants to know about the life I should have had instead.

Somewhere during her recollections the little girl vanished, and Marya had a brief moment of panic until she remembered she wasn't actually responsible for the strange child.

It's just…something about her face. I can't put my finger on it. I need to get home, sooner, rather than later, so I can tell Deb and the twins all about this crazy place.

"Well, that's probably not what he wants to hear, but we're also not going for anything as ambitious as your prostheses. Thanks for sharing with me, Marya. I hope it all works out for you."

Now that's an odd bit of phrasing. I wonder what he means by that…

"Andreison."

Marya was on her feet and turning before "Sir" even left her mouth. Captain DeMarco was standing half in, half out of the doorway to Institute Security, and he did not look happy.

"Go prep the shuttle for launch. We'll be lifting again within the hour. I've also called a troop transport down from L2, see that they gain access to the Institute when they arrive. Mr. Czgeny, a word?"

Paul stood up with a sheepish grin, and shrugged at Marya. It looked like an apology, but he still had the same amiable affect as when he was talking about his wife and that cat, and seemed to have no fear of the captain.

Marya, on the other hand, had plenty, and made her way quickly back to the lift. She thought she saw Edwin padding along after her in the shadows, but was too focused on her orders to give him a second thought.

Can this day possibly get any weirder?

MARANOVA

"Harlan, I've listened to this story three times now, and it's still the biggest bunch of bullshit I've ever heard. Even the parts of it about me are bullshit, and damned if I don't believe every word."

Looking around the storage area at the variety of gennies present, Commodore Ykaterina Maranova felt every minute of her age.

Hell, all of the gennies added together might come close to my age, and that's a generous estimate.

They were something to see, she'd give them that. Tall ones with extra arms wearing slick black bodysuits, and even bigger ones in tattered coveralls with orange skin and decidedly inhuman faces, one of whom was serving as a living chair for a little girl with impossibly smooth skin and an oversized head.

The child, Serene, looked much different than she had the first time Maranova had seen her, floating in a sleeper unit aboard Aloysius Martin's shuttle a few weeks back. She was wearing a very baggy set of shapeless cotton scrubs like the ones Harlan and the more human-looking gennies had on.

That the Alpha child and Harlan were here and Aloysius was disappointing, but Martin was a career man, principled. That he'd gone out on his own terms said a lot about him, and those he trusted.

Here and now, Mira Harlan and the strange faces she'd

surrounded herself with were watching her with a mixture of surprise and trepidation.

What the hell am I supposed to do with this lot? Harlan I have to arrest, I have to pretend Mordecai isn't committing treason against himself, and if I don't shoot the gennies for breaking the Exile, I have to find someone to arrest me!

But far and away the worst part of watching beings from another star system interacting with humans was listening to one of her prize students speak on their behalf, and as one of them.

"Ma'am, I'm just as much a part of it as you are, and I don't understand it all either. But Captain Martin brought me into this, dropped your name, and sent me the long way round here to the Harrison Institute. I was in no way expecting you to walk in that door, but I'm glad you did."

Maranova snorted.

"That's all well and good, but it still doesn't explain why I'm here. Mordecai all but ordered me to come down and play a game of chess, and when I arrived, what do I see but him giving care and comfort to not only one of my protégés but also the author of a transmission that has the fleet on high alert and me planted in orbit for the last three days trying to determine whether or not a state of war exists with the Outer Colonies.

"So here I am, waiting for an explanation no one seems to have. And let me tell you this for free, Mordecai, standing around while these children stare at me is definitely not my idea of a relaxing afternoon."

Maranova scanned the more normal faces among the gennies, in particular Jantine, or JTN-whatever the hell her number was. She'd cleaned up in a hurry, but there was no hiding her freshly fucked face, or the shit-eating grin on the one-handed boy standing next to her.

That girl would just as soon spit in my eye as shake my hand. There's some definite promise there.

"So what about it, Jantine? What's your play here?" Maranova watched Jantine cock her head, as if she was listening to something no one else could hear. If Harlan's story were true, the girl was probably asking Mira with her mind for clarification, and Maranova would be damned if she'd let one of her students speak on her behalf.

"Don't ask Harlan, ask me. I'm the one you have to convince."

Jantine's look was pure ice, but she returned her focus to Maranova while contemplating her response. Maranova thought Harlan was going to pop a blood vessel trying not to explain it herself.

"I will have my people back, or die in the attempt. What this man, this *Horass* has done is unforgivable. He will die as well. After that, it is up to you and your government."

Whore-Ass. Pretty much sums up that pissant Kołodziejski, and she's never even met him.

"That's a goal, not a plan. I need something to work with, if I'm going to help you."

"Ma'am, if I may?"

At least Harlan's voice hasn't changed. Still afraid of the sound of it, no matter how tall she stands.

"Lay it on me, Harlan. I've wasted enough time on this already, I might as well hear it all."

Mira Harlan wasn't a scared teenager anymore, nor was she a confident young woman reaching for the stars. Something had happened to her, recently by the feel of it, and Maranova didn't think it was just her transformation into a gennie.

You're half the woman you should be. You're definitely not the officer who's been trouncing my crew chiefs in fleet competency exercises the last few years, so there must be something else about your transformation that you're not telling me.

Harlan's face had some eerie similarities to the little girl's, enough that Maranova almost believed the parts of her story she'd left out of the larger briefing. She hadn't believed Aloysius Martin at first either, until she'd seen the Alpha girl in suspended animation.

But hearing how Serene's face had been changing since emerging from the sleeper unit was almost as terrifying as the thought that the T-virus inside the child could transform Maranova into something else at any time.

"Ma'am, that's not the way they think. Jantine knows she has to get a ship and some way to find Chimera. But she can't do either of those things right now, and so she's not going to waste time making plans until she knows what resources she has to work with."

Maranova wasn't ready to let Harlan off the hook just yet. There was too much at stake just to give away all her cards, and it was clear she wasn't going to get any help from "Councilor" Harrison.

Mordecai was having too much fun being in the room with his thesis subjects, drinking in every minute and preparing his next paper for publication. But the thoughtful looks he was giving the little girl when he thought no one could see told Maranova that the doctor shared at least some of her fears, and probably had a few of his own.

"More bullshit, this time with a whiff of horse thrown in. You want a ship, girl, you ask for it. You want resources and information, you ask for them. That's how this works. Or have you forgotten who I am, and what my rank actually means?"

Maranova wasn't sure if she was talking to Harlan, Jantine, or Serene, but all three of them stiffened.

Serene's look of concentration reminded her so much of Cadet Harlan that, for a second, Maranova thought she was looking back through time. It was something she'd worked for years to train out of the girl before shipping her off to Aloysius Martin.

Then the Alpha's too-large eyes narrowed, and the orange giant she wasn't sitting on straightened up.

Jantine's nostrils flared, and it looked like she was about to say something Maranova probably wouldn't like until her boyfriend put his hand on her shoulder. She bit back whatever it was with an expression of distaste, and then let it go when the big orange one with the red-striped head lumbered over.

"No, Jason," Harlan said. "I don't think that's a good idea."

Maranova wasn't sure what was more unnerving. Harlan's half of the conversation, or the big gennie reaching out a hand toward her head. That the brute was more than two meters taller than she was the deciding factor, and she took a step back.

"Harlan, start talking before I have to shoot...hell, someone already tried that, didn't they?"

Close-up, Maranova saw that what she had taken for tears in his clothing were actually hundreds of microslug punctures, but the orange skin underneath was unmarked. Somehow, the thought of a telepathic, four-eyed space monster being immune to the only weapon she had didn't make her feel any better.

"It's...it's hard to explain, ma'am."

"Simplify it. That's an order, Harlan."

Even though "Jason" had stopped advancing, Maranova took another step back. Not only did it put her out of his immediate reach, but now he wasn't blocking her view of the other gennies. The second Omega was standing up now, too, with Serene cradled in one of his huge arms like a toy. The girl still had one of Mira Harlan's expressions on her face, but Maranova no longer found it nostalgic or amusing.

"This isn't going to work, Serene. Think about what happened the last time you tried it. The commodore's a lot older than I am, and she doesn't have an active expression. This is a very, very bad idea."

"Harlan..."

Maranova drew the name out. She did not like the direction in which things were heading. Harlan was standing in front of her now, arms held up as if to fend off the advancing monsters. Then the sharp-featured gennie who'd been in the biobed earlier appeared beside her out of nowhere, with a long, jagged fragment of ceroplastic in her hand.

Katra, that's her name. She's a Gamma, one of their soldiers.

"Do not make me kill you, Jason. I will not let Mira be hurt again."

When the girl spoke, Maranova felt very old indeed. Although the gennie's voice was soft, when she spoke it was with the tones of a seasoned veteran.

The rest of the gennies weren't any more inclined to challenge her. Instead, they stood at the edges of a ragged square and tried very hard not to look at the troopers pouring into the room with their weapons drawn.

Harlan spread her arms in an attempt to capture every eye in the room. Maranova felt sunshine on her face, and swore she could taste the most delicious chocolate cake in the universe.

What the fuck just happened?

Maranova wasn't alone in her surprise; half the troopers were lowering their weapons, while the others switched their aim to Harlan. Mira's next words were right out of the Aloysius Martin playbook, and Ykaterina couldn't help but smile.

"Now just hold on, everybody. Let's not do anything we're going to regret later."

MIRA

*Oh, great. Twenty more brains to deal with, as if my head didn't
hurt enough already.*

Mira wanted to grab her induction pistol off her chest, but the
borrowed clothes she was wearing were remarkably short on
weaponry. Things were going straight to Hell, again, and this time she
couldn't even shoot back.

Mira kept transmitting her happy memories, wincing at the pain of
influencing so many people at once while at the same time forming it
into thick blocks for her wall.

≈I could use a little help here, fellas.≈

She could tell Jason was willing, but he and O-6913 were both
firmly in Serene's grasp and ready to go digging in Commodore Maranova's brain for Chimera's location. Part of her wanted to let them try,
just to see if the old lady could shrug off their attempts and give them
a mental kick in the ass. But the memory of how helpless she'd been to
resist Serene's assault, even with the Gamma memories to assist, told
her otherwise. Her next words had to be the right ones, and there
wasn't a lot of time to figure them out.

"Seriously, no one's going to do anything but Calm. The Heck.
Down. This is just a misunderstanding, isn't it Serene?"

The Alpha's face was a stone mask, and the image of her standing on O-6913's open palm with one hand on his shoulder was one Mira would never forget. Especially when Serene decided to ratchet up the tension in the room another notch. If the child was concerned by armed and armored troopers, she gave no outward sign of it.

"No, it's not. The humans have stolen from us, and as Jantine says we must have our people back. You may think you're still one of them, but you're not. Don't resist us, Mira. You won't like what happens."

Katra tightened her grip on her improvised weapon, and a few drops of blood seeped through her clenched fingers. Mira didn't think the splintered piece of Mordecai's cane would puncture Jason's chest, but there was no doubt in Katra's mind as to the outcome of the encounter.

She's already planning her second attack, and wondering if she can get to Serene in time before Jantine shoots her.

Mira hadn't seen the Beta draw her weapon, and she had even less idea where she'd been hiding it. Her Institute clothing was pocketless, and even Janbi was surprised at the sudden appearance of a Colonial hand weapon in her fist.

≈Serene, don't do this. Let me talk to them.≈

≈No. Better that we die here than do nothing while the sleepers suffer. She knows where they are, or at least how to find out.≈

"I can't say I think much of your new friends, Harlan. Although your girl Katra is growing on me. What are you going to do missy? Stab him in the eye?"

Jason's face was neutral, but he felt genuine surprise at the thought that Katra might actually hurt him. The commodore's voice was equal parts laughter and approbation.

"No, too much bone behind an eye," Katra said. "One of the ears is better—easier path to the brainstem. Plus, he'll stay in place as a shield while I take your weapon."

Jason's tiny mouth fell open in shocked realization of her true intentions. Mira's headache doubled in strength as the Omega stopped his efforts to screen her in favor of defending himself against the Gamma's imminent attack.

"Katra, you're not helping."

"She asked nicely. Just trying to be polite."

The thought of Katra developing a sense of humor was frightening, almost more so than how efficiently she'd planned to murder Jason with a piece of Mordecai Harrison's cane. The doctor was sitting on a cylindrical container, staring at the rest of it on the floor and wondering when and how she'd broken it.

Mira needed to regain control of the situation, and fast. Unfortunately, her abilities were already pushed to the maximum; anything else she tried would mean even more pain, and the very real possibility that she might lose parts of herself forever.

"Please, everyone, stand down. We don't have time for these games. No one wants this to escalate, and there's still a way for us to work together."

She knew Artemus was moving by the way the troopers shifted their attentions. Despite his size, the Delta was very graceful, and he moved between Jason and O-6913 fast enough to catch even Jantine by surprise. At the end of his maneuver, the Beta's weapon was planted squarely in the Delta's back and all four of Artemus's hands were empty and held up in surrender. Jantine snarled at him, but it was Janbi who ended up being the voice of reason.

"You're all fools. Blind, stupid fools, for convincing yourselves that your small piece of the truth is the right choice for everyone. Doctor Harrison only has one eye, and he sees more than any of you. And I've had just about enough of this nonsense."

Mira's eyes darted around the room, trying to gauge people's reactions to Janbi's words. She couldn't help but remember how close Captain Martin had come to talking down the troopers in the launch bay, and how quickly it had all gone to pieces when that pair of doomed techs decided to be heroes.

Janbi was walking very slowly over to Commodore Maranova with a pleasant expression on his face. Jantine was staring daggers at his back, and Mira wondered what this latest disagreement would do to their relationship.

Now that they're lovers in fact, she probably won't shoot him. Probably. But I've seen a face like the one she's wearing before, and I definitely don't want to be within a kilometer of those two when they have this out later.

Jantine lowered her weapon, crouching to place it at her feet. Even now, she was unwilling to let one of the mods' superior weapons out of her sight. Her emotions were locked behind her mental barriers, but she did smile as she stood back up. Artemus turned his head to look at her, stretching his lower left hand behind him and resting it on her shoulder. Jantine put her own left hand on top of it, and returned to watching Janbi.

"Hello, Ykaterina. I'm Janbi. I'm the smart one around here."

Maranova responded with a chortle.

"Well, you've got a pair of balls on you, don't you boy? Damned if you aren't the cutest thing I've ever seen. If you were about ten years older, I expect Harlan here would snap you right up."

Janbi's face became thoughtful, and Mira voiced yet another refusal.

"Please, ma'am, don't encourage him. He's bad enough as it is."

"Actually, Jantine said she liked ..."

"JANBI!"

Despite all the weapons in the room, the threats voiced by Katra and Serene, and the larger questions about their shared future yet to be addressed, the sight of Jantine blushing was something Mira could never have predicted. But the Beta was definitely embarrassed, a more genuine emotion than Mira thought she was capable of expressing at a time like this, especially considering what happened between the two of them up on the surface.

What is it about that boy that makes it so hard to stay mad at him?

Janbi just shrugged.

"The facts are plain enough," he said. "Fleet Captain Horace Kołodziejski has gained control of three hundred of our people and taken them to someplace called Chimera. While we do not know its exact location, you might. Serene and the Omegas think we should scoop the information out of your brain, but given what happened the last time they tried something like this I don't have much confidence in their plan."

Mira felt Jason's deep shame, and a lesser version of the same sentiment from O-6913. Serene was as guilt-free as ever, but Janbi's reminder was enough to shake the Omegas free of her sway.

At least for now. How does he always know the right thing to say?

"I'm not sure I'm keeping up with what you're saying, boy, but you've all got a lot to answer for."

"Oh, yes, we certainly do. But Jantine is correct; if your officer harms even one of the sleepers, we will kill him. And if his support in your fleet goes beyond the ships I saw a few days ago, he will soon force a war with our Colonies and none of this will matter."

Janbi's message wasn't lost on Maranova, and the commodore set her mouth in a frown. For the thousandth time since he flew off to his death to protect them, Mira wished Captain Martin was still here to advise her. But their shared mentor was, and if anyone could avoid a war, it was her.

"All right, then. Put your weapons down, boys and girls. Janbi here's about to tell us what happens next."

Janbi either took Maranova's mockery in stride or missed it entirely. His brain was working faster than Mira could keep up with, and she only caught small glimpses of his thoughts.

They were enough.

"Yes, I am," he said. "Commodore Maranova, I would like to request the use of your personal shuttle, several suits of that powered armor Mira likes to wear, some of your slug weapons, and a uniform that would fit Carlton. Nothing too flashy, just something he can wear without saluting everybody he meets. I'm assuming you still salute in your fleet; I never see Mira do it, but she hasn't had many chances in the last few days."

"Me? Why do I need a uniform?"

Carlton's confusion was echoed on Jantine's and Katra's faces. Serene was...pouting? Her expression indicated childish pique, and Mira wondered how many times she'd used it herself as a child.

"Because I can't go to your moon," Janbi said. "Doctor Harrison says my stump won't heal properly in microgravity."

Mira was glad to see that both the troopers and Katra were

lowering their weapons. The difference between them was that even without her encounter suit, Katra could still kill half a dozen of them before they realized she was upon them.

Even untrained, Commodore Maranova's mental barriers were on par with Mordecai Harrison's, possibly even with Jantine's. But she had much less control over her face than either of the others, and when Janbi mentioned the Moon, Mira know Maranova was holding something back.

Jantine needed more though, and she stepped in front of Artemus to get a better look at Janbi when she spoke.

"I thought you couldn't pinpoint the source of the coded transmissions?"

"I can't. Not without a few more verified sources. But there are only a few locations from which Captain Martin could have flown his shuttle unaided, and his navigational data shows several journeys in near-Earth orbit. If it was a satellite facility, he wouldn't have needed as many supplies as he had on board the shuttle, so Chimera has to be on Luna. However, I still need the exact location, which Commodore Maranova can supply."

"Anyone ever tell you you're an annoying little prick when you're right?" Maranova's grumble wasn't meant to carry, but she didn't have much experience dealing with a Beta's enhanced senses.

"Not in so many words, but yes. All the time, actually. So, Commodore, what's *your* play? Will you help us, or does everybody die badly?"

The commodore turned to Mira, who didn't need empathic senses to understand she wanted to know if Janbi could be trusted. It was a question she'd been asking herself ever since she'd first met the mods, and probably would for some time to come.

Mira nodded, which was enough for the older officer. Maranova turned back to Janbi. The move spoke volumes about her political savvy, and Mira thought that with enough time someone like the commodore was the perfect person to teach Serene some much needed self-restraint.

Assuming any of us are alive after today.

"All right, boy, you win. If you have Aloysius Martin's files, you'll probably figure it out soon enough anyway. But you have to understand that I didn't know about your missing people until just now. I definitely would have tried to stop Horace if I had."

Janbi moved forward and took the cane fragment from Katra's hand, ignoring the blood on her palm. Mira couldn't see any cuts in her skin, so the Gamma's incredible recuperative powers must have returned to full strength.

Janbi extended the piece of cane to Maranova butt first, but he didn't let go when she grabbed the other end.

"But you did know about L-A-197, didn't you? Where was your contrition when your people were experimenting on Serene's partner?"

Janbi squeezed the same splintered section that had cut Katra's palm, driving hard shards of ceroplastic into his skin. The pain was enough to overwhelm whatever medication he'd been taking, and Mira felt with him not just this new wound, but the constant ache of his stump. How he was able to keep it from showing on his face was a mystery, but Mira realized that he'd rather feel pain right now than act on his anger.

Then she felt her own rage return, along with another stolen memory. She was finally angry at Serene and O-6913 for ripping away parts of her life when they stole her implanted Gamma memories, but also at Trooper Jensen and Captain Kołodziejski and Aloysius Martin for entangling her in this mess. She was angry at her father for taking his own life and leaving her to take care of her brothers by herself.

But mostly, she was angry with Tommy for how he'd hurt her when they parted for the last time, and how he'd taken his rage out on Debbi when Mira wasn't around.

Maranova must have seen some of the struggle in Janbi's eyes, because she stepped forward until the end of the cane was pressed against her chest. "I swear to you, to all of you, that we had no idea what kinds of experiments Horace was doing. A little over five years ago, an expedition commanded by Vice-Admiral James Worthy touched down on a frozen world about 700 light years from here. He returned home with wreckage from a destroyed ship, including the two sleeper units we've been arguing about ever since. When Aloysius told me the other Alpha was dead, I wanted to kill Captain Kołodziejski, then myself for not stopping him."

Maranova looked directly at Serene, as if seeking the child's forgiveness for her subordinate's actions.

"Mordecai over there can tell you I've spent the last few days trying to keep the SDF from tearing itself apart over how to interpret Jantine's transmission. There is definitely a faction calling for total war against the Outer Colonies, and Kołodziejski is its leading advocate."

Now that she could distinguish the deep currents of rage swirling around in the Alpha's complex emotions, Mira knew the commodore would be waiting until long after the sun died before she'd get any absolution from Serene.

"But if this got out, if it gets *out*..." Maranova raised her voice, ensuring that the armored troopers could also hear her, "preventing that conflict might be impossible. Time and distance have been keeping you safe so far, but if Kołodziejski's scientists really have weaponized the T-virus, I want it destroyed as much as you do. Earth can't afford another Transgenic War. Not after how long it's taken to forgive ourselves for the last one."

The room fell uncomfortably silent, until Katra stepped up and took the cane fragment away. She twisted her hands, and the cero-plastic shattered into dozens of long splinters.

Mira regained enough composure to form the greater part of her rage into another row of stones for her wall, then buried the rest of it in her gut for later.

"Janbi, what's your plan? From what I remember of Captain Kołodziejski, he's not a very patient person."

"You've got that right, Harlan. So how about it, boy? What do you have in mind?"

Janbi took a moment and looked around the room. To Mira's surprise, all of the mods were waiting to hear what he had to say, and more.

≈*Are you sure about this, Serene? He's not that much older than you are.*≈

The Alpha's answering thought came with a wave of comfort, and a healthy dose of laughter.

≈*As you're so fond of telling us, we're on your planet now, Mira. We should pick our leaders the human way from now on. And despite his arrogance, he is the best.*≈

Janbi stood up a bit taller, and Mira smiled. Serene must have shared their conversation with him, because the devilish smile Mira had been trying to forget was back with a vengeance.

"So here's what we have to do..."

CALLAWAY

1800 SHIPTIME, SHUTTLE **V-12**

"Talk to me, Alonso. What's going on out there?" Marcus hugged himself against the cold on the shuttle's flight deck, but in truth his vac suit was doing most of the work of keeping him alive. Everything below his sealed neck collar was warm and toasty, but his face and ears were beginning to feel the effects of the shuttle's slow, inevitable death.

I wonder if the party's still going back in the Hull. Astrid definitely had the right idea there, I just wish I'd talked her into giving us a couple bottles for the ride.

Marcus' helmet was floating just within reach over the pilot's control panel, but instead of putting it on to dispel the chill, he tapped it to induce a tiny bit of spin. From his vantage point strapped into the pilot's seat, it was the most activity the flight deck had seen in some time, with tiny, reflected stars twinkling in its faceplate with every revolution.

At least something around here should do a little work. With our engines and thrusters encased in that weird space rock, I'm about as useful as a burned-out diode aboard this floating coffin.

When the shuttle's engines lost power just over a kilometer from their target, Marcus was ready to give up on the gennie hyperdrive and start chipping away black rocks with his hands. But Alonso had another miracle stashed up his sleeve, and after a bit of jury-rigging and a lot of swearing, he'd taken both their hardsuits on the coolest, and most dangerous spacewalk ever.

Over a kilometer through naked space, with no tether, and no way back if you can't get a piece of alien tech with no apparent power source operational.

They're already reserving a place in history for you, Alonso. Assuming you can get us back home in any kind of shape to tell your story.

Alonso had managed to cobble a transmitter together with a portable generator, and tethered his creation to a low-power, external antenna, a fragile construction that Marcus was sure was going to explode every time he breathed.

Thanks to whatever the black rock was doing to their power, apart from the shielded transmitter nothing else electronic on the shuttle was working at the moment—including life support. Marcus had been slowly bleeding oxygen out of a bottle since Alonso left, but without the shuttle's systems to process it—and especially without any scrubbers to sequester his carbon-dioxide-laden breaths—the resulting atmosphere on the flight deck was dry, acrid, and getting thinner all the time.

Plus, the batteries on the emergency light Alonso planted on the ceiling aren't going to last forever, so I could use some good news any time now.

"Is there ever anything you *don't* want to talk about, sir?" Ramirez's EVA was just over ten minutes in, and Marcus had asked some variation of this question several times since he'd lost visual on the young sub-lieutenant.

"I'm pretty sure this topic is the most important one in the universe to me right now. So how about it: can you see anything yet?" Marcus reached up and stopped the helmet's spin, then set it rotating in the other direction.

"I think so. I'm still making three meters a second, and there's definitely something shiny up ahead. I'll know more in about a minute." Marcus had lost Alonso's suit telemetry when he had to maneuver around some more space rocks, so he didn't know if Alonso was actually calm, or really good at hiding his fear.

From the vid I've seen of you defending yourself on the command deck, I'm fairly sure it's the latter. But no one your age should have to do this kind of stuff. I guess Mira really hit the jackpot when she recruited you out of the Academy.

"Just keep talking, Alonso. I don't really care what it's about, but keep me from going crazy back here, while you're risking your life in my stead." Marcus definitely knew that *he* was scared, and was desperate to borrow a little of Alonso's calm.

Ramirez was silent for a few more seconds, during which Marcus extended Alonso's transit vector a little farther on his clipboard. Assuming Alonso could reach the piece of gennie tech, the recyclers in his suit would keep him alive for several days after Marcus froze to death, with Marcus's suit and all the O2 bottles he could spare stuffed inside to buy him a few more.

Three-hundred, eighty-seven meters to go.

"Any forbidden topics, sir?"

"None, Mr. Ramirez. Although I think you and I are past ranks now, wouldn't you say?"

Considering that just over a shipday ago, I pulled an induction pistol on you and your Martian girlfriend while you were trying to talk me into this suicide mission, instead of the one we'd originally planned, I'm certainly willing to call you my friend.

Hell, you're probably the last person I'll ever talk to, and you're sure as shit going to be recording my last words in a few hours if you can't find a way to get us home.

"Okay, sir. Do you prefer Marcus, Mark, or Cal? I'm always Alonso, though my mother sometimes calls me Stefano, after her brother."

"Marcus is fine. Is it my turn to ask a question, or was that just a warm-up?" Marcus smiled, though there was no one around to see it."

"Still my turn, s—Marcus. How long have you been fucking Commander Harlan?"

Shit. This escalated fast.

"Well, technically, it was just the one time, none of your fucking business, and two days. And since you totally just went there, what's Astrid like in the sack?"

Alonso was silent for almost five seconds, and Marcus imagined him blushing inside his hardsuit.

"I…um…I don't rely know how to answer that, sir. It…ah…"

"Holy shit. Are you telling me you're still a virgin? After that kiss?" Marcus tried not to laugh, but the combination of surprise, lack of sleep, and serious oxygen depletion had turned off his filters a few thousand kilometers back.

Alonso was slow in replying, but when he did, it was without the bravado he'd been projecting since he left the shuttle.

"Not *technically*, sir. Not any more. I just have nothing to compare it to. Her too, that is."

Now it was Marcus' turn to be silent. He'd assumed after Alonso's opening salvo that this was going to be locker room talk, but now he had to put on his big brother voice and keep his friend from overanalyzing the coolest thing ever to happen to him.

So far, anyway. And it's just his dumb luck that all my brothers are older than I am…

"I'm sorry, Alonso. I didn't mean to make you uncomfortable. She's a good woman, a good officer, and I'm happy for the both of you. And as for comparisons, just think about how she made you feel when you were…together. That's all that really matters."

Marcus fiddled with a switch on the non-responsive control panel during the long silence that followed, praying some beep or click would distract both men from wherever it was their conversation had strayed. Nothing continued to happen, and it was Marcus who spoke first.

"Hey, are we cool, man?"

When Alonso answered, his voice was lighter than before.

"Yeah, we're cool. I was just…thinking." Marcus didn't need to ask him about what—he'd spent plenty of time thinking about Mira since he woke up in her quarters after everything aboard *Valiant* had gone to hell.

Almost makes the rest of this shitshow worth it. Almost.

"Well, it's your turn. Might want to pick a different topic this time.' Marcus smiled, and Mira's face filled his mind's eye. Everything about it was damn near perfect, and even if he hadn't been ordered to vet her for Captain Martin, he probably would have sought her out on his own.

The universe is a funny place, sometimes.

"Why did you join up, Marcus?"

The practiced lie was off his tongue before he could even think about it.

"I was tired of shoveling elephant shit." Marcus winced at the mild deception he'd been using to deflect this exact question for the last fifteen years, as the truth of the matter was still a somewhat sore subject for him. But Alonso had bared his soul just moments before, and Marcus owed him at least some version of the truth.

"I should explain. My family resettled about a hundred years ago, to a nature preserve in Kenya. My great, great-something grandfather used to manage it, and we were one of the last families dragged off the planet back in the day. So even though my father had never seen a real animal in his life, he threw himself into the role, and our family has been there ever since.

"Pretty much as soon as I could, I tested for the Academy, and got myself off the planet. It's not that I don't respect the work that my brothers are doing, it's just not for me. I've always pictured my self out here," he said, gesturing at the stars, though Alonso had a much better view, "doing something that mattered."

Plus, there was a girl, and a guy, and no real room for me in the equation.

"How about you?"

"More or less the same, I guess. Tending soya on Oaxaca Station was fine while I was growing up, but I never pictured myself doing it forever. I wanted to see the worlds, and the Fleet offered me a chance to do just that. When Lt. Commander Harlan recruited me six months ago, I thought I'd be touring the solar system, and visiting exotic ports of call.

"Instead, I got really, really good at cleaning and fixing things. It seemed like a good idea, at the time."

Both men laughed, though for Marcus it was a spectacularly bad idea. The cold, sharp breaths he was taking made it feel like he was being stabbed in the lungs with knives of ice, and he quickly clapped a hand over his mouth to stop himself from coughing. When his glove came away bloody, he stared at his palm for a while. A few dark globes separated from it and rose up toward his spinning helmet, and several more bubbled around his nostrils.

Well, shit. I do not need this right now.

Marcus had prepared himself for a lot of things before they launched from the Hull, and although freezing to death in the literal middle of nowhere was way down on the list, it was way above bleeding to death from excessive coughing.

Sadly, freezing is the best possible outcome on that particular threat chart. Should have updated my clotting factor before we left.

Not wanting to alarm Alonso, Marcus unhooked himself from the pilot's harness as quietly as he could and floated over to the medkit affixed to the wall, selected an injector, then rummaged through the kit's inventory of doses before finally admitting defeat. There weren't any factor concentrates in the kit, and even if there were, his system was likely too far compromised for one to do any good.

Looks like the docs were right. I should have joined the other pilots in Main Medical and waited this one out. A respiratory bleed in microgravity is just about the worst possible outcome for little-old-me right now, short of a surprise heart attack or a stroke.

Maybe the shuttle will blow up instead, saving the universe the effort.

"Commander, I think I can see something ahead. It's...larger than I thought, but I can't really make out any details from here. I'm going to risk a braking burn, hopefully I can find some kind of maintenance port on approach. And it's your turn for a truth, or at least an opinion. Why do you think the gennies came back?"

Marcus packed his nose with gauze as he racked his brain for an answer, hoping he wasn't doing even more damage to his mucous membranes than the dry, thin air of the shuttle had already dealt. He tasted copper in the back of his throat, but didn't feel any pressure building up inside his head, which was, in his very non-doctor opinion, a good sign.

In the past few days, Marcus had not only suffered numerous cuts, abrasions, and contusions, but he and Alonso had met and exceeded their lifetime radiation exposures many times over during spacewalks and short hops to scavenge supplies to keep *Valiant*'s crew alive

Combined with his condition, and the general lack of rescuers in the immediate vicinity of nowhere, Marcus adjusted his personal survival calculations sharply downward, while at the same time adding more time to Alonso's chances for a return trip. He shook his head, then turned to look at his remaining supply of oxygen bottles.

Not enough, not enough by far. But maybe I don't need so much air as I used to.

And as to Alonso's question, the gennies strapped themselves to a rock and jumped into hyperspace for reasons known only to themselves. Their motives since—other than survival—were unknowable, and given what I saw of their handiwork aboard Valiant, I really don't think they're here for the good of all mankind.

"I don't know, Alonso. Hopefully that big piece of machinery you're falling towards will have some answers for us. Maybe they're scouting us for something. Or they simply could be terrorists, though as far as I know they've presented us with no demands. I just don't—"

The transmitter sparked and squealed, and a small cloud of smoke bloomed around the pickup. Marcus instinctively tried to blow it away, but remembered too late what a bad idea that was with an electrical fire—especially aboard a spaceship.

The transmitter burst into flame, consuming itself—and all the nearby oxygen—in a glowing cloud of smoke. Marcus tried to smother it with his hands, but Alonso's next words set off another series of sparks that spread the blaze even further.

"Commander, I didn't catch that last part. Can you repeat?"

Marcus kept slapping at the tiny sparks, but only succeeded in fanning the flames. The fabric of his vacsuit gloves was growing uncomfortably hot, adding yet another complication to this new disaster.

Suddenly realizing there was an even worse outcome to the unexpected fire, Marcus gave up on saving the transmitter and focused instead on the generator attached to it. As he fumbled for the power cable, one more garbled transmission from Alonso sealed its—and Marcus's—fates.

"I'm coming up…the unit now. It's…utiful, sir. Some mar…lous engin…this thing. I wish I could…hold on…inute…the…Wow…"

Marcus yanked out the cable, then kicked the generator away with enough force to move him back him against the control panel. He slammed into it, hard, but still had enough presence of mind to grab first for his helmet, then a catch handle set into the panel itself.

Fumbling with just one free hand, Marcus managed to jam the helmet onto his head and seated it against his collar, wincing at the spreading pain from his abused ears. Cool, clean—and most importantly—moist air filled the helmet, and Marcus reflexively wiped away the thin film of condensation on its faceplate, only to frown a moment later at the steaks of blood and grime he left behind.

Stupid, stupid, stupid! And I should have cleared my nose before I put it on!

Taking a deep, painful breath, Marcus kept his grip on the panel and searched underneath it for one of the chemical extinguishers he'd logged during preflight. His fingers found the red, palm-sized sphere, grabbed it, then slammed it into the transmitter.

The sphere erupted on impact, filling the flight deck with a thick cloud of white powder and temporarily blinding him. Not wanting to take any chances, Marcus swung over to the copilot's station, fumbling for a few seconds until he found another sphere, and threw it as hard as he could at the deck, releasing even more flame-retardant powder into the air.

With nowhere to go, the powder was as effective a barrier to light as a bulkhead, and plunged the compartment into near-complete darkness as it expanded. Only the dim glow of the emergency light overhead and his desperate grip on the catch handle gave him any way to orient himself, and he took several more gasping breaths as he waited for his nerves to settle.

Okay, Marcus. That sucked. But let's look on the bright side here: you're alive, and more importantly, not on fire. Now get your head together, figure out how much trouble you're in, and get to work fixing it.

Marcus braced himself against the panel, and waved his free hand in the air. Nothing really changed, which meant there wasn't enough air left to either disperse the cloud, or move it away from the windows. And without the scrubbers…

Wait a minute, the windows! There may not be much air left in here, but that's a hell of a lot more than what's outside. I just need to give it a little push, that's all.

Marcus spent a few tense minutes fumbling around in the murky cloud, praying that his universe had rewarded his quick actions by actually putting out the fire. He found and secured both the generator and his remaining O2 bottles, then found his way back to the control panel.

Port or Starboard. Port, or Starboard?

Alonso's left handed, let's go with Port. As good a way to commit suicide as any other direction.

Marcus could have unsealed the flight deck aft and let the cloud out that way, but even though the rest of the shuttle had no atmosphere, it wasn't open to space. And Marcus would still have to clear and secure every hatch and corridor along the way in ever-increasing darkness, slowly bleeding body heat as he went. He needed to disperse the powder quickly, and all at once, which meant blowing the port escape hatch.

At least, I think that's what's going to happen. This could be the universe's way of telling me I've finally reached the end of the line.

Guess I'll never know until I try.

Marcus activated his boots, and clomped his way over to the side of the compartment, keeping one hand on one of the panel's catch handles the whole way. When his free hand encountered solid resistance, he slid it back and forth until he found a catch ring.

Okay. Time for step two of my not-so-brilliant plan.

It took Marcus less than a second to find the emergency release, but even though he'd resigned himself to this course of action, he took a few moments to try and think of a less explosive alternative.

Nope. I've got nothing. And when I do this, there's really no going back. Either I'm fucked inside the shuttle, or I'm really fucked outside. So really, what do I have to lose?

There's one thing I do know for sure, though. Right about now, I'm wishing I'd never heard of Aloysius Martin and his crazy crusade.

Marcus walked himself up the wall and planted his boots on the compartment's ceiling, reasoning that fewer things could come loose from that angle during the decompression. He ran through the emergency checklist in his head, clenching and unclenching his hands as he mentally gripped the first, second, and third emergency release handles in order, then slapping his hand on the big red button next to the catch ring and triggering the explosive hatch to vent what was left of the shuttle's atmosphere into space.

Maybe I don't have to do this. Maybe Alonso is cycling back I through the aft airlock, with a pack full of gennie super toys that will make all this worrying moot.

Yeah, and maybe I'm the king of…Fuck it.

Marcus blew the hatch in record time, desperately clinging to the catch ring as his plan executed perfectly. Four seconds later, the flight deck was clear and spotless, with only a scorch pattern on the deck to remind him of the ruined transmitter. He did a quick visual survey to make sure the generator and bottles had stayed inside, then edged his head outside the shuttle.

A white cloud was slowly floating away into space, a tiny new nebula orbiting around a few pieces of shining metal and ceroplast. The escaping atmosphere had imparted a slight spin to the shuttle, and Marcus dropped his gaze to the hull to avoid vertigo.

This would be the longest fall ever, so I think a little caution is warranted. But since it's such a lovely day outside, I think I'll go for a little walk. There's a few more things I'd like to see before I die.

Marcus swung himself up throughout the hatch, and locked his boots onto the shuttle's hull. Going out like this with no tether, no comms, and no backup was the most insane thing he'd ever done, and considering the catalog of impossible things he'd accomplished in the last few days, that was really saying something. But Marcus wasn't angling for a better view—he had a specific destination in mind, one that was literally impossible to see any other way.

Clomping his way aft, Marcus almost didn't see the thick layer of black rock encrusted around the rear of the shuttle until he was almost upon it. Unlike the huge slug that had killed *Valiant*, it looked like a landslide had partially buried the shuttle, a shallow layer of irregularly shaped rocks joined together by a fine layer of impossibly black silt.

It's like the stuff is literally drinking light, in defiance of everything we know about physics, geology, and every other universe-defining science I learned at the Academy. Whatever crazy stuff the gennies are into, this is by far the most terrifying thing they've come up with yet.

If this ever gets down to Earth, is there any way we can stop it?

Marcus was bending down to poke at a small piece of rock stuck to the hull a few meters away from the rest of it when the entire shuttle was illuminated in a flash of light. Marcus turned his head as far to the right as he could, and saw a new star shining brightly off the shuttle's nose. It took him a few seconds to realize how close it really was, and a few more to make the connection.

Great Mother above, Alonso. What have you done?

To make the moment even more surreal, Marcus saw movement at the other edge of his vision, and turned back to watch the piece of rock next to his hand float up off the hull, spin in place, then rise up to join other pieces as they separated from the shuttle on a long, sinuous arm, stretching towards the new point of light a kilometer or so away.

But...that's not...

Marcus stood up, watching the slow stream of rock moving through space with no apparent power source, twisting itself into a series of spiral turns, then again into concentric rings of roughly equal size.

It's...I...

What happened next was equally confusing, as the shuttle's hull thrummed to life beneath his feet. Marcus's eyes went wide as one set of running lights after another turned on around the hull, progressing from tail to stern in the most beautiful technological display he'd ever seen.

Then the grav drive kicked in, and it was all he could do to hang on tight as the shuttle began accelerating again for the first time in many hours.

I hope you've got another miracle handy, Alonso, because I sure as shit need one...

DEMARCO

2110 SHIPTIME, **EFS** *CLARKE*

Any way I look at this thing, we're fucked.

Sam had listened to Mira Harlan's story three times now, once over security cameras while he tried to think of what to tell Andreison, once in person, and once from the perspective of Janbi, the leader of the gennie crew that took down *Valiant* with their space rock. Every time he read over his notes, they seemed more and more fantastical, and every time he thought about what they were about to do, he became less convinced of his own worth in the grand scheme of things.

For a force that small—comprised of children and teenagers—to have come so far and achieved so much, Sam had to wonder if there was any chance of the Earth winning a third Transgenic War.

Or would it be a fourth? Old Earth records are a bit spotty, especially the period after the Exile.

Either way, Kołodziejski couldn't be allowed to start another one, and Janbi's plan to assault Horace Kołodziejski's hidden base was almost too simple to fail. A strike team comprised of Harlan and two of the gennie combat specialists—including Janbi's girlfriend Jantine—

would infiltrate Echo Base on a false flag courier run, along with their medic and the Alpha child Aloysius Martin had given his life to protect.

Once there, the plan was to overcome any resistance, retrieve any gennie prisoners, then signal *Clarke* for extraction—not for help—when they were done.

Without the commodore's assurance that she was immune to their mind powers, Sam would never have believed she wasn't coerced into following the gennie kid's lead. But Maranova signed off on everything he'd asked for—her private shuttle, weapons, a secure section of the Fleet's flagship in which to train, and for the *Clarke* to buy time to complete their mission, if necessary.

That kid bothers me even more than what's happened to Harlan, but I don't have to like my orders; I just have to follow them.

And now that I'm officially a traitor, it falls on me to make some even worse decisions to protect the human race.

Sam had made all the necessary arrangements but one, and she was waiting outside his office. He pinched the bridge of his nose to forestall the headache he knew was coming, but he'd already kept Andreison waiting for the better part of an hour.

Unsupervised, at that. More than enough time for her to cause all manner of problems I'm not prepared to deal with.

Making sure his command baton was secured and out of reach, he signaled his aide to let her in.

If Andreison had slept at all since they'd left Earth, her face didn't show it. Since the moment they'd met, she always appeared on the brink of collapse, and other than her new duty uniform nothing had changed. She'd spent nearly all her time aboard doing deep searches on *Clarke*'s primary core, analyzing and re-analyzing every bit of data they'd collected on the *Valiant* incident, hoping to find some clue as to her wife's whereabouts.

And it's now my job to order her to stop, lest she somehow discovers Mira Harlan is a few decks below us right now, about to go off on a suicide mission.

"Have a seat, Lieutenant."

Andreison moved forward and sat across the desk from him, in nearly the same position as she'd taken during their initial meeting aboard L6 station. Her exhaustion hadn't changed her defiant nature any, and what he was about to do to her certainly wouldn't improve it.

"Is there a problem, sir?"

Is there ever!

"Not really, but I do have a concern. You've logged a lot of hours since you came aboard, and while I appreciate your efforts to familiarize yourself with both the ship and its crew, I worry that you are overextending yourself."

"I'm just making up for lost time, sir. I pulled the same shifts when I first got to *City of Lights*. And I've written a few letters to my wife that I'd like you to approve as soon as possible."

Sam really couldn't fault her diligence—he'd done similar crams when joining new crews—but since he couldn't state his intentions outright, he had to make it her idea to stand down her investigations, and fast.

As for forwarding on her letters, that's about the worst idea ever.

"Send them to Commander Salisbury, he handles redaction for me. But I'm more concerned with you right now. You're no use to us if you burn out, Marya. You're pushing too hard to prove yourself, and I need you at the top of your game."

"Sir, I'm… "

"Tired, and hurting, and trying to make sense of the impossible. I know, Marya. I've been there. And I'm going to tell you the same thing my first captain told me. Get some sleep, and get a lot of it. The ship will keep running for a while without you, and you'll need all your wits about you when you become my operations officer at the start of first shift."

Andreison gripped the sides of her chair, trying her best to push her way through the back of it.

Well look at that. I finally found something she's afraid of.

"I'm honored, sir, but I…"

"Have the finest tactical mind I've ever seen, and the will to make things happen. I don't need a pilot for a few days, and I've already got someone I trust heading up Comms division. I trust you, Marya, and I want you in the pit at 0600 shiptime. Do you trust me?

Andreison swallowed hard, and Sam could almost see the last of her resistance crumble. She'd been awake even longer than he had, and had lived through more shit than anyone her age deserved. If anyone needed a break, it was Marya, and Sam could see in her face that she believed it too.

"I do, sir. I don't think you're right, but I do trust you. I just...I don't want to let you down."

Sam stood up, prompting Andreison to do the same.

"I'll make you a promise, Lieutenant. You get at least five hours of sleep, and I'll do the same. And if we're both still crazy by then, we'll have an uneventful shift in the command center of a ship that goes nowhere and does nothing, and then we'll both take the rest of the day off. I'll even buy the first round in O-Club. Sound good to you?'

Andreison smiled, and put out her hand. Sam shook it, and smiled back.

"Sounds great, sir. And yes, I will run Ops for you. I just hope your pit crew can keep up."

This is going to go wrong in so many ways, but at least I'll be well rested when it does.

And when I finally have to tell her about Harlan, there'll be no way for Marya to stop her from saving us all...

ANNAHKO

Caroline stared down at the frail thing that had once been Horace Kołodziejski, with fear, love, and disgust warring inside her.

Horace was laid out on a metal biobed deep inside Echo Base, hooked up to more machines than Caroline could count doing God knows what to his emaciated body. Some were helping him to breathe, some were cycling the green sludge that was now serving as his blood, and there were at least two others monitoring the slow, steady beating of his heart.

She knew he hadn't been eating much the last few days, but to see him like this, stripped of all his armor, brought the point home more directly than anything else she'd learned about his condition.

You're really dying. Fleet Captain Kołodziejski, hero of the Mars Confederation, brought low not by some enemy or battle, but by your own pride.

And the worst part of it is, I'm the only person in the worlds who knows what you were truly trying to accomplish.

What a waste.

How did we get to this place, Horace? We're so far apart, I can't see any way back. Even if you wake up, even if you're cured of the Transgenic virus, it will never be like it was again.

Thinking of her former lover also brought thoughts of Daniel Tepes to mind, standing behind her and guarding her throughout her grief. They'd renewed their physical relationship on the night she cast Horace and his lies out of her heart, but ended it the next day when she learned how deeply he was enmeshed in Horace's web of lies.

She'd almost refused his offer to bring her to see Horace, but the pull she still felt to both men was undeniable.

And if this is going to be the last time I see either of them, I might as well make the most of it.

Caroline turned to look at Daniel, encased in his white suit of powered armor, standing ever-vigilant at the compartment's door. Outside his armor, he was everything she wanted in a man, except for the part where he wasn't Horace. Daniel's goal in life was to protect his family at all costs, while Horace wanted to save the human race by eliminating the Transgenic virus from the universe, along with everyone infected by it.

One lover proposes genocide, and the other one just wants to propose. But neither man has enough vision to see what it is that I need, just how I fit into their plans.

It's not enough. It will never be enough, and I've wasted too much time living in other people's dreams.

As soon as she knew the true scope of Horace's illness, Caroline set her retainer Kurt Currano to ferreting out all the secrets of Horace's secret weapons facility. The cadet had delivered his preliminary findings a few minutes before Daniel arrived at her quarters aboard *Indomitable*, but even Currano's four-page summary was enough to ruin Horace's reputation forever.

And then there was Daniel, with his sad eyes, perfect lips, and knowledge of exactly how to push all of Caroline's buttons. Even with her induction pistol planted in the middle of his faceplate, he hadn't wavered, still faithfully serving his stricken master to the end.

"We only have a few minutes," he'd said. "If you want to see him, it has to be now."

Caroline had thought a while about what it was she did want, until finally deciding it wasn't to see Daniel's brains splattered against a bulkhead.

"Fine," she'd said, turning her back on Tepes and changing from pajamas into her full uniform while he stood in the doorway, taking extra time to dress so he knew exactly what his choices had cost him.

She hadn't said another word to him since, simply following his lead through the darkened tunnels and corridors of Horace's secret research facility inside Earth's moon, then through a forest of gently humming suspension units containing the sleeping gennie test subjects Horace had chosen over a real future with her.

This is it. This is our moment, and you're not even here to hear me say the words.

"Goodbye, Horace." Leaning closer to the biobed so Daniel couldn't hear her next words, Caroline wrinkled her nose at the sour odor rising from Horace's body. "I hope you rot in Hell for your sins, tortured by the knowledge that I'm the one who has to pay for them. And even if I can find a way out of this war you've forced on us, I'll never forgive you. Never."

Caroline wanted to pound her fists on Horace's chest until he woke up, to kick over his table and destroy all his machines and scream her rage until her throat was raw and numb. But instead, she turned to Daniel, eyes cold and face neutral.

"I'm done here. Let's go."

"Carrie, I...I never meant to..."

"What's done is done, Mr. Tepes. You've made your choices, and I've made mine. And as long as you stand here, wearing his colors, there is no us. There is no Carrie, no Caroline, or any other woman answering to those names.

"I am Captain Annahko, commander of SDF *Indomitable*, and my responsibility belongs to my crew, my god, and my planet, in that order."

Caroline tensed her shoulders, ready for a fight she wasn't sure she wanted to win. Even with his faceplate blanked, she was certain

Daniel was going to try and apologize again, to profess his love and hopes and…

…and give me everything I asked him for, once upon a time. I want him by my side, but he'll never leave Horace's, even though he knows I can release him from his service forever. But I'm the captain of Indomitable *now, and since everyone else in the Home Fleet is either a traitor or following Horace's —or rather, Admiral Worthy's orders, I'm more alone than ever.*

"Is that clear, Mr. Tepes?

Daniel said nothing, but moved aside to let her pass. The quarantine field on the door buzzed against her skin as she left, but she didn't stop to examine the controls. She had to leave now, or she might lose her resolve and demand that Daniel abandon Horace and come with her.

And the worst part of it is, I still don't know which one of us he'll choose in the end.

Caroline wandered through the suspension units, wondering who the gennies inside were, what lives they'd lived before climbing inside and firing themselves out into the universe. Who they'd loved, who they feared, and who they wanted to be.

She imagined herself flying through space, skin buffered by solar winds and arms stretched wide to encompass galaxies as she passed.

She made it almost all the way to the elevator before she fell to her knees, tears flowing freely as her heart broke all over again…

20 JULY, 2640 OER

MARANOVA

"Talk to me, Samuel. What's going on out there?"

Ykaterina was worried. It wasn't as if she expected Harlan and her gennie friends to light off a solar flare as a signal, but from what she understood about the Omegas' capabilities, it wasn't completely out of the question.

A holo of Earth's moon hung in the air beside her desk, studded with tiny bits of information about its surface and settlements collected over six centuries of continuous human habitation. From the maglev lines connecting the three megacities, to the isolated mining operations that never seemed to stop producing, Luna was alive with activity.

And from where she was seated, Ykaterina could see the northwest quadrant lit up with everything she knew about Echo Base, either from her own infrequent visits or the information smuggled out by Aloysius Martin.

Samuel looked at the projection, then eased his way around to half-sit, half-lean on the edge of her desk. If he was any other officer, this casual stance would have earned him a sharp rebuke.

Samuel's got even more to lose than I have in this scenario, and besides, it looks like he hasn't slept in a week.

"Nothing yet, ma'am. We've got eyes on every square meter of Luna. If something twitches, we'll know about it before it stops shaking. But I'm more concerned about the rest of Home Fleet. We don't take *Clarke* out for a ride that often, and that fact alone is going to raise some eyebrows sooner or later."

If you'd just let us in on your plans, Allie, you'd probably still be alive. Instead, you tried to play superspy, and look where that got you.

But then again, who am I to talk?

In the fifteen hours since Janbi laid out his grand plan, Maranova and DeMarco had brought most of the senior officers in their chain of command not named Andreison into the loop. Captain Davis aboard SDF *Planck* and Captain Mallowalli aboard SDF *Gustav II Adolf* had had even less time to process the information, and as it stood, less than ten percent of Home Fleet was aware of Maranova's plans to depose one of her senior captains.

Lucky for us, they're the ones in charge of steering the ships and firing their missiles. When the time comes, they'll be ready.

If the time ever fucking comes.

It had been over three hours since the gennies launched in Maranova's private shuttle. Even with a conservative approach, Harlan and the gennies would have entered the Lunar control sphere an hour ago, and from experience, she know it didn't take long to get down into the tunnels.

Once you're down there under the regolith, your biggest problem isn't completing a secret mission, it's getting out unseen. Aloysius managed to do both, twice, and our girl Harlan's got more than enough gumption to pull off the same feat.

"How long do you figure?"

DeMarco stood up, and walked over to the projection. He stared at the same part Maranova had been studying for the last hour, as if his increased scrutiny could summon up information as to what was happening under the lunar surface.

"They have to have encountered some kind of resistance by now, even if the plan worked. And no plan ever works—you spent enough time drilling that into our heads at the academy that none of us are likely to forget it.

"But up here, inside the hull…it's anybody's guess, though my gut tells me it won't be long."

Unlike the romantic notions of spaceship design that resurfaced every few years, *Clarke* was built along solid lines for an older kind of war. Ykaterina's stateroom had no windows facing space, nor did the command and control center DeMarco had just come from. Both were located deep inside the ship, so that the chances of her surviving a prolonged missile engagement, or even an unexpected impact like the one that wiped out *Valiant*, were fairly high.

Not her specifically, of course. Whatever flag officer was in command at the time. The trade-off was that ship's protective design also made her dependent on relayed observations for all her information, which meant either marrying herself to a bank of holo projectors or letting her subordinates do the heavy lifting.

Both officers stared at the holo, entranced by the slowly rotating globe many times the apparent size of the real thing just 100,000 kilometers away. Maranova held up her hand, then made a fist, pulling the projection down in size until it fit in her palm.

DeMarco nodded from his perch on the desk, but said nothing. He'd already delivered all the relevant information he had, and neither of them was big on small talk.

"What do you make of them, Samuel? Can they do it?"

Though Ykaterina kept her eyes on the slowly turning moon, Samuel kept his on his commanding officer. He continued his silence for almost a minute, then spoke in a candid tone she rarely heard him use.

"When we went down to the Institute, I had no idea what to expect. My mind was still full of scenarios having to do with Councilor Harrison and those damned committee hearings.

"But when I saw the gennies in that storeroom and listened to their plans, and later when I talked to Jantine and Janbi to work out the logistics, I knew everything we've been arguing about over the last few days actually meant something, even if the worlds never found out about it.

"The gennies have come home not because they were forced out, or were lonely, but because they want to help us. And the fact that they were willing to wait another hundred years in hiding until we were ready to listen to what they had to offer makes me feel...small."

Ykaterina understood completely. She turned to look at Samuel, wanting to get the full experience of his testimony. His face seemed decades younger than when he came in the room, as if whatever worries were packed into the lines on his face had just floated away.

"But it wasn't just their plans that sold me. It's the way they approach life. They're all so...young, but in many ways they're more focused than I am. Than anyone born on Earth. Even in the face of certain death, they're willing to risk everything for one another, while all we can do is plot and maneuver until something finally shakes loose.

"I'm positive that Janbi kid will be running the entire system someday. And that Alpha girl, Serene. I can definitely see why Aloysius Martin was willing to risk his career to get her out of Horace's clutches. She's just so...happy. Like nothing happening around her matters, only somehow I knew she could hear and understand every word spoken in the room."

It was Ykaterina's turn to feel younger. The gennie child had affected her in much the same way, and it was clear that Mira Harlan had been a positive influence on her. Of all the gennies besides Janbi, Serene was the only one that really smiled.

Although that deadly little Katra came close a couple times. Probably figuring out the best way to disembowel us and make little lace angels with our spleens...

"If Serene asked me to swim down to the lunar surface and collect her, I'd probably do it. She's the real future of the human race, something untouched by all of our hate and shortsightedness. And those other gennie girls are downright terrifying. If there's a few hundred more like them down there, and if Serene gets even a minute to inspire them, Horace doesn't have a chance."

The thought of James Worthy's fair-haired boy in command of a secret base dedicated to eradicating every Serene in the universe was what finally forced Ykaterina to act. She'd greenlit the gennie's suicide mission, even though it meant sending young Andreison's wife along to die.

And maybe that's why I'm so nervous about all this. If the gennies die, well, they aren't supposed to be here anyway. But if Harlan dies, I don't think Samuel can move fast enough to keep me alive if Marya makes good on her promises.

Ykaterina waved a hand to cancel the projection, then got up and walked toward the pressure door separating the stateroom from the control center.

Samuel was a stride ahead of her, opening the panel with a wave of his command baton. The silence of her private space was replaced by the sounds of an active and efficient command center, full of life and energy and everything human beings should be.

And in maybe half a dozen other ships out there in the black, there are rooms just like this one waiting for an order to kill me.

So be it.

She was the Commodore again, the War Witch, undisputed champion of the spaceways. And it was time people were reminded why she was in charge.

"Captain DeMarco." Maranova's words were spoken loud enough for all the junior officers in the room to hear, whether they were on the same level as she was or down in the sensor pit.

"Ma'am."

"Get me a transponder fix on every one of my ships. I want to know what the Home Fleet is doing today, and why."

"Yes, ma'am."

The noise in the command center doubled as officers started sensor sweeps of every relay within a million kilometers, and a few even further out. As she stepped up to a virtual terminal floating above the safety rail, a much more detailed holo of the Earth-Luna system sprung into life.

Tiny red dots representing ships, satellites, and centuries-old junk no one had found use for yet filled the display. One of her first commands was floating out past the six million kilometer mark, slowly skeletonizing as crews dissected her for components necessary to keep *Clarke* operational.

But when the holo shifted to show the silhouettes of nine Redstone dreadnaughts and their associated tenders, each with a thin line connecting its battlegroup to this very room, all thoughts of the past faded away.

All right, kids. Show me what you've got.

Planck and *Gustav II Adolf* were keeping station halfway between Earth and Luna, ready to deal with any planetside threats. *Washington Carver* and *Bonaparte* were outbound towards Neptune at a good fraction of the speed of light, and even at maximum deceleration they couldn't make a return trip for at least ten hours. She'd elected to keep Captains Dubois and Peng in the dark about her plans, even though both were part of the undertaking.

But the biggest surprise was a speck of red far above the ecliptic. Even though Ykaterina knew *Valiant* was dead in space, her transponder was still returning a signal. Mira Harlan's report had provided enough details to get the long range sensors looking in the right place, and she'd been as surprised as anyone to see it still pinging.

And finally, there was Horace Kołodziejski and *Indomitable*. The ship had officially last been sighted en route to Saturn, and her course was labeled as "projected."

But you and I know differently, don't we, Horace? You're either up there above the ecliptic pretending to be Aloysius, or hiding somewhere behind the moon.

Only two of the ships on the plot were moving toward her, Anya Goro's *Nelson* and Freida Marcaine's *Merrimack*. She wasn't surprised to see their range to *Clarke* decreasing; if anything, she was wondering why they were still so far out. Both were in Worthy and Kołodziejski's camp, and Goro in particular was frequently vocal about the need to attack the Outer Colonies.

Three hundred years gone, and you're still blaming them for Rome, aren't you Anya? But it was us that unleashed the hunter-killers, not the gennies. All that hate's got you pointed in the wrong direction.

Maranova furrowed her brow, so intent on discovering the whereabouts of *City of Lights* that she almost forgot where she was.

I could have sworn there were nine signals, but now I see only eight. So where are you, Markus? And more importantly, whose side are you really on?

Determining which of the "false" signals was hiding her missing captain's intentions was so engrossing that she didn't notice Samuel standing at her side until he tapped her on the shoulder.

Eyes still narrowed, she turned to see all the lines in his face back in place and deeper than ever.

"What? What is it?"

"Missiles. Four vectors, three Geyser spreads each, standard dispersal."

The command center's vibrant cacophony settled down to a whispered rumbling, as all eyes turned to the two officers at the rail. Samuel pulled his command baton, and used it to highlight an area in front of *Nelson*.

Sure enough, there were thirty-six Geysers in flight, but Ykaterina shared Samuel's confusion. The rebel dreadnaughts were still over 300,000 kilometers away, and the powered envelope for the missiles was less than half that distance.

Ykaterina stood in front of the plot for long seconds. *Nelson* and *Merrimack* were too far out to do any real damage, so why had they fired? The pattern was too neat, too focused, and even if the Geysers were loaded up with some fancy second stage maneuvers, the spreads wouldn't do more than piss her off.

There's got to be something else happening. Something I'm not supposed to see.

"Samuel?"

"Yes, ma'am?"

"Turn on the lights. All of them. And tell the point defense crews to fire at will."

Samuel DeMarco was a good officer, and a better captain. He knew both how to follow orders, and the order of battle. The women who'd just fired on his ship were good captains too, they'd just backed the wrong side.

But their biggest mistake was forgetting who it was that trained them all.

Samuel gave the order, and an area a thousand kilometers around *Clarke* turned into a miniature star. Work lights, navigational beacons, targeting lasers, anything capable of generating an electromagnetic frequency blazed to life, and Ykaterina's suspicions proved true.

She didn't have visual confirmation, but as the newly revealed red blobs on the plot resolved into suspiciously spaceship-shaped objects heading her way, Maranova decided they looked a lot like missile tenders.

Clever girls.

Samuel waved his baton at the plot, and it updated to show three ships slowing their approach, wobbling as they fired braking thrusters to form a staggered line of attack. But the maneuvers were too late, as was the missile salvo fired from the one ship still coming at them full speed ahead. *Clarke*'s point defense cannons blew it apart, and were already cycling for their next shots before the sparkling red dots on the plot were clear. The remaining tenders were removed from the universe in short order, and Ykaterina felt a hard ball forming in the pit of her stomach.

"Find out who was commanding that attack for me, Samuel. I want to put a commendation in their file."

"It was Dianna Aluandre, ma'am. She was on my fight team at the academy. We used to…we used to practice that maneuver."

Ykaterina pulled her attention from the plot down into the pit, where Marya Andreison had her hands ready to fire another volley. Other than her newest recruit's matter-of-fact delivery, the command center was absolutely silent. Everyone present knew the stakes they were playing for, but there was no turning back now. They had just killed sixty men and women who either believed their orders were righteous, or just didn't care.

Either way, we're at war.

"Are we launching intercept vessels, ma'am?" Marya's voice was steady, but Ykaterina could see her hands shaking just outside the interface.

Ykaterina looked around the room, gauging the resolve of the officers who had pledged themselves to her cause. But for the luck of the draw, it could have been them on the tenders, or aboard *Nelson* or *Merrimack*. Instead, they were stuck with the War Witch, and about to kick off a conflict that could tear the system apart.

"No. Fire everything. Then, fire it again."

Samuel nodded, then swept his hand across a panel depicting *Clarke's* long-range weapons status. One hundred forty-eight green icons turned red, and he was already preparing a follow-up volley when she gave her next commands.

"Helm, I want to be in close lunar orbit before our Geysers are on final approach. And someone get me a priority channel. People deserve to know what I've gotten us into."

Ykaterina gripped the support rail, and imagined the ship turning as if she could pull it in the right direction. This deep inside the hull, she couldn't feel the missiles launch or see the flashes as their propulsion systems came online. But the cloud of red dots racing across space represented enough destructive power to sink Australia into the Pacific Ocean, and it was aimed at a pair of the finest officers she'd ever worked with. She needed to feel something before she launched a second volley.

And I've got ten more volleys waiting for the next batch of idiots that come for my head. Aloysius was right. We are fools. But he's dead now, and I'm still gonna try and save his little gennie princess.

God help anyone who gets in my way.

"Ma'am? We're ready for you."

Andreison was looking up at her from the pit, hand hovering over a transmit icon and waiting for her to dictate a message.

"Marya, I want my words bounced out to every corner of Reclamation space. No one eats, gets a haircut, takes a shit or tells a bed-time story without hearing what I'm about to say, you understand?"

"Yes, ma'am. No one shits without your permission. I believe we have a code for that."

Ykaterina's eyes widened at the unexpected response. She glanced over at Samuel, whose smile was wider than normal.

Well, fuck it. No one lives forever—not even me.

"You've got some sass there, Andreison. I like it. Get ready to make some history."

"Yes, ma'am. Shit-stopping history in five, four, three…"

Okay, Ykaterina. Make this count.

"This is Commodore Ykaterina Maranova, commanding the Home Fleet. I'm currently in orbit over a secret facility on Earth's moon, preparing to blow the lid off a conspiracy that reaches to the highest levels of the System Defense Force.

"If you're wondering who the hell I am or why you've never heard of me, it's because I've been doing my job the right way for the last twenty years, keeping you safe from all sorts of nasty little secrets. But the time has come for me to tell you about the worst one I've ever had to keep, and I'm not ashamed to tell you that I'm ashamed to have ever tried.

"A little over five years ago, an expedition commanded by Vice-Admiral James Worthy touched down on a frozen world about 700 light years from here. He returned home with wreckage from a destroyed ship. Not one of ours, but one sent out centuries ago by descendants of the Transgenic Exile.

"In addition to some fairly interesting technology, he also brought back two survivors…"

MIRA

"Copy that, Control. Coming around to vector six-bravo, velocity ten meters per. Touchdown in three minutes, on your mark."

"Confirmed, Clarke Six. Black King sends his regards to the queen, and requests she join him at her convenience. Over."

Mira cut the circuit, trying not to let her annoyance show. The woman responsible for bringing the shuttle in had either defeated Janbi's scramble program, or some bright-eyed officer was following procedure for a change and looking out a window.

Either way, it meant trouble. Mira turned her head and shouted down the shuttle's main corridor to Jantine.

"Get everyone closed up; they're going to go with the gas."

Jantine responded mentally, and Mira winced. The Beta was completely enamored of using that form of communication, no matter what difficulties it caused anyone else.

≈*Noted. I hope the filters on these suits are everything you say they are.*≈

Mira sighed, added another stone to her wall, and sent a reply though the pain.

≈Just keep your eyes open and weapons loose. We'll be completely helpless until we're tractored all the way in, and they might already have eyes on us.≈

≈Understood.≈

The lunar surface was speeding beneath the shuttle as Mira sent the disarm codes to the hidden missile platforms lining the approach to Chimera base. Both her instruments and eyes told her she was flying straight into a crater wall, but she was on the beam with no deviation. Since she hadn't been blown out of space yet, the codes were authentic, and there was still a chance that whoever it was on the other end of the comm wasn't mobilizing the entire base against her.

Lots of variables. Still so many things that can go wrong.

"Control, sorry for the confusion. This is Clarke Three, not Six. No flag this trip, just pawns dropping off the mail. But I will convey Black King's regards, over. One minute to surface, the ball is yours."

Mira activated the autopilot and gave a sigh of relief as Chimera's computers took over the approach. She imagined the maneuvering jets firing to slow the shuttle, but she didn't check the instruments to confirm. She was already out of her chair and floating aft to join Artemus on the cargo ramp, sealing her helmet as she went.

Commodore, I sure hope your intel is good on this one. Because we'll make one messy terrain feature if they decide to divert us now.

Mira passed Carlton and Serene standing in the door of a state-room, breathers on and ready to go. She knew they couldn't see her face inside the helmet, but she smiled at them anyway, knowing that the Alpha would pick it up and relay the sentiment.

Serene was, for the most part, cocooned in a hazard bag, waiting for Carlton to seal her in and carry her down to the mobile contain-ment unit in the cargo bay. It was sweet irony that she'd be the most protected member of their group inside the unit, but completely shut off from the rest of the team while there. Even with an inactive stasis field, something about the unit's construction completely blocked mental communications, something she'd need to remember if they ever had to pull this stunt again.

For now, Mira had to keep her focus on the next few minutes, and the numbers counting down on her helmet display.

≈Mira, we just crashed into the lunar surface. It's fairly dark where I am, but I feel quite alive.≈

From her position on the hull, Katra had a much better chance of surviving the next few minutes than anyone else. Mira was depending on her eyes to tell her when it was safe to act, and part of her wanted to be out there with her. But no one else could fly the shuttle, and despite their combat training none of the mods could pass for a fleet officer over a comm.

"Touchdown, Clarke Three. We have you in the green. Initiating core shutdown. Be advised you'll be on your own for a few minutes—you caught us during shift change and we're still trying to find some loaders to help you."

"Roger that, Control. Tell those crane monkeys there's a little something extra in it for them if they can get me back in the sky in under an hour. I left something simmering back home, and I'd hate for him to get cold, if you know what I mean."

Mira wished her abilities worked over comm lines so she could tell whether the laughter on the other end was with her or at her. Careers were going to end because of this op, but Mira still wanted to keep the body count as low as possible.

"Understood, Clarke Three. Welcome to Echo Base. I'll try and get you back in your own bed as soon as possible. Control out."

Something grabbed the bottom of the shuttle, causing a vibration strong enough to register through both the deck and her boots. The lights went out in the cargo bay, and Mira switched over to her suit's internal sensors while at the same time borrowing the use of Jason's eyes for Carlton and Serene. Artemus was still in his encounter suit, and from her experience sharing Katra's perceptions in the tunnel, she knew the Delta's visor was even better suited than hers to lightless combat.

≈We are moving through a tunnel now, zero tolerance. I repeat, zero tolerance.≈

Katra's check-in increased the pain in her head. Mira tried to shove it away, but acting as a communications relay again was stretching herself too thin. Her skull felt like an eggshell, and even though they'd be leaving Artemus and the Omegas behind for a while, this mission was only just beginning.

What Katra was saying seemed right; it made sense that the hidden entrance to a hidden base was the same diameter as a flag shuttle, and not a meter wider.

Even though she worried about increasing the load on her poor brain, she chanced a message to Carlton.

≈*Are we ready?*≈

If there was even one sleeper hidden inside the base, Carlton was the only one of the team who could bring them out of suspended animation safely. And for Janbi's plan to work, he'd have to do it in record time.

≈*She's locked in. Mira, can you explain something for me?*≈

≈*Make it fast.* ≈

≈*Serene kissed me on the cheek before I sealed the hazard bag. Is all this kissing going to become a thing?*≈

Mira smiled at the image he unconsciously transmitted with his question, then blinked her eyes when the Alpha's chaste kiss on the cheek was replaced with a very sensual scene of Carlton walking in on Jantine and Janbi while they were having sex.

She wished he hadn't seen that, or that they'd seen him before he backed out of the room. From what she understood about Betas, they'd likely have invited him to join their lovemaking, and it couldn't have been easy for the emotionally isolated Carlton.

If Mira hadn't known better, everything she almost remembered or had been told about the social structure of the Outer Colonies would identify Carlton as a perfect Gamma. But he was born into a Beta crèche and came from a genetic line of incredibly talented technical specialists. In many ways, he'd had even less choice about his future than Janbi. Even so, only his superior skill with machinery had kept him on the mission rolls once some of his crèche-siblings were selected.

That, and his expendability. One more thing for the two of us to be angry about.

Mira moved closer to Carlton, opened her visor, and put a hand on his shoulder. What she had to say was probably better relayed mentally, but her head was already pounding, and the Beta could probably use some physical comforting.

"It's called being human, Carlton. You'll get used to it, and with the right person it's a lot of fun. I wouldn't worry about Serene, though. She was just wishing you luck, and trying to tell you how much faith she has that you'll keep her safe. I'm going dark now, so tuck in and hold on to something until I give you the all-clear."

Carlton sent her a wordless acknowledgment, and as she dissolved the sensory link, the edges of the whirlwind pulled back enough for her to add another stone to her mental wall. It was getting taller all the time, but she kept finding new ways to add fresh layers to the top.

For example, though she needed to keep her attention focused on the base of the cargo ramp, Mira couldn't help but think about Carlton's confused emotions. He said the Omegas had helped him deal with Harren's death, but when she asked Jason about it, the Omega told her that O-6913 had done what was necessary at the time. And since the other Omega wasn't very receptive to her mental communications, she'd let the matter drop.

I definitely need to get all of these kids hooked up with some of Harrison's psychoanalysts. They've got a lifetime of bad programming to unlearn if they're ever going to fit in on Earth.

Mira returned her thoughts to the vibrations under her feet. Whatever was going to happen, it was going to be soon.

≈Mira. We are approaching a barrier of some kind, and have travelled approximately four hundred meters on a declining slope.≈

Mira did a quick calculation on the distances Katra supplied and realized that she was missing some information. Despite the pain, she pulled Katra and Jantine into a single conversation, careful not to overwhelm the former lest she lose her grip on the shuttle's hull.

≈Katra, Can you send me your last clear memory of the crater wall? I'm trying to figure how deep we are, and—≈

Katra replied at once, not only with the memory she'd requested, but with a real time image of her suit visor display. It was Jantine who provided context, though, and Mira gave herself a mental kick in the backside for not thinking of it sooner.

≈Seven hundred eighty meters. Janbi interfaced our handhelds with both the encounter suit grav systems and the sensor suites of this Earther armor. I didn't see any reason why we should be as clumsy as the humans, if it comes down to a running fight.≈

Although she approved of Janbi's initiative, she didn't like that neither he nor Jantine had told her about it, or Jantine's continuing derision of humans as being, well, sub-human.

≈We talked about this, remember? We're all human no matter what the T-virus has done to us. We have to keep that in mind, or we'll never make this work.≈

≈As you say. Perhaps if we survive this mission you can remind me again. Katra, can you see any enemies from your position?≈

≈Negative. The barrier has opened, and there is a lighted chamber beyond with a track on the floor and what look like blast doors on the other side. There are neither any visible weapons systems nor any unloading equipment.≈

The rumbling under her feet stopped, and Katra's head moved enough for Mira to watch the bay doors grind shut after the shuttle was clear. Atmospheric sensors on her visor showed increased pressure in the chamber, and Katra triggered the gas canisters.

As power returned to the shuttle, and the lights came on in the cargo bay, Mira dissolved the three-way link and sent one last message to the group.

≈Get ready everybody. It's time.≈

Ignoring the pounding in her head, Mira resealed her helmet, stepped forward, and activated the ramp controls. Through her external pickups, she heard a hissing sound as the shuttle's atmosphere started mingling with the thinner air outside, and sent a silent prayer into space.

All right, Commodore Maranova. Keep your eyes peeled for our signal, because no matter how friendly we get, we're not going to fit three hundred more people on this boat for the return trip...

ANNAHKO

"I don't care what they're doing, if they're not at their stations in five minutes, they'd better not be anywhere on this ship or there'll be hell to pay! And would somebody *please* get back to me with that force assessment."

Caroline preferred not to shout her orders, but with *Indomitable*'s crew assignments still in flux and her people adapting to unfamiliar duty rosters, she'd had to adopt a more forceful approach to discipline than usual. Maranova's broadcast had thrown the Command deck into disarray, and she was still trying to figure out whether the moron who'd left an outside comm channel open was aboard her ship, or among the remnants left behind on Echo Base.

Captain Kołodziejski would know, but at the same time, it's his secrets that got us into this mess. I should never have agreed to this, but Indomitable *is mine now, and with the obvious proof of his claims bearing down on us, there is no other conclusion than the scenario he and Admiral Worthy laid out in their private communications: the Reclamation government cannot be trusted, and no matter who started it, we are well and truly at war.*

It was getting easier not to use Horace's given name, or to think of Daniel standing faithfully by his side instead of at hers. With every passing hour, she thought less about their past and looked forward to her own future, unfettered by the chains foisted upon her by the men in her life.

And if I tell myself that lie enough times, maybe someday it will be true.

A holo formed in front of her, with Illyana Tepes's face superimposed over a Lunar defense grid.

"Ma'am, all ship's personnel are accounted for, and our external sensor relays report Geyser detonations in near orbit. EFS *Clarke* is still inbound, and has at this time not reported any flight information to Argo City, Tycho City, or any of the satellite domes."

Caroline flicked it away, leaning forward in the chair and taking in the windows hovering over as many of the duty stations as she could.

Captain Kołodziejski would know what to do here, would probably already have done it. But she was no Simak, and had to make do with merely human perceptions and intuitions.

"Mr. Kirk, systems check."

"All divisions report combat readiness, ma'am."

Caroline pursed her lips, and bent her head to Chief Kirk at Munitions.

"Is that true, Guns?"

"Yes ma'am! Let me know what you want gone, and I'll make it disappear."

Caroline smiled, and sat back in the chair. Kirk's reply was exactly what she'd expect from a veteran of first shift. She had at least a few good people to work with, and with their help, she'd return *Indomitable* to the glory she rightly deserved, untainted by the sins of her former commander.

Caroline opened an intraship channel, and gave the order her crew was waiting for.

"All hands, suit up and prepare for maximum acceleration. I repeat, prepare for full acceleration, condition Alpha 1-1. Today is the day, people. Let's not keep our destiny waiting. Mars, Together and Strong!"

There was a small cheer in the command center as the crew answered her call, which Caroline didn't bother to squelch.

They should be happy. This is what we've been working for, a Martian ship crewed by Marsborn, answerable to no-one but ourselves.

There was one thing still bothering her, though, and Caroline reopened the message window Alex had sent her. The defense grid showed *Clarke*, and only *Clarke*, on approach to the north polar region.

So who was it fired those missiles? Or if it was Clarke *doing the firing, at whom?*

"Ms. Monahan, I want everything you can tell me about those detonations, and I want it now."

Caroline didn't wait for confirmation, but instead threw the grid from the window up to her panel. It wasn't that she didn't trust Monahan, but she wanted as much information as she could get before entering a potential firefight, and the fastest way to get it was to look at it herself.

The display was still set for Captain Kołodziejski's eye-line, but Caroline didn't mind sitting up a bit straighter to review it.

Just one more reminder of the mess that I have to clean up because of that asshole. Whether he lives or dies, everything about this ship is a testament to his grand, maniacal plan.

A situation I intend to remedy as soon as I get that doddering wreck out of my sky.

She ran the grid telemetry back ten minutes, then scanned it for any information that might give some clue as to *Clarke*'s plan of attack. She found nothing other than a flash of light—no, multiple flashes, all centered on or around *Clarke*, but with no definable purpose.

Just what are you up to out there, commodore? Why commit tactical suicide by giving away your exact position in hostile space, and what do you hope to gain by this display?

A few seconds later, the grid had recorded nine detonations against *Clarke*'s hull, which the venerable flagship shrugged off without any change of course. There was a brief flurry of energy weapons fire, some secondary explosions, then nothing.

Caroline narrowed her eyes, searching the footage for anything she could use to her advantage. It was only on Monahan's second attempt that she noticed the younger woman was trying to capture her attention.

"Ma'am, I have something you should hear."

Caroline pulled her attention away from the plot long enough to acknowledge Monahan, and the command deck was filled with screams a second later.

"…repeat. This is Captain Goro aboard SDF *Nelson*. We surrender. I repeat, we surrender. For God's sake, turn the missiles around. I've shut our weapons down, please, spare my crew. We're no thr—"

The transmission cut off, and *Indomitable*'s Command deck went silent. Caroline closed her eyes in an attempt to summon up Anya Goro's face, but all she could see were Daniel's sad, perfect eyes.

This is it, isn't it Danny? This really is goodbye. The time was never right for us, and now we're out of time.

"Guns, I want a firing solution on EFS *Clarke* right now, and don't let her out of your sight until I tell you otherwise."

"But ma'am, we're… "

"I know where we are, Chief. But they don't, and I'm counting on you to use that to our advantage. Mr. Currano, spin us up."

"Yes ma'am."

Caroline programmed the chair's dispenser for a stim capsule, then batted away the mandatory SDF holo warning her of the drug's harmful effects. She crushed it between her back molars, feeling the near-orgasmic rush of power flow over her tongue, down her throat, and into her lungs, savoring the burn as her sinuses carried the stimulant's effects directly to her brain.

All her senses came alive, and the compartment came into sharp focus as *Indomitable*'s main thrusters rumbled to life beneath her.

"Final status checks, people. All divisions."

Okay. Time to go to work.

KOŁODZIEJSKI

"…him up. Wake him up now!"

Daniel's voice came to him from somewhere far away, but Horace loved it all the same.

I'm still alive. Do you hear that, you gennie bastards? I'm still alive!

"I'm trying, I'm trying! His system doesn't react to stimulants the same way with the blood substitute. You have to give it more… "

"Time, doctor?" Horace's mouth was drier than he could ever remember, and he scraped his tongue across his front teeth to try and bring some life back to it. A few of them felt loose, and he added this indignity to his list of punishments to exact on Watson when this was all over.

"Time is precisely what we don't have. How long have I been out?" A warm something rushed into his left arm, and Horace snapped open his eyes to see very concerned Daniel Tepes in a fully sealed hardsuit, holding a very frightened Thomas Watson a meter off the floor at the foot of a diagnostic bed. The Earther was still wearing his Fleet Medical costume and pretending he was real people.

I swear, if he pisses himself again…

On the bed, Horace was covered from his neck down to his feet by a thin blanket, pressed-skin-tight around his body with wires and lights leading off to machines on either side. He had barely enough strength to lift his neck, but with every passing second he felt more like himself.

Daniel, of course, would be strong enough to lift Watson even without the suit, under any gravity.

"Twenty hours, sir. This one wanted to keep you under longer, but there are some developments you need to be aware of."

"It was n-n-necessary. The v-v-virus m-m-mutated again. I had t-t-t-"

Horace's eyes went wide, his heart beating so fast several monitoring devices started screaming in protest. He tried to push himself up in the bed, but the blanket would not move, and he felt a band of resistance across his bare chest. Fearing the worst, he began thrashing against his restraints, until strong hands rested on his shoulders.

"It's ok, sir. I've got you. Let me undo these straps, and we'll get you out of here and someplace safe."

Craning his neck upward, Horace could barely make out Andrew's smile through his faceplate, but it was enough to reassure him.

Collins promised me he wouldn't let Watson try one of his "cures" on me. Didn't he?

Daniel returned Watson to the floor, and the Earther gripped the foot of the bed like his life depended on it.

"You're at a crisis p-p-point, Captain. I can stabilize you for another t-t-twenty-f-f-four hours, at which time you will have no options at all, or we can try the new serum and hope for a c-c-cure. The newest pair of gennies haven't died yet, and I'm still reviewing their bloodwork. I'm c-c-confident that I..."

Once his right arm was free of both restraints and tubes, Horace dismissed Watson with a wave. Daniel used his now free hands to undo the band holding Horace's legs, and with both men's assistance, Kołodziejski was able to sit up on the bed. Andrew kept a steadying hand on his shoulder, unwilling to let him fall again.

"Thank you, Andrew. You were saying, Daniel?"

Collins smiled at the recognition, and stood up a little straighter. There was concern in his eyes, as was Horace's due. But it was Tepes he wanted to hear from, and he didn't have long to wait.

"Sir, an unauthorized shuttle docked about thirty minutes ago. We voice-locked the pilot as the traitor Mira Harlan, and thermal scans count at least five troopers with her, possibly more. We deployed gas as per protocol, but to no effect. They've been disabling our security feeds at random intervals, and we're having problems tracking them through the corridors."

Horace swallowed what little spit he had, and beckoned for a bulb of water. He didn't like what he was hearing, but he hated not being able to talk. He bit off the nipple and sucked greedily at the bulb, over Watson's strenuous objections. Another glare was sufficient to shut him up, and Horace motioned for Daniel to continue.

"Not long after, Commodore Maranova broadcast a message that got through our lockdown, accusing you and Admiral Worthy of war crimes and calling for your arrest. Our people now have comms completely under our control, but with the compromises we made to crew *Indomitable*, we're spread a little thin."

So you've finally made your move, Ykaterina. I can't say I'm surprised. But how in the worlds did you rescue a dead woman, and get her up here now, of all times?

The answer came to him a second later, adding more fuel to an already raging bonfire of hatred. Horace slipped off the table and shuffled towards the examination room's desk, clutching the thin blanket to cover his nakedness. The last few monitors tore away from his chest and left arm, but he was beyond pain now.

The fucking gennies. She really was colluding with them, and somehow they got her off Valiant. *I should have blown that wreck out of existence when I had the chance.*

Horace sat down at the desk, and swiped a bloody hand through the activation field. The motion send oddly-shaped droplets flying against the back wall, and Horace saw points of red inside the green slurry Watson had been pumping into him.

The desk's menu didn't seem affected by the cast-off, and he'd been sure that Watson would leave it unlocked. But just thinking about another of the doctor's failures made his head pound.

Useless, Earther, fucking piece of shit gutter rat!

Each word pushed his temper higher, and Watson picked exactly the wrong time to start talking again.

"Please, captain, you have to rest. The v-v-virus is still active, and unless you go back under, I can't—"

"Shut. Up. Earther! I've had it to here with your excuses and promises. You had one job. One fucking job! Instead, you fucking killed me, as surely as the gennie filth you failed to remove from my body!"

Horace didn't remember standing, and barely felt the impact of his hand against Watson's chest. Watson flew across the room, bounced off the far wall and into Daniel's armored arms. Horace felt a rush of adrenaline, and heart pumping, he hopped across the room to grab Watson by the neck and lift him out of Daniel's arms with one hand.

"Tell me, Earther. Tell me why I shouldn't snap your fucking neck right fucking now!

Watson's eyes bulged as he writhed under Horace's grip. His doughy Earther hands clawed at Horace's arm, drawing green-red lines across his skin that sealed up almost instantly.

Horace threw Watson to the grating with a strength he'd never had before. The doctor was gasping for air as Horace stepped away, unwilling to believe his eyes as he turned his hand back and forth under the lights.

"No, no, NO! What did you do, Watson? What did you do to me!"

Daniel and Andrew pulled the doctor roughly to his feet, each taking one arm and holding the sputtering man half a meter off the floor.

"Noth...nothing. That's w-w-what I'm trying to s-s-say. The virus has gone t-t-too far, and I c-c-can't s-s-stop it any m-m-more. The c-c-coma slowed the advance, b-b-but it's now or never. You either change, take the cure, or d-d-die."

Hearing Watson stutter out his cause of death wasn't exactly a new experience, but this time Horace finally believed him. He could feel his body changing with every beat of his heart, his thoughts slowing down at the same rate his strength increased.

A wordless shout tore his throat, which obediently healed in an instant. The sound of it echoed in his ears as he stumbled back to the desk.

"No. Not yet. I have a few things to do before I die, and killing you is mostly likely one of them. So be a good little boy, and shut up while I'm working. You may still have some value to me, and I'd hate to accidentally beat you to death while I figure it out."

Watson finally took the hint, and other than his labored breathing, remained silent. Horace turned his attention back to the desk, and pulled up the files for the two gennies Watson had experimented on while he was asleep.

Both were male, and thankfully still alive. But according to their readings, they were also still transgenic—just less so.

Perfect little Earthers, in fact.

Well, that's not going to be me.

Horace entered his personal code into the terminal, temporarily transferring control of Echo Base's comms to himself. He then selected the emergency frequencies used by all Fleet fire control teams, and began transmitting on every one of them.

"Hello, Miss Harlan. I don't know what you and your gennie friends did to our cams and internal sensors, but there are only so many places you can hide before I'll find you and put an end to this ill-advised mutiny of yours. Enjoy what life you have left, and here's a little something to watch while you wait. Be seeing you."

Horace uploaded Watson's failed experiment to the channel, and savored each moment of the gennie's death. When it was over, he typed one more message for Harlan and her mutant scum, and then locked the system down for good.

<<<293 MORE TO GO>>>

"There, that should do it. Now, put the good doctor back in his hole, and leave the gennies to me. I don't think they'll refuse our invitation now, do you Andrew?"

When his guard didn't answer right away, Horace turned his head and sneered at the fear in Andrew's eyes. The guard looked almost as scared as Watson, and the sight of a true believer mirroring the Earther's revulsion was more than Horace could stand.

He flew across the room, tearing an induction pistol off Daniel's chest and jamming it under Andrew's armored chin. It discharged with a roar, blowing out the back of his helmet and splattering red across the wall and ceiling.

Out of the corner of his eye, Horace saw Daniel going for his second weapon. But his new gennie reflexes were much faster than those of a Marsborn, even one trained to Horace's exacting standards. He emptied the rest of the ammo canister into Daniel's chest, painting the walls bright red with his blood.

Droplets were still bouncing around the room when Horace registered Watson's screams. He shoved the pistol in the Earther's face and pressed the firing studs, but instead of the mini-sonic booms that normally accompanied that action, there was only a high pitched whirring noise.

Horace tossed the pistol away in disgust, then grabbed a double handful of Watson's blood-drenched tunic and dragged him to his feet.

"Let's you and I go get some fresh clothes, Doctor Watson. After all, we've got company coming, and I can't wait to show them how well your new virus works up close and personal."

KATRA

KATRA DROPPED FROM HER POSITION UNDERNEATH THE HULL TO THE TOP of the cargo tender holding the shuttle fast, reinforcing Mira's suspicion that they would not be using it as an escape vessel.

Still on the lookout for enemies, she reclaimed her slugthrower from where it was racked next to the gas canisters, and waited. Jantine would join her soon if the bay was clear, and if it was not, then she would find an enemy and kill it.

Katra wished she'd had more time to train with the unfamiliar weapon, but she'd seen enough of them in action aboard the *Valiant* to know the basics. Once Mira showed her how to maintain it, she was as ready as she'd get without several days of living with the weapon.

And if we're not successful in several hours, I won't need weapons or anything else anymore.

There was no need for speculation at this point, either they would be attacked soon, or they wouldn't. At least here they'd be able to see the enemy coming.

As the cargo ramp lowered, Jantine skipped down the ramp with a tight grip on her own borrowed weapon.

Jantine's boots attached to the tender, something Katra had forgotten to do. It was a minor lapse in discipline, but she still didn't trust the Earther suits.

Katra inclined her head to Jantine, who repeated the gesture until the two mods' faceplates touched.

"Anything?"

"No."

The suit pickups recorded the sound of Mira's footsteps on the ramp, and then Katra heard the Earther's voice in her head again.

≈*Jason says the securecams are on, but there's no movement in the corridors toward us. And no one's talking to me on the comm channel. We've been made.*≈

Katra and Jantine rolled out from under the shuttle and into firing positions, which they held only long enough to verify the landing chamber was empty.

The Earther was already racing for the blast doors, and she pulled a round object from one of the pouches on her hip. Aside from her handheld, Katra's pouches contained only additional ammunition and replacement weapon components, but whatever Mira was carrying opened the hatch within seconds.

Katra sprinted for the opening, paralleled by Jantine from the other side of the shuttle. But while Jantine continued out into the now-revealed corridor of carved regolith, Katra put her back to the manufactured wall of the room she was in and looked back at the shuttle.

Carlton came rocketing down the ramp at the controls of the mobile stasis unit. It responded to his deft touch like a personal transport, and Katra smiled at the thought of the dour Beta riding into battle atop an armored duo-cycle.

A schematic of the base's corridors appeared on her visor, just ahead of Mira's voice in her head.

≈*Jason says he's redirected the securecam feeds and also sent a map to your handhelds. I don't want to know how he did it, just that it worked.*≈

≈*Confirmed. I see Jantine down the corridor.*≈

Jantine sent her own response a second later.

≈*Clear. Tell Carlton to come ahead. We have one hundred ten meters of passage secured.*≈

Katra waved Carlton ahead. Mira had probably relayed Jantine's order to him as well, but as long as the Beta complied, it didn't matter how he'd received the message.

Over his shoulder at the shuttle, she saw Artemus and O-6913 come down the ramp. The Delta took up a defensive position at ramp's base, while the Omega crouched under the shuttle and examined the clamp preventing their escape. It would be good to have more options, and the Omegas had already demonstrated their ability to deal with Earther technology. Once Carlton hummed by on the mobile unit, Katra looked to Mira. The Earther held up a hand with four fingers extended, and started folding them in toward her gauntleted palm. When she made a fist, Katra rolled forward into the corridor, noting that Mira had used her suit's maneuvering jets to clear the blast doors before they closed.

Once on the other side, Katra felt her perceptions expand to include Jantine's, and then she heard the Beta's words in her own voice.

≈*Katra. One hundred meters left.*≈

Katra skipped past Carlton as he glided up to Jantine's position, then she lengthened her strides. It only took a few jumps to reach the next junction, and she used the last one to push off the corridor's ceiling and then activated her boots. She touched down on one knee in a secure firing position, letting the encounter suit inside the powered armor take the brunt of the impact.

She looked down both sides of the corridor, comparing what she was seeing to the map projected on her visor. The right passageway ended in another set of doors fifteen meters away, while the left branch curved around a corner and out of sight twenty meters in the other direction.

≈*Clear. Map is accurate. Do you see the indicator?*≈

Jason had placed a green dot on the nearer set of doors, indicating it as the most likely route to the lab complex. The corridor was almost five meters wide, and much better maintained than the roughly excavated one she was crouching in.

≈*Yes. Mira, we have a path.*≈

≈*Copy that. Before he moved out of range, Jason said he'd try to give us door control, and enough advance warning as he could of troop movements. Ykaterina's estimates have two hundred troopers stationed here, plus an equal number of scientists and a small cadre of fleet officers.*≈

Katra noted that Mira had not said "non-combatants." Unlike the *Valiant*, there would be no innocent casualties here. Just unfortunate ones, and she'd deal with them as they came. There was more than enough ammunition secured about her person to handle that many enemies, but she still longed for the pulsers and energizers they'd left with Artemus to maintain their disguises as troopers.

But we can't use them on this op anyway. Might as well wish for Crassus, Jarl, and Malik to return to life.

Katra felt a vague sense of unease, and she wondered if she'd transmitted that last thought inadvertently. But neither Jantine nor Mira offered any comment, and she dismissed the feeling as what Mira referred to as "the jitters." She felt exposed like this, carrying around an extra hundred kilos of gear and unable to use her active camouflage. But this was the mission, and she'd carry it out to the best of her ability.

A red light flashed on her visor, and at first Katra was unsure what Jason was trying to tell her. Words appeared, and the jitters doubled:

>>*INCOMING TRANSMISSION.*

She recognized the voice instantly, even though she'd only heard it once before. And despite her earlier statements, Katra felt very real hatred come through the link from Mira, a sentiment she had no problem sharing.

"Hello, Miss Harlan. I don't know what you and your gennie friends did to our cams and internal sensors, but there are only so many places you can hide before I'll find you and put an end to this ill-advised mutiny of yours. Enjoy what life you have left, and here's a little something to watch while you wait. Be seeing you."

Though she had never seen Captain Horace Kołodziejski's face, Katra imagined it was wearing a smug grin. A vid image appeared on half her visor, and she imagined filling that face with a few hundred micro-slugs.

A tall, dark-skinned human wearing a uniform like Carlton's was leaning over a sleeping mod attached to a tangled web of monitoring devices. He touched something to the mod's skin, then backed away quickly. Katra saw the shimmer of a transparent shield on the human's face, but her attention was drawn immediately to the mod on the table when the sound of the devices changed from a sedate, rhythmic beeping to a screaming staccato.

Black veins rose under the mod's skin, and he sat up screaming. Katra gasped when his forehead split open, revealing half a dozen black and vaguely eyelike growths. Then his chest burst open, heart and lungs extending outward on a blackened arm of flesh.

Mercifully, the screaming stopped, and the mod slumped forward over his legs. The devices switched over to a continuous tone, but the horror had not yet ended. The body kept twitching for several more seconds, skin cracking open over the veins and oozing dark fluid.

Katra dropped her weapon and removed her helmet just in time to avoid filling it with vomit. Luna's lower gravity sent her vomit bouncing everywhere, but she didn't care. All that mattered to her now was surviving long enough to reach the human in the vid and kill him with his own poisons.

Katra spat the remnants of her last meal from her mouth and used alternating fingers to blow her nose. When she was done, she heard something moving behind her, and she grabbed for her slugthrower as she spun around to face it. But she misjudged the distance and forgot that her boots were magnetically locked to the metal floor. The weapon went sliding forward on a tide of vomit, leaving her empty-handed and on her back, staring up into Carlton's shocked face.

≈*He doesn't know. Mira, don't share that transmission with Carlton! He can't know that his*—≈

The three-way link dissolved before Katra could finish her warning, but over the direct connection she had with Mira came a painful jumble of images and feelings. Arid landscapes, lightless caves, and the taste of something sweet and frozen spun around a male Earther face that she never could make out before it faded away into another memory.

A fresh wave of nausea punished her chest, and as she lay coughing, Carlton's eyes went wide behind the transparent lenses of his breather. The Beta had climbed down from the mobile unit and was kneeling beside her, turning her head to the side. Katra caught a glimpse of Jantine bounding up the corridor before a new series of images began whirling inside her head.

Loss and pain Katra could deal with, she'd known more than enough of both in her short life. But there was something deeper binding Mira and the Earther together, and every time she caught a glimpse of his face it got worse. Finally, Mira returned to the images of the mod's death, but instead of the body on the table, she was focused on the dark-skinned man.

Katra watched as a lifetime of faces stacked together: smiles and frowns and shouts and ecstatic utterances. She felt content and scared and resolved and unhappy, until the faces solidified into a cruel glare of hate hidden behind a shimmering mask.

Jarl died in her heart all over again, but this time it was much worse. It was as if Jarl was on the table, while Horace Kołodziejski's mocking voice rang in her ears.

Mira's emotions vanished from Katra's head, leaving behind the deepest disappointment she'd ever known. But what confused her wasn't the sentiment; it was Mira's mental lament.

≈*Oh, Tommy. How could you?*≈

MARANOVA

"Multiple contacts. Bearing 1-1, 2-6, 119!"

Ykaterina gripped the rail tightly, careful not to use her hardsuit's full strength. She'd long ago learned the best way to survive any encounter was to be as prepared as possible, and even though the chance of a hull breach this deep inside *Clarke* was remote, the hardsuit was not only a good idea, but a requirement for a flag officer.

Her boots were already locked in place, and using both her suit's internal displays and the battle holos of the command center, she finally felt connected to what was going on "outside."

If Samuel was similarly affected, he gave no sign. This latest threat was due to hit them in less than ten seconds. While *Clarke* was busy disabling Luna's ground-based defenses, Markus Maddsen and SDF *City of Lights* emerged from hyperspace in a burst of hard radiation that not only scrambled *Clarke*'s external communications, but also panicked the people of Tycho City. In response, the moon's oldest colony launched every missile they had at whatever target they could see.

And since *Clarke* couldn't tell them what was really going on, as the closest ship, she was by far the biggest threat.

I'm sure the Geyser spreads City of Lights *just fired at us might change their minds, if there's anyone still within 200 meters of the surface to look. Guess there's no need to ask you what side you're on, eh Markus?*

"Puoliz, I want ten degrees z-spin. Chief Lewis, fire PDCs seven through twenty-one, and get the tubes in Quad 4 cleared. We're too deep in the gravity well now to make any mistakes. Murkel, tell Commander Harris I need full power in three minutes, even if he has to get out and push. No more excuses."

Samuel's words were spoken with a calm Ykaterina tried to instill in all her cadets, but few ever developed. Less than two percent of her advanced students made it through a full year of study, and even those who didn't complete the course quickly found positions in the Home Fleet when their marks were posted.

Many of them were here aboard *Clarke*, but more than enough were aboard *City of Lights* to give her pause.

Since *Clarke* first started firing missiles, DeMarco had been locked into every data feed his staff could send him. Her flag captain's face was a wash of color inside his faceplate, as lines of light drew themselves directly onto his retinas. He was in complete control of his vessel, and watching him in action filled her with pride.

The only thing I can do here is watch and coordinate the other elements of the Fleet. But since most of it is shooting at me, all I've got to work with is Clarke.

And she already has a captain.

Planck and *Gustav II Adolf* were conducting rescue operations near the wrecks of *Nelson* and *Merrimack*. Though Anya Goro's surrender came too late to stop the spreads that killed her, she at least had time to get most of her people into the escape pods before *Clarke*'s punitive strike hit. *Nelson* was dead in space, nothing more than a collection of radioactive spare parts that might someday cool down enough to be re-purposed. And unlike *Valiant*, completely unreachable yet still shining brightly, her death was confirmed.

I wish I knew what was going on there, but we have bigger problems.

Merrimack had died a much different death. Whoever Frieda Marcaine had running her defenses was a wizard, and Maranova was already composing another posthumous letter of commendation. He or she had stopped all but three of the Geysers, but *Clarke*'s fire control division knew their business too well. Though the dreadnaught's hull was mostly intact, its primary power systems were completely offline and no one was responding to *Planck*'s hails.

Two of the SDF's finest captains, wiped out in seconds. If I could have stopped the missiles, I would have. They waited too long to make the right decision, and now we have more friends to kill.

The pronouncement from the pit caught her completely by surprise.

"New contact! 0-0...0. My god, that's not possible!"

Andrieson's last words were almost a whisper, and Ykaterina had to agree with them.

That's from inside the moon...

Samuel muttered something she couldn't quite catch, even with the suit's pickups. *Clarke*'s captain stabbed his command baton into the battle holo and blanked a small section in front of him. Curiosity got the better of her, and Ykaterina clomped over to stand behind him, even though it meant sacrificing her God's-eye view of the battle.

The holo wasn't blank for long, and her quick nav calculations were confirmed. Just over three kilometers behind *Clarke*, *Indomitable* emerged from the lunar surface in a great cloud of dust and light.

It was like nothing she'd ever seen, but Ykaterina couldn't take time to enjoy the sight. Horace Kołodziejski wasn't wasting time with missiles, and although he was completely vulnerable to a similar attack, he opened up with every point defense cannon that could be brought to bear.

"Full power NOW! Punch it, Murkel!"

Warning lights went off all around the command center. The external pickups Ykaterina had slaved to her suit's visors burned away in a flash of brilliant white light, and the battle-holo flickered and died. There was a deep rumbling she could feel in her bones, and the officers down in the pit bounced in their seats.

Half blind from the instant of hell she'd seen as *Indomitable*'s point defense cannons found their targets, she was still trying to make sense of Horace's choices when a much larger vibration shook the command center, this one hard enough to dislodge one of her boots.

That can't be good.

Too much was going on to describe the command center as silent, but Ykaterina did a quick scan of the faces in the room as they pulled themselves back into their chairs. No one seemed seriously injured, but she saw the same expression of shock on all of them. Alarms were sounding from nearly every console, and the strobing warning lights were so intense that her visor dimmed.

Through it all, Samuel's voice retained its solemnity, even as his ship screamed around him in response to the beating it was taking.

"Give me a bearing, Mr. Puoliz. Gravitics, dead reckoning, anything you've got. Guns, was that what I think it was?"

Mariel Lewis was bent over her console, with several curls that had escaped from her normally tight braids hanging in front of her face. Intent on whatever report she was reading, *Clarke*'s senior non-commissioned officer just shook a hand in his general direction.

But it was Jakob Puoliz's halting response that commanded DeMarco's greater interest, and irritation.

"Sir, I..."

"Tell me what I want to know or get out of that chair, mister!"

Puoliz's mouth worked several times, but no words came out. Ykaterina didn't need any gennie powers to see he was terrified, not only of whatever was displaying on his console but at the very real displeasure of his captain.

"Dolan, get in there!"

"Sir!"

Another of Samuel's fresh-faced crew climbed out of the pit and relieved the stunned lieutenant, pulling him out of his chair and tossing him at an unused station. Puoliz slid past it and was halfway to the deck before another too-young officer caught him and led him away.

Dolan gave a quick scan of the nav console, then chimed in with a report just as someone realized decided that the blaring klaxons weren't helping and killed them. As such, his words fairly boomed across the command center.

"Sir! We're accelerating freely on our last heading, but flying blind."

Lewis turned from her console and pushed back an errant curl with her left hand. It fell back into her face immediately, but she gave her report as if nothing happened.

"Sir, my crews are reporting multiple impacts. The launchers in Quads 3 and 4…they're gone, sir. One of the blocked tubes must have kicked off. And…we're venting."

A ruptured hull during battle was every captain's worst nightmare. *Clarke*'s triple-hulled construction was a paranoid response to generations of attacks by orbiting hunter-killers, and was built such that damaged sections could be isolated as fast as possible. By necessity, her weapons systems were on the outermost layer of the ship, but even though half that surface was apparently missing, one order would seal that wound and allow the ship's remaining sections to recover.

And doom anyone still out there without a properly shielded suit.

Ykaterina had no doubt as to what Samuel's decision would be, but it didn't mean either of them had to like it. She thought she felt something humming through the soles of her feet, as if the ship's power was collecting here at its center before moving onward. It was an impossible scenario, but as she imagined herself as a part of *Clarke*'s heart, the sound of it beating was Samuel DeMarco's voice.

"Shut them down, Guns. We'll mourn later if we have time. Mr. Dolan, what's our present sensor capacity?"

"Sir, sensors are down, or rather, gone. The blast burned away our outer shell, but the core systems are intact. Maybe an hour?"

Ykaterina turned to see Samuel's face, wanting to see his reaction to the news. She was unprepared for his wolfish smile.

"That's good to know, son, but I'd assumed as much when we didn't explode. I needs eyes as soon as possible, or we might as well surrender."

"Sir, if I may"

Ykaterina turned to look at Andreison, and the younger woman's face looked as though she'd just swallowed a rat. But Samuel was in full crisis mode, and wasted no time in getting whatever she had to say out of her.

"Whatever it is, Marya, do it. You more than anyone know what's at stake here."

Andreison nodded, then addressed her comments to the increasingly fatalistic Dolan.

"What's our launch status?"

Dolan half turned to Lewis, who pointed to the nav console with a gauntleted hand. The lieutenant shrugged and pulled up what looked like a weapons schematic from across the compartment.

"There was a full load in the tubes, and a second ready to go. It's like the chief said, all the Quad 4 tubes blew, but the magazines were untouched, and I can detail crews to shift the remaining missiles over to Quads 1 and 2."

"No, not the missiles. I mean the ship's boats. How many transfer bays are still operational?"

The brilliance of Andreison's plan dawned on Ykaterina in an instant, and despite her suit's environmental controls she felt colder than she had in years.

No wonder she's got such a sour expression. That's some serious next-level thinking, girl, and wherever you've been hiding for the last few years seems to have toughened you up just fine.

Dolan—*George, I think, although that might be Murkel's name*—hesitated a second time, long enough for Samuel's smile to harden.

"Lieutenant, she knows what's going to happen to them when they clear the hull. But it doesn't change what we have to do. Can we launch shuttles or not?"

Ykaterina didn't have to see Command deck's faces to know what they were thinking. None of them were used to making this level of decision; they were just too young to wrap their heads around the fundamental loneliness of command.

People they know are dying, and Samuel's about to order even more to sacrifice themselves to keep us flying. They might think he doesn't care, but he's feeling it stronger than anyone else, with the possible exception of Andreison.

Dolan recovered quickly though, and turned back to his console. It took him less than half a minute to respond, and when he did it was with no hesitation whatsoever.

"Sir, ma'am, I have four ready to launch, and another six coming online."

"Thank you, George. Marya, pick three and patch me in, and let the others hear us."

Andreison swallowed hard, but nodded her understanding. One by one, the faces of two men and one woman sprung into life above the pit.

This time the room did go silent, as the three pilots selected acknowledged their commanding officer with a chorus of "sirs." Samuel was studying their faces, committing every feature to memory so that his nightmares would be accurately populated. Marya's projections supplied their names, but Ykaterina knew from experience that it was the faces that would haunt him forever.

You can't go in their place, Samuel. No matter how much it kills us inside, we usually survive our orders long enough to regret them.

"I'm not going to lie to you, *Clarke* is in bad shape and getting worse by the second. We're flying blind, and I need fresh eyes out there to get us through this. Once you clear the hull, I want you to boost hard away from us with every sensor you've got running at full power. If you can get free of this mess, rendezvous with the *Planck* and tell Horatio Davis what's going on back here. He'll take care of you, no matter what happens."

Ykaterina saw all three pilots nod. There wasn't any purpose in discussing what to do if they couldn't get free, and each of them was already working up their launch sequence.

"We'll give you as much cover as we can, but we'll need at least ten seconds of flight data for an accurate point defense. As for the rest of you, we'll work up your courses as soon as we know what's out there. Good luck everyone, and Godspeed."

Marya cut the transmission, but her hands were still moving

though control interfaces. A new holo formed above the pit, with *Clarke*'s bloated starfish shape at the center. The damage to Quads 3 and 4 was indicated, and gently curving lines stretched out from her center as the doomed shuttle pilots submitted their flight plans. The names of the pilots were floating around *Clarke*'s core, waiting to follow their virtual shuttles on onto the plot.

Maxwell. Inyoke. Park. However this turns out, I'll make sure you kids and your crews are remembered properly.

"Birds 3, 7, and 10 report ready to fly, sir. On your mark."

Andreison was doing her best to ape Samuel's calm, but there was a hint of sadness in her voice.

Samuel closed his eyes, and gave one of the hardest orders any commander could.

"Send them."

ANDREISON

Marya couldn't stop her hands from shaking, so she grabbed the bar in front of her and held on tight.

I just killed another twelve people. That's over seventy on the day, not counting anyone in the ground stations on Luna. And if I can't get my shit together, everyone left aboard Clarke *will be on me too.*

It's probably a good thing I haven't been promoted until now. I really suck at this.

A line of sweat ran down her hairline scar, tickling the too-sensitive nerves above her implants. She wanted to brush it away, but holding onto the bar was the only thing keeping her together.

I should have commed Deb. Said goodbye to the girls, at least. Instead I just have her letter, and the memory of our last family dinner.

Her wife had been understandably nervous when she shipped out for *City of Lights*. Years of therapy and reconstructive surgeries hadn't made life any easier on her, and now both parts of Deb's support network were far away in space, where nothing she could invent would save them.

At least this time, she's protected from Thomas Watson. The compound's guards have shoot to kill orders, but even though a living prisoner may mean another court martial for me, I'd risk it for another crack at that bastard.

Gorsky signaled his readiness from Transfer Bay 4, and Nelson and Armbruster were right behind him. Marya sent a quick message to Captain DeMarco, and went back to gripping the rail.

It should be me out there, not those kids. They deserve better than to be data points—sacrificial lambs for the greater good.

If that's even what we're about, anymore. Even with what the Commodore told the worlds, there's still a chance that Captain Kołodziejski is right.

Marya looked at the faint point of light representing SDF *Valiant* all alone in the night. Either Mira was aboard her, or she was dead, and no amount of wishing could change that.

Captain DeMarco danced around the subject every time she brought it up, and the commodore had all but ordered her to accept her loss and move on. But Marya still felt the same connection to Mira she'd had the first day she saw her at the Academy, which was the only reason she hadn't collapsed into a screaming mess by now.

She was so beautiful, and so alone. She needed a friend, and we both just knew. I took her under my wing, as it were, but it was Mira who taught me how to fly.

And if she really is dead, I can't even cry for her.

Marya reflexively blinked away the tears that would never come. There was work to do, and she couldn't find her soulmate out among the stars if she was dead.

Okay, baby. Time for me to go to work.

MARANOVA

The seconds ticked by as Ykaterina, Samuel, and the rest of the command crew held their collective breaths. The shuttles were thrusting outward at maximum power, and every instant of flight expanded their knowledge of the universe.

Andreison tapped at a holographic button, and the plot gained the countdown the rest of the officers in the pit were afraid to voice.

5...4...3...2...

A panel in front of DeMarco switched from red to green, and in a voice almost too soft to hear the Captain gave the order everyone was waiting for.

"Weapons hot."

Indomitable appeared first, or rather, her missiles did. Just at the edge of *Clarke*'s improvised sensor net, they would have been fired just before or just after the shuttles launched. DeMarco's board started flashing as the gunners picked their targets, and a second countdown started alongside the first.

+8, 30...+9, 29...+10, 28...

Ykaterina gripped her support railing harder, and through the suit's pickups heard it creak in protest. There was nothing anyone could do but wait for the dreadnaught's next volley; without something to shoot at *Clarke*'s remaining missiles were just so much dead weight.

Andreison's carefully chosen words were the next ones spoken aloud, and what she said made Ykaterina's gut churn.

"Shuttles 5, 6, and 11 are go. On your mark, Sir."

Samuel's response was instant, and just as devastating.

"Send them. -45 for 11, +45 for the other two."

Andreison nodded, inputting the course changes that would send Lieutenant...Gorsky, and his crew of three straight into the teeth of the next wave of missiles, while his colleagues on shuttles 5 and 6 would race ahead to give *Clarke* a better set of navigational data to work with.

From the first flight, Lt. Maxwell's data now included real-time images of the lunar surface, including laser ranging. Lt. Inyoke had an optical fix on Earth, and Lt. Park sent a magnified image of deep space, specifically the area in which *Planck* and *Gustav II Adolf* were conducting rescue operations.

Anyone within two million kilometers should have seen our hull cook off, and if we can hold out long enough for one of the other captains to reach us, we might just live through this.

Ykaterina released her grip on the railing, surprised to find it intact. But it wasn't concern for *Clarke*'s infrastructure that motivated her, but rather a desire to remove her helmet. The regulations were more suggestions than guidelines, and the desire to see and feel something real was overpowering. She really didn't need to maintain suit integrity this deep inside the hulls, and taking off her gauntlets had other advantages. While many officers were able to manipulate holos with armored fingers, she needed more precision for close up views of the feeds as they came in.

I don't have a lot to do on this boat, but my eyes still work fine.

So did Mariel Lewis's, it seemed. Her announcement came a good two seconds before the plot updated, making Ykaterina wonder if the frazzled woman had a direct line to God. Either way, her estimates were as exact as they were alarming.

"New contact! Sorry, contacts! Multiple drive signatures in z7, bearing 1-3, 2-3, 4. Looks like *City of Lights* sent everything, sir."

The missiles were an angry red swarm, aimed at *Clarke*'s unprotected back half. It made no sense to roll the ship away from threats it couldn't see, and Markus Maddsen knew that as well as anyone. But his spreads were fired from even farther out, meaning they were relying on hard-wired evasion protocols, not live control. They'd start individual attack runs in a few hundred kilometers, taxing *Clarke*'s diminished point defense system well beyond its capabilities.

We're going to take some hits, bad ones. But if we can stay ahead of their acceleration curve long enough for a few more batteries to come online...

Samuel DeMarco had attended the same lectures as Markus Maddsen, and as Ykaterina recalled, had lower test scores. But in the simulator, it was the calculating man at her right who was the best in his class, rather than the hot-tempered one firing on her.

And I knew that going in.

Mariel Lewis added a new column to the running countdown, taking into account *City of Lights*'s probable launch window. It was longer than the one already running for *Indomitable*, and Ykaterina furrowed her eyes at the numbers.

+30, 12, 45...+31, 11, 44...+32, 10, 45...

"Murkel, give me everything you've got on my mark, including as much spin as the chief is unwilling to give me. I want us chasing Maxwell's beacon full speed as soon as the shuttles launch. Guns, give me some good news. I don't like the kind I'm seeing over here."

"Sir, I can't rewrite physics just to save our sorry butts. I can charge the point defense cannons in just over fifteen seconds, but we need a full twenty-five between shots or the barrels will fuse solid. Tell me what parts of the ship you want unprotected, and I'll make it happen."

Ykaterina wanted them both to be wrong, but unfortunately Lewis's figures just couldn't be argued with. *Clarke* was already missing a full third of her cannons, and the defensive spin would cut her accuracy down by at least half. They were unlikely to suffer anything like the damage done when their own missiles cooked off, but it was still going to hurt.

If only there was some way to increase our odds a bit...

No, that won't work. Will it?

Hating herself for jumping on Samuel's plan, Ykaterina called out over the commotion.

"Belay that spin prep. Chief Lewis, how fast can you evacuate your remaining crews in Quad 3?"

Lewis's head spun around, curls flying and eyes wide. She looked to Ykaterina, then DeMarco, whose own eyes were narrowing even as he nodded permission.

"If you don't want those missiles, ten seconds, tops. Half of them are securing the first round of Geysers in Quad 1."

"Leave them. Pull the crews back and tell them to find a shady spot. What's the status on our cannons there?"

"Ma'am?"

Ykaterina couldn't wait for the woman to figure it out on her own, not with one ship's worth of missiles bearing down and another likely on the way. She'd been tapping in commands while Ykaterina talked, but now her hands were as still as she was silent.

"Can you fire those cannons or not?"

"Ma'am, I can push all sorts of buttons up here, but it won't do a bit of good. The firing ports are slagged."

"She didn't ask if you could hit anything, Chief."

Samuel's voice was weightier than ever, so much so that Ykaterina imagined his words punching holes in the deck as the dropped from his lips.

"Birds are clear, sir. Bringing the next three up to the deck."

Another precious second passed after Andreison's announcement, then Lewis nodded.

"They'll fire, all right. I have no idea what you're planning, ma'am, but I'll do it."

Ykaterina turned her head to DeMarco, whose grim expression told her that he did.

"Samuel? She's still your ship."

"Not if those spreads hit. Let's do it."

Ykaterina's mouth pulled back in a vulpine grin, and her hand hit the belt control keeping her boots fixed to the deck. She didn't have time to clomp over to Lewis's station, and she certainly wasn't smart enough to reprogram the one in front of her to accomplish what she needed to happen.

Free from any external restraints, she ran as fast as she could with one hand on the curved support rail, dragging her holo along with her. When she was close enough, she left it behind and took the last few steps to Lewis's panel, shouting out a brief history lesson on starship construction while inputting commands.

"People, you're about to see something which has never been tried before. You already know how tough these Cheyenne class battle cruisers are, but you may have forgotten why they were built in the first place. We have three hulls instead of two because a bunch of too-smart scientists designed giant death machines that could chew their way into just about anything."

Lewis realized what Ykaterina was doing in enough time to help, starting in on another part of the panel with much faster fingers.

"The reason *Indomitable* flashed our outer hull was to seal us in and deny us a portion of our defensive capability. But what Chief Lewis and I are doing now—thank you dear, that's the last one—is jettisoning one of the damaged hull sections entirely. And...Go!"

Lewis tapped in one final command, and one-eighth of *Clarke*'s total mass separated in a shuddering blast. But it was still intact, floating alongside the ship for a few seconds before the ship's continued thrust left it behind.

New data from the second flight of shuttles updated the plot, and Ykaterina stepped up to the rail to watch it. As missiles fired almost a minute before from *City of Lights* made their attack run, they zeroed in on the ship-like mass and detonated.

There was complete silence in the command center for a few seconds, then a ragged cheer rose up from the junior officers in the pit. But the voice behind her was silent, and across the chamber Ykaterina saw Samuel's nod of approval for her next magic trick.

"Do it."

Ykaterina couldn't hear Lewis activate the control, but the results on both her holo panel and the much larger plot were immediately apparent, though in reality it took a few thousandths of a second for the firing codes to reach the point defense cannons still operational on Quad 3.

What was left of the hull transformed from a tumbling mass of twisted metal to an expanding cloud of very angry ions a hundred kilometers across, a state change assisted by the warheads Ykaterina and Lewis had activated in the seconds before jettisoning the section.

Indomitable was traveling far too fast to change her course, and entered the cloud less than a second later with her reaction drives firing at full strength. Hungry for free hydrogen atoms to fuel her thrusters, the dreadnaught's scoops drew in superheated plasma instead, with catastrophic results.

If anyone aboard had time to pray, Ykaterina hoped that whatever higher powers they believed in would forgive her.

I just turned 200 people into a miniature star, and maybe saved the human race.

The cheers stopped, and the only sound in the room was an insistent beeping from Lewis' tactical station.

"New contacts. Another full spread from *City of Lights*."

DeMarco nodded, and amended his earlier order.

"Mr. Murkel, evasive maneuvers at your discretion. Unless I miss my guess, we won't need to fire back at those, but I want as much distance between us and that next volley as possible. Andreison, find a way to get a message through to Captain Maddsen, and offer to take his surrender. I don't want a repeat of what happened with..."

RAMIREZ

"Are we ready, Alonso?"

"Yes, Sir. All systems are go."

"Punch it!"

MARANOVA

"Sir, hyper emergence detected!"

What?

Ykaterina expanded the holo in front of her, trying to see any hint of what Madison was announcing in it. Most of the data they had was obliterated by the explosion—if that word could even apply to what they'd done—and there was nothing new on her plot.

"Talk to me, Madison. What do you know?"

"Relayed from Lt. Inyoke, sir. Faster if he tells you himself. Marya, have you got it?"

"Affirmative. Audio only, on tightbeam."

There was a slight delay while the pilot collected himself, then Inyoke's shaking voice filled the room.

"Are you seeing this, Matt? Tell me I'm not imagining this."

Samuel patched himself into the channel, eyes intent on the plot. "Shuttle 3, this is DeMarco. What are you looking at, son?"

"Sir! It's... It's *Valiant*, sir! Half of her anyway. She made hyper emergence, jettisoned something, and then fired twenty, no, thirty-two

Geysers straight into *City of Lights*'s engines. She's done for, sir. Floating dead."

Ykaterina almost collapsed with relief. Whoever was commanding *Valiant* had clearly studied at the Mira Harlan school of miracle working, and had impeccable timing to go along with their skill.

"Captain DeMarco, I have Captain Maddsen and a Commander Callaway wanting to talk to you. Do you have a preference?"

Samuel's eyes were closed, head bowed in silence. In the air between them, vid matching Inyoke's description of events was playing for an audience of stunned junior officers and one very tired commodore, and Ykaterina almost missed his response.

"Put Captain Maddsen on, Marya. Let's see what he has to say for himself."

SERENE

Serene's eyes went wide at the first thoughts she'd detected in many minutes, and at the thumping sound that came through the top of the mobile unit. It was peaceful inside the doubled obfuscation of biohazard bag and isolation chamber, and for the first time since she'd awakened from deep sleep, she was alone with her own thoughts.

Mostly alone. The memory shards in her head were urging her to practice mental defenses, but all Serene wanted to do was play. Little Mirabelle Harlan was her favorite, and the two girls had danced in virtual sunlight often since the mission started.

Serene felt bad about having stolen the Gamma memories from Mira, especially since the longer she had them, the more indistinguishable they became from her own. Jason and O-6913 didn't want to tell Mira the process was irreversible, since it shouldn't have been possible for the human to get them in the first place. But as the hours and days went on, Serene knew that to rid herself of them would likely kill her.

And I so very much want to live.

The murmuring almost-voices in her head went silent, waiting for more input to start formulating Serene's next actions. From what Serene could tell from Doria's memories, they hadn't been this insistent with her, but the Gamma had been raised a first class crèche system on Colony D that prepared her from birth to be a facilitator.

That was supposed to be us. Our colony, the first one attempted after the Earthers exiled us.

According to Commodore Maranova and Captain Martin's files, L-A-197 had died a year ago, most likely somewhere here in Chimera base. With so many other people in her head, it was hard to remember his features, but that didn't make her miss him any less. All she could summon up were vague impressions, which kept forming themselves into images of Mira's father.

≈*...st do it, Carlton. We can't get the unit through this room anyway...*≈

The thoughts had no real "voice" to them, but Serene knew they were Jantine's. They didn't have the guarded chill she was used to in the Beta's mind, but Katra was much more direct in her statements and rarely dwelled on her words before speaking.

And Mira shouts all the time. Still, I should thank her for being able to hear them at all. I won't thank her for the headaches, though. Those are no fun!

There was a hissing sound above her, and the pleasant darkness outside her bag became a murky gray. A mod-shaped shadow broke the homogeny, but from the nature of its thoughts she already knew it was Carlton.

A very, very nervous Carlton.

"What's wrong? What's happened?"

Her voice was muffled by the emergency breather, but as Carton undid the seals on the hazard bag and lifted her out, the device fell away to the floor. Serene watched it drop lazily to the sterile metal panels, then bounce up nearly to his knees.

Wherever they were, it was cold and dark and a little bit scary. She clung tightly to Carlton until he set her down on the floor, and it took a few seconds to pick out Jantine, Katra, and Mira's thoughts from the humming machinery around them.

When Carlton didn't answer her, the Gamma memories decided he either hadn't understood or didn't want to tell her. One of the memory shards suggested disciplining him for his lack of obedience, but Doria's counseled patience.

"Carlton, what's going on? Where are we?" Serene asked.

Her voice was a bit louder than she'd intended it to be, but she didn't detect anyone else present besides Mira and the mods. There was something else nearby, though, something almost as omnipresent as the humming.

"We've found the sleepers. Most of them, anyway. Jason's trying to get an accurate count now, but he and Artemus are having a bit of difficulty with O-6913."

His words let her put meaning to the shapes surrounding them. The containers were far too small to be the sleeper units she was familiar with, but the deep, unformed dreams of those within resonated inside her. These were Carlton's people, and somewhere in the darkness were some of his crèche siblings.

Carlton's excitement was tempered by fear, but his thoughts were unreadable. Sometime in the last few hours, Mira must have helped him with his control. Doria approved, several of the shards tsked, and a few others let their appreciation of Carlton's fine jawline momentarily cloud their judgment.

Serene pushed away all the other voices save for Mirabelle, who really never left. What she wanted to say was nothing any stern, half-remembered mentor could help her with, but having a friend "nearby" made her less afraid.

But still, I have to ask.

"Are any of them my people?"

Carlton's emotions shifted to a dull shame tinged with dread, and she knew his whispered answer before he gave it. Despite days of close contact, the Beta still wouldn't look her directly in the eyes. In fact, he was looking pointedly away from her face.

"I don't think so, Serene. From what I understand, the units are all the same."

It was a slim hope, if any. She understood from Ykaterina that the humans had only found two viable suspension chambers in the wreck, but they did like to keep secrets. She nodded and held up her hand to

Carlton.

The Beta stared at the floor, uncertain as to what he was supposed to do. She folded her fingers into her palm several times, and sent him an image of herself holding his hand while they walked. Carlton shrugged and took her hand, but was neither pleased nor displeased to have physical contact with an Alpha.

So very different, this century. So much to learn.

Carlton led her carefully through the maze of units, pausing briefly at each one to scan its ID code. As they walked, Serene felt Jantine and Katra's emotions getting stronger, but nothing from Mira.

This made her frown, and Carlton must have picked that moment to look down at her face. His fear increased slightly, adding her possible displeasure to his ever–growing list of worries.

"What is it?"

Serene had several answers at the ready, but the one she most wanted to give was one she was sure he wouldn't understand. She wanted to speak directly with Mira's mind and gain some mature context, but the other woman had closed herself off completely.

Serene settled on her third most pressing problem.

"I still don't know what's going on. Why are we being so careful?"

Carlton knelt down beside her. At first she thought he was finally going to talk to her as an equal the way Mira and Jantine did, but instead he rubbed away a spot of grease from a metal plate to reveal a mod designation.

Serene wanted an answer to her question, and the longer she had to wait, the more the memory shards directed her actions. She sent a probe at the sleeper's mind, surprised at how easy it was to decipher his true identity. The plate gave her his designation, but with shards' help she learned his identity much faster than Carlton could access the Colony manifest through his handheld.

"TRN-G272489-A prefers to be called Trahn. Agricultural workers should not be your concern right now. What are you not telling me, Carlton?"

Serene's voice rose as she spoke. Not quite to a normal conversational level, but enough to indicate she was serious. Carlton's fear jumped to the front of his mind, and she caught a glimmer of his thoughts as he hurried to answer her question.

≈*...at am I supposed to do? Mira, can you hear me? Hello?*≈

"The humans know we're here, but not exactly where. Jantine wants us to be as careful as possible until we can secure this area."

Serene gave Carlton a hard stare, fighting the urge to force him into giving a straight answer. In the end, she borrowed from both Doria's and Mirabelle's memories for the right response.

"Carlton, you're scaring me. Please tell me what it is that you are afraid of. It's alright, I won't be angry with you."

Before the Beta could answer, a sound from the darkness sent his fear to new heights. She caught a terrifying image of a giant machine crawling on the ceiling, and of herself running as fast as she could from whatever else was hiding beyond the next row of sleepers.

But that fear was tempered by the arrival of Katra, who held out her right hand to Serene without lowering the Earther weapon in her left. It bothered her a little that Carlton was almost as afraid of the Gamma as the killer machine in his memory, but then she realized it was the powered armor Katra had on over her encounter suit.

He thought she was an Earther!

Then Katra's faceplate lit up from within, and Serene could see her smiling. All the voices in her head save for Doria and Mirabelle were on a high state of alert, and Katra's carefully modulated words did nothing to calm either them or Carlton.

"Come with me, Serene. Carlton, Jantine says this room is secure. Get started."

Doria's memories helpfully supplied that Gamma infiltrators spent more time in their encounter suits than any other mod, and even wearing an Earther hardsuit over the top Katra was probably capable of some amazing feats. Mirabelle just wanted to put one on herself.

Serene didn't want to leave, not until she had an answer from Carlton. Mirabelle supplied an image of planting her feet and refusing to move, but Katra's gentle tug got Serene's feet moving, and rather than be dragged along Serene hurried to keep up.

≈*Katra, what is Carlton afraid to tell me?*≈

It was much easier to speak directly to Katra's mind than to use words. Mira, real Mira, had said it was because Katra had a "highly developed super-ego."

≈*He doesn't know for sure. We haven't told him what we saw.*≈

Serene pondered this for a few seconds, with the Gammas screaming in her head for more.

≈*Show me.*≈

Katra obliged her instantly, supplying not only the horrifying image of the human injecting the mod, but the effect it had had on Mira.

Several things Carlton had said made more sense now, especially if his unconscious intuition was working toward the truth Katra had just revealed. If the three soldiers had been shutting him out, he was bound to know something was going on, and it was only a matter of time before he realized the truth.

≈*He's almost there now. Was there something special about that mod? And have the Builders seen this?*≈

Katra and Serene emerged from between two sleeper units to see Jantine and Mira crouching on either side of a clear pressure door. In the room beyond, the human from Katra's memory was standing in front of a workstation and looking in the other direction. Serene felt nothing from him, but she had access to Mira's memories, and already knew much more than sight alone could tell her.

Thomas Sullivan Watson. Mira's Tommy. And given what he did in the transmission Katra shared with me, I can understand part of why Mira is so upset right now.

Jantine and Mira crouched at the hatch as it opened, and Serene could tell from their thoughts that they were ready to rush in. Beside her, Katra crouched down to Serene's height, and looked at the Alpha for several seconds before her visor went dark. In those moments, Serene saw that the Gamma's smile had changed, and her thoughts now had a distant feel to them.

≈*Yes, and yes. We're about to deal with both, provided Carlton can get us a little bit of backup.*≈

Serene didn't understand what Katra was saying at first, but then she saw it. A stray image of the Gamma rolling into the room with her weapon firing—not to kill, but to maim.

She means to punish him. Good. But if I've learned anything from Mira, it's that punishments must be tempered with mercy, and we'll need to keep him alive long enough to figure out everything he's done.

Besides. Mira always liked Tommy Watson. At least, I think she did.

A quartet of new minds came to life behind her. They were hard, and cold, and Carlton was more than a little afraid as he spoke the same words she'd heard after emerging from deep sleep.

"MAR-G250698-I. YHS-G267980-I. HJR-G259612-I. KAR-G262234-I. I am CRN-B3410-T. What are you called?"

This more than anything made up her mind. Today, everyone would live. The newly awakened Gammas needed to see the best of humanity in action, and a revenge murder, however justified, did not exemplify the life in the Colonies she remembered.

Maybe the ones that exist today are different, but I think we lived better lives when I left Colony B. And Mira has certainly shown us how to make more of ourselves than our genetics.

Serene ran toward the portal just ahead of Katra's grasping hands. Jantine tried to stop her, but Serene dropped to the floor and slid feet first under her arms. Mira stood up and slapped a device with red and green lights to the side of the portal, and it dissolved into a shower of golden particles just before Serene's soft slippers passed through.

WATSON

Tommy tried his best to look busy cleaning an already pristine lab, but his thoughts kept straying from his assigned role. Instead of being a decoy for Captain Kołodziejski's plan, all he could think about was when his unhinged patron would be back to kill him.

The man's descent into madness is accelerating nearly as fast as his transgenesis.

If only he'd listened to me. If only I'd made him listen.

Tommy looked up from his pointless busywork, hoping to catch a glimpse of Kołodziejski through the observation windows. But the space outside the lab was completely lightless, again according to Kołodziejski's plan.

I'm all alone up here.

I'm going to die, on the moon, and nobody will ever know.

Turning his attention back to the bio beds, he keyed in a diagnostic sequence that would eat up at least ten minutes, and prepared himself to run it again if nothing else happened. It was hard to stay focused under the threat of constant death, but right now his only way out was to prove his worth to Kołodziejski.

And in all the years I've been under his thumb, I still don't have a clue how to do that.

With the bed whirring and chirping at his back, Tommy shuffled over to a workstation and opened a new holorecord.

I should leave at least something behind. Preserve my side of things. I'm the victim in all this, and I deserve better.

Tommy leaned forward until his face was fully in the capture field, then picked up a throat recorder from the workstation and fastened it around his neck. It was easier to do this sort of thing sitting down, but Kołodziejski had demanded he keep his hands in full view at all times.

He didn't say a thing about talking, though, so that's what I'm going to do.

Looking around one more time for his tormentor, Tommy was satisfied that wherever the captain was, he'd have at least a few seconds to record his thoughts. Centering himself in front of the recorder again, he began dictating in a hurried whisper.

"My name is Doctor Thomas Watson. For the last five years, I've been a p-p-prisoner of Captain Horace Kołodziejski, who is forcing me to w-w-work on a cure for the transgenic virus. I have been p-p-partially successf-f-ful, and am p-p-prepared to share my research w-w-"

A hissing sound made Tommy pause, and he turned to look at the bio bed. He was turning back in the other direction when he saw the lab door was open, with an armored figure standing in the entrance.

Then something slid past him on the floor, taking out his knees as it went. He fell down hard, hitting his head on the workstation. He lungs emptied in a yelping gasp, and as he fought to stay conscious, he saw the armored figure take a step toward him.

No. Please, God, no.

"Help...me..." was all he could say, and even that minor effort sent stars dancing across his vision. A heavy weight settled onto his back, and the sweetest voice he'd ever heard sounded inside his head just as the alarms went off.

≈Sleep≈

SERENE

Even though he outmassed her by a considerable amount, microgravity had clearly taken its toll on Tommy's muscles, and Mira's memories painted him as more wallflower than warrior. He bounced hard both against his workstation and the floor, but remained conscious enough to gasp out two words.

"Help...me..."

The lights in the room started flashing as an alarm sounded. But she was close enough now to do what she wanted, and aided by Mirabelle and Doria, she slid easily into Tommy's dazed mind and turned it off.

It took her only a few seconds to find what she needed in his brain, and another to figure out how to make his mouth work.

"Alarm off. Secure from containment. I slipped, nothing more. We have enough people here to handle things."

≈*What are you doing?*≈

Mira's thoughts were relieved, incredulous, and shocked. Serene turned toward the doorway and saw Jantine and Katra push Mira to the side. Jantine won the skipping footrace to Tommy, and she hauled him up by his uniform and shoved him roughly into his console, but Serene's mental hold on him was absolute.

And although the Gammas as a whole were aghast at what she'd done, Serene caught the slightest glimmer of approval from several of them.

Looks like I can do something right on my own, at least for now.

Though Serene was expecting questions, she didn't expect Jantine to shout at her.

"What did you do? What were you thinking?"

Serene stood up and took several steps away from Jantine, who was trying to shake Tommy awake. Firmly under Serene's control, he was aware of what was happening to him, but unable to react in any way.

"Jantine, please stop. I'm sorry if I disobeyed, I just didn't want Katra to shoot him. Not in front of Mira."

Jantine's furious thoughts quickly returned to the cool, neutral state she worked so hard to maintain. But before the Beta could speak, Mira's voice reminded Serene there was still a lot about humans she didn't understand.

"Oh, honey," she said, "you have no idea what he's done. Not just to the mods, but to me personally, and to the people I love. Tommy is nothing to me but a handful of good memories and several I wish I could forget."

"But, the river…"

"Was a long, long time ago. And while you think you understand that memory, you're far too young to really know what…"

≈Katra, NO!≈

Mira's ability to control others was not as precise as Serene's, and Katra was fighting her every step of the way. She raised her weapon slowly, and Serene knew that even though it might destroy her, the Gamma was prepared to kill all of them for a clean shot at Tommy's unprotected head.

"He has…to pay…"

Everyone seemed to move in slow motion, and the lights dimmed again. But this time there were no alarms, and Serene felt another four minds join those assembling in the sleepers' chamber.

What have I done? And how can I stop it before it goes too far…

WATSON

Tommy watched helplessly as the troopers talked, completely frozen in place and lungs burning for another breath. There was a fluttering sensation inside his brain, extra pressure in his ears and a taste of harsh, filtered air moving sideways across his tongue. This last bit was an even crueler torture than when one of them was speaking with his voice, but other than the one holding him, they seemed to have forgotten about him entirely.

At least the trooper's stopped shaking me, but unless they remember to let me breathe, there's not much I can do to get myself out of this.

He was frozen in place, head flopped to the side and staring straight ahead at the third trooper in the room. Everyone was shouting, but the only voice he could make out was that of the little girl who'd tackled him, with her big eyes and strange head.

What bothered Tommy most about the little girl was not her age, but the words she was saying—one in particular.

Mira? But Captain Kołodziejski he said she was dead! Promised me. I...

One of the troopers kneeled down, and lit up her faceplate. The woman inside looked a lot like Mira, but it was hard to tell from his angle.

Mira! Oh thank you thank you Thank you! Please, Mira, get me away from these people, I have to get out of here before someone kills me!

Tommy had the distinct impression of two people listening to him, even though he couldn't move his mouth. All he could do was watch as the third trooper raised a weapon of some kind, and even with frozen eyes Tommy could easily draw a triangle from the ground, to its muzzle, to his face.

No, no. Please, stop her. She'd got a gun! Someone, anyone, please look. She's right there!

ohgodohgodohgodohgod

The trooper with the gun froze, mostly. It was still coming up to kill him, but she was struggling against some force, perhaps the same one that was holding him in place.

Mira, please save me. I'm sorry, so sorry, don't let me die pleasepleaseplease...

Out of the corner of his eye, Tommy saw another suit of white armor step forward, hand raised in front of it. Unless there was someone else in the room, it had to be Mira, but she moved nothing like the girl, then woman he used to love.

Do you remember how good it was with us, Mira? It can be like that again. Just please don't let them kill me. Please, I'm begging you. Please.

Then the woman holding him dropped him to the ground. This time, Tommy's head was bent awkwardly back, with an excellent view of the ceiling, the laboratory door and the gennie woman standing over him.

He watched as she took off her helmet, dropping it to the floor right beside his head. Her smooth, unlined face and her perfectly proportioned eyes answered all the questions he was afraid to ask.

Fuckfuckfuckshe'sagenniesorrysosorryhemademeit'snotmyfault

Tommy wanted to crawl away and hide, but his arms and legs were still frozen. All he could do was lie helpless on his back and watch as one of the new gennies removed their friend's helmet, revealing another beautiful face twisted in an angry scowl.

JANTINE

JANTINE STARED AT THE WHITE SUIT OF EARTHER armor containing Katra, more specifically at the weapon in her shaking hands. She'd never seen a Gamma this far out of control, and if Jantine couldn't bring her back from the edge it was unlikely either mod would live long enough to see anything else.

Is it too much to ask for just one thing on this mission to go according to plan?

"He has…to pay…for what he did."

Katra's voice over the suit's speakers was ragged, as if she were fighting herself for each word. Given Mira's fixed stance, outstretched hand, and abrupt mental silence, it was reasonable to assume Mira was somehow holding her in place.

"Katra—"

"No. Mira. No more forgiveness. He and his captain have declared war on my entire people. He will kill all of us, and that includes you. We have to stop him!"

Jantine saw herself and Mira mirrored in Katra's faceplate, and she realized that Katra was staring down a reflected image of herself in Jantine's. Whispering inside her helmet, Jantine hoped things had settled down enough in the landing bay for someone to come to her rescue.

"Jason, Artemus. I need you."

As soon as she spoke, she regretted not including O-6913, but it was hard to think of the Omega as an ally at the moment. That he cared for Serene was plain enough, but his loyalty to the rest of the mods was more than a little suspect. Jantine raised her hands to her suit's neck seals and released them. The inrush of cold air was just what she needed to help focus her thoughts, and she turned back to face down her de facto second-in-command.

Mira and Katra hadn't moved from their spots, though the Gamma's weapon was still struggling upward. Before Jantine could move forward and disarm her, Serene padded forward in her ridiculous Earther shoes and pulled the muzzle of the slugthrower up until it was pointed at the center of her forehead.

It was exactly the distraction the newly awakened Gamma infiltrators needed to swarm Katra and immobilize her. Unlike Serene, they'd entered suspended animation fully mature and in peak physical condition, and the more modern sleeper units had been conditioning them for Earth's gravity for nearly a month. Even if she'd had complete control of her body, Katra was no match for eight other Gamma infiltrators in their primes, especially when they picked her up and held her off the ground.

Mira slumped against a metal table that looked a lot like the one in Captain Kołodziejski's transmission. But Jantine had little time to wonder if it was the same surface, as Katra was now in full control of her mind once more.

"Release me at once! I am Senior Scout KTR-G245980-I. That human is a war criminal, and he must be executed immediately."

The Gammas holding Katra were a mix of genders and crèches, and though they were older by a few years, several reminded her strongly of Jarl. But while she didn't know all of their faces as intimately as Malik would have, they certainly knew hers.

One of them worked the seals on Katra's helmet, revealing her wide eyes and snarling expression. The Gamma's hair was slick with sweat, and Jantine thought she detected a faint odor of bile.

The Gamma who'd removed Katra's helmet looked up from the

disheveled mod in front of him, meeting Jantine's eyes from across the room. Ignoring Katra's curses and threats, he spoke in a strong, clear voice.

"Commander? I am MAR-G250698-I, called Marius. Carlton tells me that we are inside a hostile Lunar base. What are your orders?"

"Put her down. I have the prisoner under control. Serene, how long will he be like this?"

"He'll wake up whenever you want him to. Hello, Marius. Hello Yesha. Hello Hajira. Hello Karen. Hello... "

"You stupid girl, there's no time for this. He has to *die!*"

Katra surged forward, this time using her full, suit-assisted strength. But Jantine was prepared, and she met Katra's charge not with strength, but leverage. She grabbed a wrist in one hand and caught her under the shoulder with the other, using her own momentum to spin the Gamma into Mira's waiting arms. Mira reached down and touched a control on Katra's belt, and its gauntlets and joints locked into place.

Katra had knocked Serene to the floor as she passed, and it took all of Jantine's self-control not to backhand the Gamma. But the memory of Janbi's ruined face was enough of a reminder of how ragged her own emotions had been over the last few days.

Mira's voice sounded in Jantine's head, and for a second she shared in the entirely righteous rage that had consumed Katra. She felt her hand tightening on the Earther weapon in her hand and decided to return it to the holder on her chestplate.

≈*Katra. Katra. Listen to my thoughts. Let your anger go, this is not our way. I'm here with you. It's going to be all right.*≈

Jantine returned her attention to Marius and the awakened Gammas. One of the new arrivals was helping Serene up from the floor, and Jantine was about to thank him when she noticed his face wasn't quite right.

It was a mature face, not a fresh-faced mod just out of deep sleep. A human face, pressing a very human device against Serene's neck.

"You are a very bad man," said Serene, "and soon you will be dead."

"How sweet. You gennies always say such nice things. I'll assume this is my missing test subject, and that's Harlan over there in the sealed suit, yes?"

Horace Kołodziejski was as loathsome in person as Jantine had imagined. He was a thin, shifty-looking man, who'd somehow acquired a Colonial jumpsuit identical to the ones the Gammas were wearing. Given the transmission he'd sent earlier, it didn't take much imagination to figure out where it had come from, and as he pulled Serene close to his body, Jantine saw a designation on his chest that made her blood run cold.

DRN-B34316. That would make the mod in the vid one of Carlton's…

Jantine's jaw clenched, and she silently cursed herself for putting away her weapon. Marius turned at the sound of the human's voice, and Kołodziejski started at the motion and backed himself into the wall. As quietly and with as little movement of her lips as she could, Jantine mouthed, "Not yet. Wait until she's free," and the Gammas took a step back.

Now that she could see Kołodziejski's face she wondered what his plan really was. Despite his stolen garments, no one would ever mistake him for a mod. His face was too angular, his eyes too close together. In general, he gave off the impression of a skeleton trying to push its way out of an ill-fitting suit of skin.

Is he trying to escape? To free the other human? What's his play here?

Mira must have been thinking along similar lines.

"You won't get away with this, Captain. Commodore Maranova is—"

"A cloud of expanding atoms by now, I expect. When last I checked, she was flying blind straight into the teeth of my best two ships. And don't you lot get any ideas, you've seen my new T-virus in action, and I'm more than a little curious to see what it does to your little Alpha here."

Kołodziejski couldn't have frozen the mods in place more effectively if he'd used liquid nitrogen. Even Jantine was afraid to act, and she had no doubts whatsoever that the human would kill Serene anyway once he felt he had the upper hand.

But for now, she's alive. And he's not going anywhere.

The scenarios she could see resolving weren't at all to her liking, so Jantine decided to consult with her more level-headed advisors.

≈*Serene. Mira. Can you hear me?*≈

≈*Yes.*≈

Mira's thoughts were tinged with pain and fear, but Serene's were as cold as ice.

≈*Yes. Don't worry, Jantine. Help is on the way.*≈

≈*What?*≈

Before Serene could answer, Kołodziejski started sliding along the wall toward the portal leading to the sleeper chamber. To her dismay, the crowding Gammas parted and let him pass. Katra gave out a strangled moan, and Jantine's heart raced.

Then Jantine heard two clicks in her left ear, followed by Artemus's breathy rumble.

"Commander, I'm sorry. He got away from me and Jason. We're almost—"

The scattercomm squealed in her ear as a competing frequency came into range. She spared a look around the room to see if anyone was using an Earther comm, and in the split second her eyes left the doorway, O-6913 appeared crouching on the other side.

The Omega's face was a mask of fury, mouth open wide and lips trembling. Jantine eyes widened as she realized the interference on the comms was not coming from any device, but was, in fact, a scream.

Oh, no.

Jantine's was about to think a warning to Mira and the other mods when she heard the hiss of the injector.

"I warned you gennie freaks, and now this is on y—"

Kołodziejski's head exploded in a spray of bone and blood as the Omega's hands came together. Serene slumped to the floor, and it was Katra who voiced the scream in Jantine's throat as the Omega's ultrasonic wail of agony intensified.

The interference in Jantine's ear rose up past her ability to register it as anything other than pain. She felt her heart skip in her chest, and denied the double protection of SDF armor and colonial encounter suit, her exposed face grew uncomfortably hot.

She dove behind the instrument console the dark skinned Earther had been working at, pulling his unresisting form after her. On the floor and out of the direct path of the Omega's scream, she felt its effects subside. It felt like a fire was burning inside her left ear, but her vision was unaffected and unblocked, giving her an ant's eye view of the very messy end of Captain Horace Kołodziejski.

Not satisfied with simply beheading the murderous human, O-6913 seized his corpse in his large orange hands and squeezed. Blood fountained from the human's neck and bounced off the ceiling, and when the Omega pulled his hands apart, what was left of Kołodziejski came apart with them.

Katra's screams continued, and Jantine turned to look at the Gamma. Her skin was red and flushed as well, but Jantine could do nothing to help her but think one word over and over again.

≈StopstopstopstopStopSTOP!≈

Whether Mira relayed her order, or the Omega heard it himself, O-6913 slumped to his side and closed his mouth. Katra's screams became sobs, and fell to her knees as Mira deactivated her suit's restraints. Mira's own suit fell away from her as she raced to Serene's side, hard plates bouncing off the floor as she took two short hops across the blood-drenched room.

Jantine returned her eyes to Serene's still form. The child was covered in human blood, with an angry red welt spreading on her neck. She heard two voices rise above the growing confusion. The first was Mira's, calling for Carlton. But the second was a stranger's, and it took her a moment to realize it had come from behind her.

"W-w-what happened?"

A cold rage built behind Jantine's eyes, and she drew the pistol from her chest plate as she rolled over and slammed the human scientist's face into the floor. He was still groggy from Serene's mental control, but he recognized the muzzle of a weapon pressed into the back of his neck well enough.

"Shut up, human. Or you're next."

MIRA

Mira knelt down next to O-6913, watching as Carlton worked furiously to transfuse a barely conscious Serene from a device attached to his arm. That Serene wasn't dead already was a good sign, and the lack of black veins or exploding organs meant that either Kołodziejski was lying about what was in the injector, or that Tommy and his team of mad scientists had developed more than one T-Virus variant from the captured Alpha's blood.

Damn you, Tommy. Damn you for ever making me believe you cared about anything but yourself.

"Get back. All of you."

Artemus's basso rumble drew Mira's attention, and she saw him push through the group of Gammas crowding around Carlton while he worked. The Delta's voice was enough to deter most of them from interfering, but more than a few were offering to help, and the confusion over what had just happened was whipping them into a frenzy.

I can't do this. There's just too many of them.

"Mira..."

Serene's voice was barely a whisper, and from the scowl on Carlton's face, her brief return to consciousness wasn't what he'd hoped for. There was an SDF emergency kit open beside him, and the Beta was filling an injector with a green liquid of some kind. Mira had vague memories of an emergency medical seminar during which the instructor had warned about certain compounds that were only to be administered as a last resort.

The noise of the crowd intensified, as did their thoughts. Mira closed her eyes against the pain, but if dealing with a double handful of mods over the last few days had been stressful, several dozen was overwhelming.

"Mira...help...him...you need...to—"

Carlton pressed the injector to Serene's upper arm, and the child's fear spiked. Serene's eyes widened, and her unfocused panic was stronger than that of the crowd's emotions. Despite the pain, Mira reached out and brought both of them into a link. She regretted it instantly, but she borrowed some of Carlton's impossible calm to help her through the worst of it.

"Carlton. Wait. Let her finish."

The Beta's eyes narrowed, but he paused.

"There is no wait, Mira. I'm going to lose her if I don't intubate. Plus, the longer she's awake, the worse her pain gets. It's already making the rest of them crazy. Do you think we can deal with them if she dies?"

Mira's thoughts went immediately to Serene. She knew it was bad, but through Carlton's eyes, she saw just how close to death the child was. But Serene's fear of the injector was stronger even than her fear of death, and the Alpha bolstered Mira's efforts to remain calm. O-6913 seemed to relax a bit as well, but the Omega's shattered mind threatened to suck Mira in at any moment.

Think about clouds, Mira. Big, white, fluffy clouds. That's all they need right now: something to distract them. But you have to help O-6913. It's all too much for him—what he did, what he wants to do. You have to—

The injector hissed in Carlton's hands, and Mira felt the child's mind floating away.

"Dammit, Carlton! Not yet! Serene, I can't do this on my own. I don't know how—"

Yes you do. You just don't...remember...

Mira screamed as thoughts and images from dozens of lifetimes exploded in her head.

Again. And this time, she had Serene's memories of the last few days as well. She was vaguely aware of Carlton yelling, but she couldn't make out the words over the rush of information trying to find a home in her already battered brain. It was worse this time, much worse, and even though all of her own memories were settling back into familiar places, they didn't quite fit the same way as they once had.

Mira collapsed onto O-6913's chest. That she no longer heard every stray thought in the room was a small comfort, but the continuing chaos in the Omega's mind was mounting a serious challenge on her renewed mental defenses.

So she thought about clouds instead. Billowing, fluffy clouds, dancing across the sky and sparkling in the sun. Above them was the deep blue of a Colorado sky over the mountains, and the feel of the wind in her hair as she sailed an ultralight over the plains helped smooth out the rough edges of two dozen very scared mods.

The storm in O-6913's head dissipated, as did the rumble of the crowd. Mira felt another mind nearby, and she opened her eyes to see Jason staring down at her, his right hand extended for support.

Mira smiled and sent him her thanks, taking another small pleasure in his realization that for the first time communicating directly with her mind didn't include pain. With the Omega's help, she sat up and took in the room.

Artemus had pushed the Gammas back, and on the other side of the crowd, Jantine had Tommy sprawled facedown on the floor with one induction pistol pressed into the middle of his spine and another against the back of his head.

A fresh wave of anger toward her former lover almost undid her newfound calm, but the Gamma memories were back and offering suggestions about how deal with her emotions. Mira found it amusing that almost all of them suggested using her rage to build a wall, and then went a step further by expanding her previous efforts to include a courtyard, a moat, and a grand dining hall.

If I'm going to save a princess, I might as well have a castle.

Carlton rolled Serene onto her stomach and began massaging her lower back. Despite O-6913's distress, and the very real possibility that Serene might die from whatever had been in the injector, it was Carlton and Katra who were Mira's immediate concerns.

The Beta was sweating profusely, and though his hands were fast and sure as he worked to keep the Alpha alive, his emotions were running wild. Mira recognized the symptoms; she'd experienced them herself when Jason activated her latent T-virus as they fell from orbit in a stolen shuttle. Whatever Serene had done to give her back her memories must have affected him as well, and there wasn't anything she could do to help him with the extra voices in his head other than to continue projecting an aura of calm she didn't share. His thoughts were more focused than ever, and the one that was foremost in his mind was also in Mira's.

She looks so small...

Katra was on the verge of fighting her way through her own people to kill Tommy, and although Mira mostly agreed with her, she owed it to Serene to find a peaceful solution.

"Katra," she said, "please come help Carlton. You can't do anything there."

The Gamma turned to her, incredulous, as if by even suggesting that she not carve her way through the press of bodies and wring Tommy's neck Mira was guilty by association. But after a moment, Katra's thoughts fell into a pattern that Mira had learned to associate with risk assessment.

"Trust me," Mira said, "he will face judgment for this. But if we kill him now, no one will ever know what he's done. I claim his life—for this, and other harms done to me."

Katra's eyes widened, and Mira wasn't sure if it was her use of "we" or "me" that most affected the Gamma. Whichever it was, Katra approved, and the visions in her head about what she wanted to do to Tommy were enough to add a drawbridge to her castle.

Mira drew back into herself, clinging desperately to Jason's towering sense of identity. Now that she was whole again, or at least mostly so, she could finally appreciate the incredible journey the Omega had taken in the last few days. From being the elder statesman of a doomed expedition, to a marginalized outsider, and back again to a trusted counselor, his transformation rivaled Janbi's in its completeness, and the Omega still didn't consider himself exceptional.

My friend, will you help me again? Our brother needs us.

In lieu of an answer, Mira found herself on a broad white plain, with her castle at her back and Jason by her side. The child version of O-6913 was several meters away, blurring in and out of sight. Mira reached one of her hands up to Jason, who shrank until one of his hands was barely larger than hers. Hand in hand, they walked forward and knelt beside O-6913's flickering form.

One of O-6913's arms stretched out, and Mira opened herself to his perceptions. She was already accustomed to the confusion and pain in his mind, but she was not prepared for the thought-image he was trapped inside.

Kołodziejski was alive, and threatening Serene once more. But the Alpha's face kept shifting, becoming Crassus, then Jarl, then Doria.

"It's not his fault, you know," said an almost-familiar woman's voice from behind her. "He's so young, to have all this thrust upon him. His mind is shutting down, and you have to help him move on."

Mira expanded her perceptions until she could see the speaker without taking her eyes off of O-6913. To her surprise, it was a young girl with dark eyes and a wide smile whom she'd seen only in other people's minds.

"Doria?"

A slim boy about as tall as Jantine appeared next to Doria and spoke. "She worries a lot, doesn't she? It's a shame that she can't accept her strength."

"Hush, Malik. She's still alive, still finding her way. The clarity we have is denied her. For now."

Mira manifested another arm so she could take one of O-6913's hands in two of her own without letting go of Jason's. Drawing on the experience of the Gamma memory shards, she left the greater part of herself with the Omegas, and let her inner self rise up out of her body.

Mira turned, reveling in the freedom of an unencumbered mind. She could go anywhere, do anything, but fought the urge to spread herself across the universe. Standing naked above the Omegas and herself, she was finally free to confront the one voice in her head that all of her friends wanted to hear.

"See," said Malik. "She understands now. Can we go?"

"No, Malik. We still have more to do, and in any event, I must stay behind."

"That hardly seems fair. Let the living sort out the living. Haven't we done enough?"

Mira smiled, taking in the truth of Malik's words. The image of Doria smiled in return, and the memory of the Beta dissipated, flowing back into her subconscious mind where it belonged.

"Hello, Mira. I'm Doria. I'm glad you're here to help my friends. None of this is your fault, but if I'd known of your existence, I'd have approved."

Doria floated over to Mira, impossibly beautiful and far more corporeal than a memory had any right to be. Mira felt awkward and ashamed and unworthy in comparison, until Doria touched her on the shoulder, and Mira realized that all her doubts were holding her back from a deeper understanding.

Doria flowed into her arms, kissing her neck and whispering into her ear.

"It's all right. I'm here with you. And we have work to do."

Mira had no idea how long they stayed like that. In the mindscape, it could have been a heartbeat or a lifetime. She had no memory of breaking their embrace, but her next thoughts were of O-6913, and how weak his thoughts were.

The Omega was still reaching out for Serene, Crassus, Jarl, and the rest of his fallen comrades, but he could no longer articulate his desires. Mira felt a sense of deep responsibility for those deaths, and when O-6913 recognized the tenor of her thoughts, she sensed his inescapable guilt.

"It's all right," said Mira. "Doria helped me, just as you did. We're all here with you now, and you don't have to face this alone."

Serene's three-day old sense of self separated from Mira, keeping one hand on her shoulder and reaching toward the Omega with the other.

"I'm going to be all right. He was a bad man, and if you hadn't done it, one of the rest of us would have. It's not your fault, and no matter what happens, we will be together always."

Mira wondered how much of Serene's words were her own, or carried over from the Alpha's inexpert attempt to heal her. Doria's image knelt beside Mira, and guided her hands to the Omega's face.

"Rest now, my friend. Let us carry your burden for a while, until it is time to pass it on."

Doria and Serene and Mira and a dozen other memory shards took form and placed their hands on the dying Omega, taking away his pain and confusion and sifting through all of his happiest memories. Mira saw her Doria-self as a child, reaching up with a shaking hand to greet him for the first time. Saw Jason pulling him from the floor of the crèche and enveloping him in a warm sense of belonging, explaining to him about Jantine and Janbi and Carlton and Katra and Artemus. As Mira watched O-6913 fade away, Doria hugged her, pulling all the parts of her mind back into one coherent whole named Mirabelle Agnes Harlan.

Kneeling alone in front of her castle, Mira spoke to no one in particular. "He should have had a name. Serene never needed one for him, and he didn't want the rest of us to know. But I refuse to remember him as Grumpy. He deserves better than that."

"Mira Darling, we all do."

The sound of her father's voice filled her mind, and despite the pain of her last memory of him, she looked up to see Captain Emmanuel Rogers Harlan in his dress blacks.

"There's my girl."

"Daddy, I—"

"It's all right, Mira Darling. I'm always here, just like Doria and all the rest. Ask us for help, and we'll give it."

Mira stood, now wearing a set of her own blacks. Mira thought she could see Captain Martin peeking around the corner of her castle, but she kept her attention on the man who was never there.

"Daddy, I'm not sure I can do this. I'm not a Gamma, not like she was. They need more than I can give them, and even though I have the memories, it's just too hard."

Emmanuel gave one of his infrequent smiles, and Mira saw more than a little of Brian in his face.

"I thought you understood, daughter-mine. Of course you're not a Gamma. That's not what they need. You're an Alpha. A new kind of Alpha, just like the rest of them. Jantine, Carlton, Katra, Janbi, they're so much more than their programming now, and it's all because of you. You've shown them another way to live, a way to choose their own futures.

"Jason will help you make them understand, as will Serene. But you have to go back now. She doesn't have much time left, and Carlton will need help understanding what's happening to him."

Mira knew he wasn't real. She knew her father was ten years dead, and that Doria and Aloysius Martin and Malik and all the others were just memories trying to help her get by. But the thought of letting her father fade away into white nothingness was too much to bear, and she crushed him to her with all her strength.

"I love you, Daddy. Please don't leave me alone again."

"You're not alone, Mira. I'm with you, now and forever. But you have to go now, before it's too late."

Emmanuel Harlan's embroidered chest melted away, shifting into a bloody and tattered coverall. Mira looked up into O-6913's face, and a despite the chaos around them, a sense of absolute peace spread through her.

"Goodbye, Brian. I forgive you."

The Omega's thin mouth closed in a smile, something his living flesh could never do. Then he was gone too, leaving her alone.

No. I'll never be alone again.

The real world snapped back into focus around her, but this time the chaos of the lab was well within her ability to cope. The hurricane in her head was gone, and everything was exactly as Mira had seen it last.

Damn.

"Carlton?"

≈*Mira? I'm losing her. I can feel her slipping away. Doria says not to worry, and Harren is here and —*≈

≈*I know. It's going to be all right. I'm here with you. Here's what we have to do.*≈

JANTINE

"Marius, Katra, help us get her on the table. We don't have much time."

Mira's sudden order startled Jantine, and she nearly pressed the firing studs on her weapons. It wasn't that she'd have minded killing the human, but Serene and Mira seemed to think he was worth keeping alive, and he was probably the only one left alive who knew what was in that injector.

From her vantage point, it was hard to see exactly what was going on, but then a crowd of legs parted and Serene rose up from the blood-soaked floor in Carlton's arms.

≈*Jantine, are you with me?* ≈

≈*Yes, Mira.* ≈

≈*Take a couple Gammas and secure Tommy in the next room. If the information Serene got from his mind is correct, there's maybe a dozen people left on base, and only a handful are troopers. The rest are either away in Tycho City, or launched with* Indomitable *a few minutes ago.*≈

Jantine pulled one of the hand weapons away from the human's back and returned it to its place on her chestplate. Using her now-free hand, she grabbed the human's neck and pulled him from the floor. The room spun around her, and she altered her stance slightly to adjust for her damaged ear.

Still pressing the other weapon into his back, she leaned in and gave her best impression of Jarl's threatening whisper.

"One wrong move, and you're dead, human."

Whether out of fear or enlightened self-interest, the human complied, letting Jantine turn him away from the carnage and push him toward an exit on the far side of the laboratory.

Jantine gestured for two of the Gammas to follow, then shoved him a shuffling step forward. Even with the room spinning around her, Jantine was more graceful than Tommy, though being unable to hear out of her left ear would be a problem in a fight. She felt blood running down that side of her face, and wondered if Janbi's miracle doctor could build her a new ear.

"Open it. And no tricks, or you'll join your captain in whatever hell you two have made for yourselves."

The human raised a shaking hand to the door panel, but he paused before activating it.

"He wasn't my captain. He made us...this isn't what we set out to do. You have to believe me, I never meant to—"

Jantine smashed his face into the door and shoved her weapon into his back so hard she worried that she might push it all the way through.

"Intentions mean nothing, human. I saw what you did. No one had a weapon to your head, though if you'd prefer that I'll be happy to comply. Now open the door, or I'll press these studs and leave you to drown in your own blood. One more death isn't going to matter today."

The human's fingers fumbled blindly with the panel, opening it on his second try. The door opened, and he fell through into a sparsely furnished office. Keeping her weapon trained on him, Jantine waved one of the Gammas forward to cover the room's far exit. Jantine tipped her head toward the other mod, careful not to take her eyes off the blubbering human on the floor.

"What are you called?"

"Yesha, Commander. Are we going to execute this human?"

"No, please! It's not my fault!" Tommy whined. "They made me do it. I was trying to help you, honestly! Oh, God, please don't kill me pleasepleaseplease…"

"It's always excuses with you, isn't it, Tommy?" Mira's voice from the doorway was flat and hard. "Never your fault. Well, fuck you and your excuses. This time, you're the helpless victim, and it's us women who are in charge. Tell me where the antidote is, or I'll let Katra come in here and finish what she started."

"M-Mira?" The man—Tommy—sounded surprised to see her.

"Yes, that's right. M-Mira. Are you going to give me an answer, or do I have to go into your mind and rip it out?"

Jantine's eyes widened, and she turned away from the human to gauge Mira's intentions. The look of pure fury on her face was more pronounced than it had been at their first meeting, and even Jantine was surprised when she stepped forward and hauled Tommy to his feet.

"Well? Nothing to say? Oh, that's right, you don't speak Decent Human Being, do you? Only Chickenshit. Well maybe this will jog your memory."

Even without her suit, Mira was stronger than most humans, and her slap knocked his head back. Her next blow was a punch to his midsection, then her knee smashed into his groin. He dropped to the floor and curled up into a sobbing ball, but Mira wasn't done with him yet.

"Where is it? Where is the antidote! If that girl dies, they'll tear this system apart, and the universe will run red with blood. Tell me where it is!"

Mira punctuated each sentence with a kick, the last one coming dangerously close to the human's neck. He was barely able to speak, and what words he did get out weren't what she wanted to hear.

"I'm sorry…I'm sorry…I'm sorry…"

"Mira. Enough."

Mira spun around, rising half a meter from the floor. The look in her eyes was familiar, and when she spoke, it struck Jantine that this is how she must have looked when she was beating on Janbi.

"It will never be enough, Jantine." Mira waved a hand at the man on the floor. "This...this *thing* doesn't deserve to walk around like a human being, not after what he did. Serene's going to die if he doesn't help us, and I'm about out of options."

Jantine gave her weapon to Yesha, and then stepped forward to place a hand on Mira's shoulder.

"There has to be another way," she said. "You taught me that."

"No. Not with him. He deserves all this, and more."

"I don't underst—"

"Commander?" Yesha's voice drew Jantine's attention back to the man on the floor. "He's trying to say something."

"Only had... one dose. Kołodziejski barged in, grabbed...Couldn't stop him. Please, don't hurt me anymore. There isn't any more...please... "

Even with only one working ear, Jantine could make out what the human on the floor was saying, but Mira's perceptions went beyond the purely physical. From the look on her face, the human was telling the truth, but his words made no sense.

"Mira, what's he saying? I don't understand."

Mira shook off her hand and started back toward the other room. There was some sort of commotion behind her, and Jantine was tired of not knowing what was going on.

"Yesha, keep that safe for now," she said, gesturing to the human on the floor. "I'm sure we'll have more...questions for him in a minute."

"Yes, Commander."

Jantine followed Mira, and part of her was pleased by the grim smile on the Gamma's face as she passed. Yesha had clearly enjoyed Mira's abuse of the human, and Jantine wondered if she'd have felt any different a few days earlier. She certainly hadn't cared when Katra struck Captain Martin, and this wasn't much different.

What was it Jarl said? I have to do better.

Mira was standing just inside the doorway, looking at something in the laboratory. Jantine slid around her, and saw Serene was sitting up on the table, arms around Carlton's shoulders and crying. Katra was crying too, something Jantine never imagined was possible.

"You bastards. You had no right." Mira's voice carried across the room, and Serene turned at the sound of it. Her eyes were red and puffy, and her skin several shades darker than it had been just minutes before. But what grabbed Jantine's attention were the child's eyes. Brilliant blue eyes, set in an otherwise unremarkable human face.

Understanding came in a flash, and Jantine was torn between weeping and returning to the office to finish kicking Tommy to death. But it was Mira who said the words aloud, and when she did everything changed.

"The injector. It wasn't the virus, it was the antidote. But the active strain in her blood...our blood...it didn't distinguish between the two."

Across the room, Carlton nodded, his own eyes brimming with unshed tears.

"Yes. Congratulations, everyone. The humans finally found a way to reverse the effects of the Transgenic virus."

MIRA

MIRA COULDN'T BELIEVE THEY'D ACTUALLY DONE IT. CAPTAIN MARTIN
had hinted at the possibility of a vaccine, but not an actual cure.

*They've created a more terrible weapon than the virus variant that kills
instantly, and they have no idea what a good job they've done. We have to
shut this place down, and pray no other samples have made it off the base.*

If she didn't have the memories of an unchanged, happy, and
transgenic Serene in her head, Mira would never assume the little girl
in front of her was ever anything more than human. Her head was
already rounder in shape, and her eyes near copies of Mira's own.

My old ones, anyway.

Mira was almost afraid to be near her, ashamed of her birth planet,
of Tommy, and the uniform she once wore with pride. But Serene's
need for companionship was apparent even without empathic abilities, and Carlton had no experience with human children.

*At least, none of his own. Not sure how I feel about being on intimate
mental terms with him as well, but we'll figure it out, in time.*

Mira stepped forward, glad that she'd shed her armor earlier. The
Gammas had removed the Omega's—Brian's—body, but Kołodziejski's blood still coated most of the exposed surfaces in the room,
including Serene. When the little girl leapt awkwardly into Mira's
arms, the impact was enough to force her back a step.

Mira just held her, letting Serene cry herself out against her neck. Nothing she could say would make up for what she'd lost, just as there was no real way for Serene or Brian to apologize for ripping apart Mira's mind.

If she hadn't given them all back, my memories would be lost now. But thanking her for it seems so petty, and no matter what, I still love her. How can I not? Like she said, I'm a part of her, and she of me.

"What do you want to do, Serene? How can I help you?"

≈*Can you still hear my thoughts?*≈

Serene gave no response to either query, and Mira did not press her for one. She could remember her being cold and scared and feeling like the world was ending, and although there was no going back for Serene, she was still part of a larger community that loved her.

Larger. Right.

"Carlton, I need you to take Serene for a while."

"Why?"

"Jantine, Katra, and I still have some work to do. Artemus and Jason can help you deal with her, and I'm sure some of the sleeper Gammas can as well."

Mira could tell from his reaction that Carlton hadn't thought of that possibility. She wanted to tell him it was going to be okay, but if experience told her anything, it was that there were dozens of other voices in his head giving him advice right now, including one that sounded a lot like her.

Mira shifted her right arm to support Serene's weight, and used her left hand to gently pry the girl's arms from around her neck. As she'd expected her to, Serene resisted, burying her face into Mira's neck.

"No, I want to stay with you."

Even her voice is different now. So young.

"I have to go, Serene. I still have work to do. But when this is over, I promise we'll spend time together, all right? Just you and me, for as long as you like."

Serene sniffed, and she pulled her head up to look at Mira's face. It could have been a trick of the light, but her hair looked a few shades darker than before, and Mira had an urge to ruffle her fingers through it.

"Can Jason come, too?"

Mira gave in to her impulse, adding a smile to the action.

"Of course he can. If he wants to. Jason's got a lot of work to do as well, helping Carlton with the sleepers, but I think he'd like that. Can you be strong for me until I get back?".

Serene sniffed again and nodded. Mira nodded back and offloaded her into Carlton's waiting arms. He laid her down on the biobed and gave her a mild sedative. Serene tucked her hands under her head, closed her eyes, and fell asleep.

Carlton looked up at Mira and smiled.

"I don't think I'll ever be able to do that as well as you."

"Well, I've never done it before just now, so I think you'll be okay. Whatever you do, don't let her out of your sight. There are still hostiles in the base, so don't use any tech you're not sure of. I might be out of mental communication range, so send a Gamma to ask for help if you have to."

"All right. Hurry back."

"I will."

Katra bristled at the side of the room, her thoughts easy to read. She wanted to kill something, or specifically, someone, for what was done to Serene. Kołodziejski was dead, so Tommy was the only target left for her anger.

And since I just kicked him half to death, it wouldn't take much to finish the job. We'll have to leave by the other door.

Mira collected the scattered pieces of her armor and began reassembling her hardsuit. The emergency shutdown she'd performed didn't seem to have damaged any of its components, and while she snapped the familiar white and red pieces into place, she watched Katra for any change in her demeanor while keeping a cadence in her head.

Right shin, left shin, front and back. SDF troopers got the knack.

Right thigh, left thigh, up the leg. SDF enemies gonna beg.

By the time she'd finished, Jantine had reclaimed both her helmet and Katra's, but the Gamma refused to take it from her. Instead, Katra withdrew the supple black hood of her encounter suit from a hard pouch and pulled it over her head. A second later her visor appeared from another pouch and snapped into place without ceremony.

Jantine simply shrugged and put on the glossy white helmet that matched her suit. When Mira pulled her induction pistol from her chest plate, both Jantine and Katra did as well, following suit when Mira checked the ammunition canister, triggered the acceleration module, and watched the indicator light cycle from amber to green.

Awarding each of them forty points for following proper weapon discipline, she nodded to her new strike team and prepared herself for action. They might not win the Clarke Cup, but Mira would take them at her back any day.

"All right, ladies, let's go."

Jantine fell in behind her, but Katra didn't budge. Mira was two steps from the portal leading to the sleepers' chamber when Katra voiced her objection.

"No. There are still threats here."

"And Artemus and eight other Gammas to deal with them," Jantine said, speaking up faster than Mira expected. The Beta was back in command mode, at least for a little while.

"I...we need you with us. And after the beating Mira just gave that one," she said, hooking a thumb over her shoulder, "he's not going anywhere for a while."

Katra scowled and remained where she was.

"There are still at least a dozen people in this facility," Mira said. "I don't know what side everybody's on yet, but I do know that they can't lie to me. And if I can save more lives today, I have to at least try. Serene sacrificed a lot to get us this intel. We need to put it to good use. I need you at my back to do this. Can I count on you?"

Katra simply nodded. Her scowl did not diminish, but at least she started moving. Then, proving that she was always paying attention, Katra triggered a belt control and her hardsuit came apart as she took her first skipping step, and her second one carried her past Mira into the sleeper chamber.

There was a clattering sound as the induction pistol hit the floor, and Artemus tossed her both a pulser and a Colonial hand weapon. The latter disappeared almost instantly, then a second later there was a shimmering effect as Katra passed one of the suspension units. A second after that, she melded into the darkness as if she'd never existed.

Mira formed a three-way link between herself, Jantine, and Katra. The other mods were calm and focused, and they sent her their readiness for orders. Mira was pleased that their emotions no longer threatened to crack her skull open, and she moved into the larger chamber with Jantine a step behind her.

≈*Jason's map indicated a control chamber one level up. Katra, do you think you can find it?*≈

A wordless affirmation was the Gamma's only reply, and quicker than Mira expected, she slipped out of her mental communications range. All Mira could do was follow, pausing at the corridor entrance and scanning the opposite direction for anything Katra might have ignored.

There was nothing there.

≈*Jantine. I hate to even ask it, but can Katra hold it together?*≈

≈*Of course. Katra's the best. It's why she's here. Jarl was better at takedowns, but no one matches her on patrol. Those mods back there are going to be the best trained infiltrators this side of the colonies.*≈

Jantine's response was tinged with amusement, and Mira was pleased again to note that it held none of the contempt it might have a few days earlier.

Is this my command, then? I still feel like an SDF officer, but other than Commodore Maranova, everyone from the fleet I've met since leaving Valiant *has pulled a weapon on me. They've branded me a traitor, and if being a patriot means associating with trash like Kołodziejski and Tommy, I don't think I even care.*

The realization of her fall from grace stung, but Mira heard Emmanuel's chuckle in the back of her mind. If her mental father figure approved of her choices, then the rest of the fleet didn't matter.

As they approached an autolift, Jantine pulled up short, and through her eyes Mira saw a different view of an emergency panel Mira had seen earlier and dismissed. She'd entirely missed the pattern of scratches Jantine had seen from meters away, and Mira resolved to enroll herself in Katra's scout school when this was all over.

≈*What does it mean? Does she want us to follow, or is it a warning? None of my mod memories are combat-related.*≈

≈*You're doing fine. We follow. This is one of Jarl's marks, actually. She really cared for him, and I guess this is her way of keeping him alive. I'll lead for now.*≈

Mira still remembered the depth of Katra's pain from the few seconds she'd let it overwhelm her that first night, and the echoes of it when they'd spoken on the train. Mira had never met Jarl save in battle, and she still didn't know if any of the slugs that killed him had come from her weapons.

If Jantine was still grieving for Jarl, or *any* of her dead, it didn't show. Her mind was focused on the task at hand and nothing else. The panel came off the wall easily, indicating Katra hadn't secured it from within. This part of the base wasn't on Jason's map, but Jantine skipped ahead into an accessway of pressure-sealed moon rock as if she'd been walking it for months.

Each new set of nearly invisible scratches she saw sent them moving in a different direction, until the map overlay appeared again in Mira's visor, just as Jantine finished climbing a slanted shaft to the next level. Katra's position was marked on Mira's display, just out of communications range.

≈*Jantine, wait up.*≈

The Beta paused at the top of the shaft for Mira to join her, then turned her head toward her. Mira leaned close and touched faceplates, only speaking after verifying all her comms were off.

"We've still got a long way to go, haven't we? To trusting one another, I mean. Until now, there's always been another goal, some-place we had to be and reasons why we couldn't talk about what's happened and heal."

Jantine paused for a moment before speaking, and Mira tasted rich notes of sunlight and chocolate in her thoughts.

"Mordecai Harrison said something to me before we left. I was angry at Janbi for staying behind, angry at you and Serene, and a bunch of other things that aren't important.

"Harrison told me that he believes each of us makes our own universe and peoples it with our own fears. He said that the reason why I was angry, why I'd lost control not once, but twice, is because I didn't believe in myself. Not my abilities, or training, but myself. And until I did, I'd never be the person I wanted to be."

It didn't happen often, but when Jantine spoke like this, Mira could see why the Colonial Alphas had shaped an entire generation of mods to follow her.

Jantine gestured at a section of wall with three small dots carved into it, each smaller than the other.

"This way, but quietly. Use your abilities."

Mira tried to keep her steps soft, wondering if her maneuvering jets would exceed the sound threshold Katra was trying to maintain. She thought about Harrison's once-removed advice, and then remembered another conversation she'd had with Jantine.

Or, more accurately, one she'd had with Doria.

≈*Do you remember what Doria told you, about what to do when things go wrong?*≈

An image of herself and Jantine sitting in folding chairs while the Omegas worked behind them formed in Mira's mind, and she shared it with Jantine. She felt Jantine's appreciation of her effort, tinged with a bit of sadness.

≈*Yes, and that's exactly what sprung into my mind when he said it. I was trying to be strong, but nothing was working right. I hated Janbi for how well he was adapting, and I loved him and feared him at the same time. But Serene was right: he's the best of us, and he was meant to be the person I turned to for help.*≈

Jantine crouched at a corner, her hand a few centimeters away from a curved, arrow-like symbol. Mira could feel Katra moving in and out of the edges of her perception, and sent her an acknowledgment. To her surprise, it wasn't the Gamma who answered, but Carlton.

≈What is it? Are you back already?≈

Mira's eyes widened, and she checked her location in the visor display. They'd traveled almost six hundred meters from the lab, well beyond her normal range.

≈Carlton, how are you hearing me? Is Serene …≈

Mira didn't even know how to ask the question, but Carlton supplied the answer she was looking for anyway.

≈No. She's completely virus-free, even the normal human variants are missing from her system. As for empathics, other than surface reads, I can't get anything from her. Harren says…Sorry, I'm not used to this.≈

≈Hold on for a second, will you? I'm with Jantine. Jantine, did you hear Carlton just now?≈

≈Carlton? Why would I…is he in the tunnels with us? Has something happened?≈

Mira tried to make sense of what was going on, but before she got anywhere with her thoughts, Katra came back into range and sent words and images into the shared link.

≈I have five hostiles in hardsuits guarding a collection of civvies and one female SDF officer. How soon can you tell me who to kill?≈

Mira sat down in the passage, trying to concentrate. She and Carlton shared more than an ability to communicate and read emotions. They shared the *same* ability, and more than a few of the same memories to boot.

And if I'm right, perhaps something else as well.

≈Carlton, I know the answer's probably yes, but do you still have Serene's scans from the Institute on your handheld?≈

≈Of course I do. Why?≈

≈Tommy's… that lab should have a genetic sequencer. You should run a scan of yourself and compare it to those readings. And mine, if you have them. Wait till I contact you to give me the results—I have an idea about what's going on.≈

Carlton sent her an acknowledgment, and then his thoughts disappeared as suddenly as they'd arrived. There'd be time enough to puzzle out why she was connected to the Beta like this later. Katra and Jantine needed her full attention right now.

≈*Katra, what's your position?*≈

≈*One hundred ninety-five meters from you. That's your range, yes? The humans are thirty meters from here.*≈

≈*Copy that. Head back over there, we'll be up with you in a minute.*≈

Jantine started to move down the passage, but Mira reached up and grabbed one of her arms. She held her still until Katra was back out of range. Jantine sent her caution and surprise, but she stopped anyway.

≈*They can wait a minute. What did you do? Did Mordecai say anything else?*≈

≈*I told him about Janbi. About who he was, both to me and the Colony. Can you see it in my mind? I don't want to get the words wrong.*≈

≈*I'll try. I've only ever done it with the Builders, so if it hurts you have to let me know.*≈

When Jantine signaled she was ready, Mira opened her mind, and pulled Jantine with her onto the white plain. They appeared standing at the edge of Mira's mind castle, bare feet resting on green grass. Mira was surprised to see a second towering structure nearby, and also when Jantine's hand reached out to touch her cheek.

There was a look of wonder on the Beta's face that never seemed to reach her real one. Her hand was cold, like glass, but it warmed instantly when it moved across her skin.

"I like your new face better. But this one is all right, I guess."

Mira smiled, and Jantine did the same. She looked younger in the dreamscape, as if the cares of the real world never touched her here. Unlike Mira's castle, Jantine's tower was built to keep things in, and there were no doors.

"Who you are here is who you are inside. It's the universe Mordecai was talking about, created by your thoughts and desires. Just think about him, and we should—"

An image of Mordecai Harrison appeared beside them, mouth open as if frozen mid-sentence. Jantine raised her hand to touch his face, and the old man's mouth pulled back into a smile.

"Good. It's not right to be alone. My wife and I were together for almost eighty years. In all that time, I never felt good enough for her, and when she died, I was lost for a while."

Mordecai's voice was warm and soft, and it seemed to fill all the space around them. His right hand gestured to his eye patch, and then down to his leg. Jantine mirrored the gesture, and her lips were moving when he spoke again.

"We caught the men who killed her—who did this to me. They were separatists. Young fools who didn't want old men like me telling them what to do with their lives. They killed my wife and burned my body, and instead of doing the same to them, we locked them away and put happy thoughts back into their heads.

"But no matter how long they live, no matter what kind of productive lives they might someday lead, Almira will still be dead, and I had to let her go before I ended up the same way.

"My universe is full of possibilities, and if you want to be more than whatever thoughts were stuffed in this fragile thing..." Both Mordecai and Jantine reached up and poked the other in the forehead, "...you have to forgive yourself for being alive. It's not your fault. You didn't choose to live, you just did. And if you're anything like your young man, your universe is going to be a very, very interesting place."

Mordecai smiled, and his face faded away into whiteness. Jantine rose off the ground, arms stretched wide, and she flew around Mira in ever-tightening circles before touching down in front of her.

"I've always wanted to do that. Your hardsuits, they can fly, yes? Once you learn how, that is."

Mira laughed, remembering her very similar urge the first time she went out on *Valiant*'s hull. She and her team were there to check on power conduits, but every one of her people was watching to see what she'd do. Instead of giving them a show, she'd given them orders, saving her zero-g acrobatics for the Fleet Games.

"Oh, yes. And so much more. So what are you going to do?"

"Janbi wants to live on Earth. He wants us to be old, and tell people what to do. But I want this, all of this..." Jantine gestured, and the mindscape became the blackness of space, with stars and galaxies blazing in all their glory.

"And Janbi. He was right about that, too, when he offered to let me go. But I want him, so I'll kill more people and fight as hard as I can until I can be with him again. I believe in me, in him, and us. And you as well, so you'd better be right about who we can trust."

Mira returned the mindscape to white, and then dissolved the link and returned them back to reality. According to her visor, only a few seconds had passed, which boded well for Katra's mood. Mira released Jantine's arm and carefully stood up.

≈*Well, let's go see about that.*≈

JANTINE

JANTINE SETTLED IN NEXT TO KATRA'S SLIM FORM, WISHING SHE'D thought to shed her Earther armor as well. With full respect for Mira, it was awkward and bulky, though there were a few features she wished to try out someday. The maneuvering jets for one, but once interfaced with her handheld, its sensor suite was truly impressive.

As she shifted to get a better look at the rendered scene on Katra's handheld, a spike of pain from her ruined left ear made her wince, and an accompanying wave of vertigo caused her to lean into the Gamma. Luckily, the humans below them were too busy arguing with one another to hear the two mods tumble into the side of the passage, but it was definitely more noise than she'd intended to make while observing them.

≈*Jantine, are you all right?*≈

Through the three-way link, she saw Mira's view of the pressure door leading into the compartment, and could also feel Katra's concern and fierce devotion to her. The Gamma set her handheld down and helped return Jantine to a crouching position. After a moment, the dizziness and pain subsided, and she returned her attention to the surveillance.

≈*I'm fine. Another of them is gesturing at the door now, but the civvies are still in restraints. I don't think the female officer is with them, given her posture.*≈

In truth, it was hard to tell anything from an image rendered from ultrasonic sensor data, but Jantine had made do with less information in the past. The armored humans were definitely arguing, and the others were either tied to chairs or refusing to leave them.

≈*I'm definitely picking up mixed emotions, but it's hard to distinguish who's who from this side of the door. I'm going to have to get line of sight for an accurate read. Are you two ready?*≈

Katra nodded, powering down the handheld and stowing it in a thigh sheath. She checked her pulser's charge one last time before turning on her active camouflage, and faded from sight.

True infiltrators like Katra didn't simply blend in, they *became* the space they inhabited. Jantine had never been this close to an active system before, at least not one she was aware of in advance. The urge to poke Katra to see if she was still real was strong, but their mission had to take precedence.

And since I'm the distraction of the hour, I need to focus on the fact that while there are only a couple of drawn weapons in there, all of our enemies are probably as heavily armed as I am.

The natural passage the two mods were in was separated from the mechanical crawlspace above the control room by one of the omnipresent magnetic grates the Earthers used to build this base instead of proper grav plating. It was easily removed, allowing Jantine to slip into the crawlspace and move forward to retrieve the sensor Katra had placed earlier.

It was impossible to tell exactly where Mira's thoughts were coming from, but the Earther's eyes told her she was about a meter away from the pressure door leading from the main corridor to the control room.

It was Mira's eyes she needed now, or more accurately, her experience.

≈*I'm in position.*≈

Jantine was lying prone next to a gently humming machine, and she imagined the air it was circulating running over the skin of her suit. While she had no direct information on where the people in the room were, all of them had to breathe something, and once she installed the gas canister, the humans in suits would either have to come up here through the maintenance hatch into Katra's line of fire, or open the hatch and step into Mira's.

≈*Okay. Jantine, press the red switch on top of the unit, and then pull the handle on the side toward you. The control center's systems are independent from the main base recyclers, and with that many people moving around down there, the CO2 alarms will go off almost immediately. They'll revive as soon as they're exposed to fresh air, so we'll have to move fast.*≈

≈*It's cycling now. And Mira?*≈

≈*Yes?*≈

≈*Thank you for letting me fly.*≈

Mira's answer was the memory of a smile. Jantine edged forward on her elbows until she was at the edge of the maintenance hatch, and then she drew her induction pistol from the suit's chest plate before lying flat again.

≈*Something's definitely happening in there. Tempers are flaring, and… the hatch is opening! Get ready to go in.*≈

Katra appeared at the hatch with her pulser in one hand and the release handle in the other.

≈*Go, Go, Go!*≈

At Mira's signal, Katra twisted the handle and threw the hatch open, and Jantine slithered down into the room. One of the armored humans pointed a weapon straight at her, but was shocked enough by her appearance that she was able to easily knock it out of his hands and force him to the floor.

The suited human at the door took a step forward, but then crumpled into a heap, and Jantine felt Mira's satisfaction through their link. Another was turning to see what happened when Mira's external speakers sent her voice booming into the room.

"This is Lieutenant Commander Mira Harlan, ordering you to stand down. I know some of you don't agree with Captain Kołodziejski's methods, and you probably already know that there is a fleet in orbit prepared to utterly destroy this base unless you comply. Put

down your weapons and deactivate your hardsuits, and you will not
be harmed."

≈Mira, which ones can I shoot?≈

*≈None of them, it seems. Jantine dealt with the leader, and the three still
active don't want to be here any more than we do.≈*

Jantine smiled at Katra's flash of disappointment. The Gamma
dropped to the floor, and a moment later, the humans followed Mira's
order. Jantine removed her helmet, relishing the feel of cold air on her
face.

"Identify yourselves for the record."

The three standing troopers kept their attention on Mira as she
came into the room, following her weapon with their eyes as she
waved them toward the wall. Once they were up against it, she aimed
the pistol at the chest of the man on the far left. He swallowed noisily
before answering.

"Sergeant James Hardesty," he said.

The other two quickly followed suit.

"Trooper Nils Mikkelson."

"Trooper Janice Walters."

Katra moved to the black-clad human woman sitting at the control
console and shoved her roughly to the floor. She came to rest
awkwardly on pieces of the troopers' discarded armor, but she made
no move to adjust to a more comfortable position. Jantine shot Katra a
questioning glance.

"She was about to activate a control," Katra said. "Now she
cannot."

Jantine shrugged, and then she collected weapons from the floor
and tossed them out into the corridor. When she reached the other
side of the room, she turned and looked at the humans who were still
seated. As they'd suspected, all six were secured to their chairs with
their hands behind them. Some sort of clear material held their
mouths shut.

≈Mira, what about these civvies?≈

*≈Two of them are—or rather, were—Kołodziejski's spies. The woman on
the floor had a spike of fear when she heard my name. I think she's the control*

officer I was talking to before. She wants to tell me something, but she is terri-fied of Katra.≈

While she couldn't sense Katra's underlying emotions like Mira did, the Gamma's response gave Jantine a fairly good idea of what she was feeling.

≈*Good. Shall I shoot the spies?*≈

Jantine was only mildly surprised by Katra's bloodlust, but it had been a trying day for everyone, and the Gamma's opportunities for physical release had been few.

≈*Not just yet. We want them to confess first. Jantine, there's a belt control shaped like a…I forget sometimes. It looks like this.*≈

Mira sent an image of a pair of slightly raised concentric circles, and of her hand turning it two rotations to the left. When Jantine turned the first of her downed opponents over to reach it, the man's face was slack and lifeless. Assuming he was somehow incapacitated by Mira's abilities, she activated the control as she'd been shown, and the man's suit went completely rigid. She picked him up and moved him away from the uniformed woman on the floor.

Once he was safely out of reach, she removed the helmet from the second, revealing a bald, dark-skinned woman. Jantine repeated the process, then stood where she could see both the corridor and the humans standing against the wall.

"So, who wants to tell me their story? My friends and I have come a long way to hear it, and we appreciate your cooperation."

≈*Jantine, Carlton is sending Artemus and three Gammas to our position. He also wants to know how you're feeling.*≈

≈*I am fine. You will tell me about how you know this when we are finished, yes?*≈

≈*Of course. We're still trying to figure it out ourselves, but I don't think it's something you need to worry about. It may…no, I don't want to speculate.*≈

Jantine sent Mira her confidence and looked down the corridor for the other mods. But an unfamiliar voice behind her brought her attention back to the uniformed woman on the floor.

"Your fleet? It's gone. We recorded a massive explosion a few minutes ago, about the time we lost contact with *Indomitable*. But we had nothing to do with that, I swear. And the whole time I was talking to you before, that pig Washburn"—the uniformed woman said, gesturing to the trooper Jantine had disabled—"had his pistol jammed into my ear. When I couldn't raise Captain Kołodziejski, he went crazy, and sealed us all in here."

Mira didn't directly acknowledge what the woman was saying, but Jantine had a sense of great sadness from her friend that could have meant several things. She hoped that whatever it was that was bothering Mira was something she'd share before too much time passed.

Katra moved forward and nudged the woman toward the other humans, and she crawled over without further complaint. As she moved, Jantine noted an angry bruise on the side of her face, far too developed to have been Katra's doing.

≈*Jantine, the lieutenant on the left wants to say something. Take the tape off his mouth.*≈

Jantine stepped past Katra to the bound SDF officer and tore the transparent covering away.

"It's true, ma'am. When Captain Kołodziejski arrived a few days ago, he evacuated pretty much everyone to Tycho City. And when your voice came over the comm from the shuttle, Washburn kind of lost it. This base has been staffed primarily with officers from *Indomitable* since we arrived, and they all cleared out when the ship lifted. We're alone down here, and it seems we're...what the hell is that!"

Artemus wedged himself through the portal, and once inside, had to duck his head slightly to avoid scraping it on the ceiling. Mira slid to the side as he approached, and all three prisoners tried to press themselves into—and through—the wall. Jantine saw Marius and Yesha take up station outside.

"I am Defense Guardian Artemus, and you humans are now subject to the Interstellar Compact." When he spoke, he spread his arms wide, making sure the humans could see the weapons in all four of his hands.

"If you attempt to escape, you will be punished. If you attempt rebellion against my authority, you will be punished. If you take any action against my comrades in arms, you will be punished, and most likely killed. Do you understand these conditions of captivity?"

The troopers nodded, but Jantine added her own warning to that of the Delta.

"He needs to hear you say it. Otherwise, you are still enemy combatants, and he's a very good shot."

Artemus turned both his lower arms and one of the uppers until each of the weapons was pointed directly at a prisoner's head. All three were quick to respond with "yes" and "yes, sir", but Artemus wasn't done having fun just yet.

"I am Defense Guardian Artemus! There is no *sir* to *yes* at! Will you comply or not!"

"Yes, Defense Guardian Artemus!"

Artemus gave one of his rare smiles, showing his massive white teeth. "Good. Scout Marius, secure these prisoners, and those two on the floor as well. I will follow directly. Scout Yesha, up."

The slim female Gamma tossed one of the captured induction pistols up through the maintenance hatch, then followed it herself a moment later. Jantine heard her settle in next to the circulating machine, and several seconds later, she felt fresh air blowing on her face. Marius led the prisoners out into the hallway.

Why Artemus, you have a positive gift for command. We will need to work on this, but I see new opportunities ahead for you.

"Commander. Lieutenant Commander. Will there be anything else?"

Jantine shook her head.

"You have performed admirably, Defense Guardian Artemus. Please see to our guests, and we'll talk soon."

The Delta nodded, and reversed his complicated entrance.

Mira waved Jantine to the command console and began activating controls. By the time Jantine sat, several holo displays were active, one of which showed the repeating signal they'd agreed upon with Commodore Maranova before launch.

Mira rested a gauntleted hand on Jantine's shoulder.

"If they're out there, any of them, this should do the trick. All we can do now is wait. Carlton says we'll need to get you down to Earth as soon as possible to deal with your ear, but he thinks the damage isn't irreversible."

Jantine thought about what Mira was saying, her eyes on the slowly bouncing signal announcing their presence to their allies. She didn't doubt that her friend was in contact with Carlton, but Mira hadn't indicated that the prisoner was lying earlier either. If Commodore Maranova's strike force really had been destroyed, the only vessel they had access to was the shuttle they came in on, and it was far too small to accommodate the sleepers.

The chair she was sitting in was much like the ones in the shuttle's control center, as was the console in front of her. She hadn't had time to familiarize herself with it completely, but if it was anything like the other ones she'd seen, there would be an internal transmitter.

Jantine swiveled to face the uniformed woman on the floor. The woman shot her an angry look, but while Jantine was not quite as threatening as Artemus, she still liked to think she inspired respect.

"You, human. What is your name?"

"Lieutenant Lydia Daniels."

"How many humans can this base support?"

"I'm not sure I like the way you say humans."

Katra stepped forward, raising her pulser. Jantine stopped her with an upraised hand, which was enough to change the look in the human's eyes.

"Shall I call Artemus back in here to explain the rules again? Or can we discuss this like rational people?"

Before Daniels could answer, Mira removed the tape from another prisoner's mouth.

"Quit playing around, Lydia. These gennies mean business, and they probably saw that transmission the Captain sent. Five hundred. It can support five hundred of us for almost a year, indefinitely if we can get enough oxygen out of the walls."

Yes, that will do nicely.

ANDREISON

"Sir, ma'am, Lt. Inyoke is picking up a signal from the north polar region. No audio, but definitely repeating, and on a Fleet frequency. Shall we respond?"

Marya's head was still reeling from the magnitude of what had just happened. Every few seconds since her old ship had surrendered, she'd logged another request for clemency from another vessel, each with some variation of, "It wasn't me; I didn't know."

Save it for your court martials, you fucks. I know some really lousy advocates, and I'd be happy to make a few recommendations.

Captain DeMarco had been answering each one in the order it arrived, and so far, most of the Home Fleet had surrendered to their force of one antique battle cruiser and one and a half dreadnaughts.

One of which belongs to Mira, or at least should. But still no contact from Valiant, *and I'm about to lose my mind.*

"Hold off a moment on responding to that, Andreison. There's something we need to talk about first."

Commodore Maranova swung herself down into the pit, and clomped over to stand behind a very confused Marya.

Oh no, you don't. I've seen that look on your face before, and it always means more bullshit duties on behalf of your secret cabal.

I'm out, and after the last hour you'll have to shoot me before I'll agree.

"Ma'am, with respect, Comms division can field these messages going forward. I'd like to fly over to *Valiant*, and help coordinate the rescue ships. I need to see my wife, ma'am, and as soon as possible."

Maranova added a few more wrinkles to her smile, and Marya got ready to end her career.

Again.

"That's what I want to talk about, Marya. Your wife's not aboard *Valiant*, and hasn't been for a couple days. You were right: she and Captain Martin made it off alive, along with the gennies you identified for us."

Alive. She's alive, and…

You fucking bitch!

Marya's eyes responded to her burst of anger and adrenaline, narrowing her focus to pinprick apertures with just enough room to record Maranova's every action. Attack vectors and pressure points filled the space around the older woman's face, and Marya was half out of her chair before Captain DeMarco leaned over the railing to put one of his huge, gauntleted hands on her head. Marya shook it off immediately, but the distraction was enough to let Maranova slip out of reach, and Marya punched her chair instead.

"I know, Marya. I know it was wrong to keep this from you, but we needed you calm and focused on the task at hand. Once we found her at the Institute, we…"

Marya stepped away from the chair, fists clenching and every muscle in her neck and arms as tight as a drum. DeMarco's words had done nothing to calm her down, and now she wanted to punch him as well.

"Where. Is. She? Sir." Marya refused to look at the commodore as she scrambled back up the stairs on the opposite side of the pit. She didn't care about how this looked, about what it would mean in the long run. She just wanted to see Mira again, to hear her voice and drink in the smell of her hair.

"She's under our feet, so to speak." DeMarco was crouched down with his hands on the rail, helmet off and eye to eye with her for the first time since they'd met. "She went down to Echo Base with the gennies to get back their people. And before you go flying off to rescue her, that signal means she accomplished her mission. So, can you hate me a little later, and tell her we're ready to come get her?"

"Do you still have my transfer request on file, sir?"

DeMarco's expression was somewhere between surprise and terror, but he wasted no time in replying.

"Yes. If that's what you want, I'll approve it as soon as…"

"Get rid of it, sir. Someone has to teach you people some fucking manners, and I can't think of anyone but me who can do the job. What's the code to reply to Mira?"

Marya stared down the captain with one eye, and set the other on the commodore on the other side of the compartment. Maranova was smiling again, which pissed Marya off even more.

"Better give it to her, Samuel. I think she means it this time."

The captain didn't say anything, just manipulated his baton for a few seconds and waved it at her board. A holo panel appeared in front of her dented chair, and Marya sat down as fast as she could. It took her a few seconds to set up a secure relay through Inyoke's shuttle, and a few more to swallow as much of her anger as she could. Heart pounding, hand shaking, she pressed the send button and prepared herself for the worst.

"Aggie? Is that you?"

The transmission was a bit spotty, so Marya did her best to boost the signal. But the voice that came back to her was definitely Mira's, and the most beautiful thing she'd ever heard.

"Mar? Where are you…are you on the *Clarke* now? When did you leave *City of Lights*?"

They didn't tell her either. Fucking shit! How much of our time did they fucking waste to save their secrets, and how much danger did they expose her to when they had me broadcast them to the fucking worlds?

Marya set the channel to auto broadcast, and gripped the rail in front of her as hard as she could. She wanted to scream, to cry, to break everything she could lay her hands on. But the only thing Marya could do was the one thing she wanted most, so she did.

"There's a story there for later, but it's been a few days now. When you...when *Valiant* went dark, Captain Maddsen transferred about half his crew planetside. I was on L6 station when Captain DeMarco and the Commodore arrived, and the Captain seconded me to run his comms. I have him for you now, if you're ready."

"Give me a minute, Mar. I have something to do down here first."

Marya smiled, and suppressed a chuckle.

Typical Mira. I spend four days in Hell, fought a fucking war to bring her back to life, and my wife wants to put me on hold.

"Copy that. Ping when you're ready. And Deb would want me to tell you that she never believed what they were saying. You should come visit her and the girls, when you get a chance."

"I will, Mar, thanks. See you soon."

The circuit cut out on the other end, and Marya leaned forward to rest her head on the rail. Visions of Mira swam through her brain, of their first meeting at the Academy, of her hand being the only real thing in the universe as she screamed through the radiation treatments, of saying goodbye as she lifted for *Valiant*.

Of patching a transmission through every relay she could suborn between Earth and Saturn, to tell her about what happened to Deb.

The comm went live again, but before Marya could say a word the commodore jumped in.

"Harlan? Harlan, what's going on down there? What's the big idea about making us wait? Do you have any idea what's been going on up here? Well?"

"I'm here, ma'am. We've been a bit busy as well. The base is under our control, and Captain Kołodziejski...well, let's just say he's paid for his crimes."

"Well good. And everyone else?"

Did, did she just say...

A second, unfamiliar voice came over the relay "We are well, Commodore. I wish to make a statement, not just to you but to your planet. Can you facilitate this?"

Marya turned both eyes to the commodore, whose smile was wider than ever. Sensing what the older woman was about to say, Marya said it first.

Almost.

"We have a code for that, yes." Maranova's barking laugh filled the command center, and despite her righteous fury, Marya let the commodore just the slightest bit back into her heart.

"Go ahead when you're ready, Jantine. Marya here will make sure everyone with two ears and a heartbeat gets your message."

The relays she'd set up for the last systemwide message were still more or less in place, but it took a couple seconds to patch them through Inyoke's shuttle. Marya almost missed the start of the message, because once the woman started speaking she just about fell out of her chair at the realization of who Mira's new friend really was.

"This is Governor Jantine. In accordance with Interstellar Compact and the Magellan Accords, I claim right of conquest over the section of Earth's moon known as Echo Base, in response to war crimes perpetrated against myself and my people by rogue officers of your military.

"In cooperation with the legitimate leadership of your System Defense Force, my forces have occupied this base, and hereby declare it to be an independent colony. Our ambassador is already in negotiations with the highest levels of your government, and we will not be displaced.

"Attempt no landings here without our permission. Do not seek to challenge our sovereignty. We have come to heal the rift caused between our two peoples by the misguided actions of our ancestors, but if necessary will defend ourselves to the utmost of our abilities.

"You have been warned..."

MORDECAI

Mordecai stared across the chess board at Janbi, who was grinning wide enough to split his face in two. His nose was still a tad crooked, but something about it seemed to fit his face, giving it a comfortable imperfection that the rest of his people seemed to lack.

The Beta was waiting patiently for Mordecai's next move, with most of Mordecai's white pieces arranged in front of him. On the board, only four of Mordecai's wooden army remained, surrounded by a besieging force of black he'd barely managed to scratch.

It's not like I have much choice, now is it?

Mordecai moved his rook back to take the pawn threatening his king, unwilling to take direct action with that piece and be blocked by his own knight from escaping.

Janbi quickly moved his bishop in for the kill, pulling the captured piece off the board and placing it into its correct position with the rest of the queen's retinue.

Neither player had spoken since hearing Jantine's announcement, though Janbi's smile spoke volumes as to his intentions.

Ambassador. Hah! Can't even tie his own shoes, and he's one of the most important people on the planet. Who would have thought?

Mordecai felt a slight twinge of guilt for belittling Janbi's struggles on Earth, but it was hard to find anything not to like about the boy. In order to maintain the upper hand in their "negotiations," he had to at least think of him as an opponent, instead of someone he'd been waiting to meet all his life.

Besides, I'm not entirely sure he's not reading my mind. Did you hear that, Janbi? Smile if you're cheating...

Mordecai moved his knight to take the bishop, and Janbi's response was to move another pawn forward into the eighth rank. Mordecai scowled at the move he'd seen coming for at least fifteen minutes, and he waited for Janbi to ask for his queen back.

"How long have you known, Mordecai?"

"What? Are you reading my mind after all?"

Janbi shook his head.

"No, just your archives. And your personal journals, as well as those of your father. The analysis finished a few minutes ago, but we've been having so much fun, I decided to wait to ask."

"Ask me what? Paul, did you have anything to do with this?"

Paul didn't shift from his position across the room, where he was waiting with a pair of dinner plates that by now must have been stone cold.

"Don't drag me into this, old man. I told you to take black."

That you did, my boy. That you did.

"The virus, Doctor. How long have you known where it came from?"

Mordecai's blood ran cold, and his heart leapt into his throat. Janbi had somehow uncovered his family's deepest secret, on his own, in only a couple of hours.

It took me sixty years, and I only confirmed the hypothesis this afternoon. Hell of Bad Reasoning, I haven't even written that down yet.

"Janbi, I'm not sure I like you anymore."

Mordecai's voice was calm, but it did nothing to disturb the Beta's smile.

"That's all right. You don't have to like me. Just tell me the truth. How long have you known?"

Mordecai picked up the black queen and exchanged it for the intrepid pawn. Leaning back in his chair, he nodded at Paul, and the younger man left the room quietly. A few seconds later, convinced that all electronic records of their conversation were now scrambled, Mordecai leaned forward and made his confession.

"To be honest, I don't know that I do. But I've suspected it for the last few years, and the samples I took of Serene's and Harlan's blood were the pieces I was missing."

"So it is the ice world, then. Where they found Serene?"

"If not there, then wherever that colony ship stopped before it. We have no records of ever visiting it before, but Serene's virus was still active, in a way that we haven't seen since the very first expressions. It was changing her as we watched, adapting to whatever challenges she was facing. At first I thought it was because she was an Alpha, but Harlan was born right here on Earth and had the same strain of virus in her."

Janbi nodded.

"But even Harlan was an anomaly among anomalies. There had to be something else-some other factor that linked them together, and not the rest of you."

"It was the Omegas, wasn't it?"

Mordecai nodded.

"Even your Type 6s, the Deltas, they're still recognizably human. But the Omegas are so far removed from the baseline genome that they definitely qualify as an alien species, no matter what their origin. They were the first line to express on a planet other than Earth, and it would explain a lot if they had something to do with that ship crashing. Both Serene and Harlan were in near constant contact with one or the other of them since you kids landed, and despite the reverence your people have for them, I think they know a lot more than they're telling you."

Janbi nodded and pushed himself away from the table with his good arm. Mordecai's eye went to the sensor coupling on his stump, wondering what it was that Janbi was going to do if the T-virus proved incompatible with a prosthetic nerve graft.

"That much is certain. I think Mira will be able to help us with that when she returns, but for now I think we should keep this between us.

There may not be other Omegas among the sleepers, but if what you say is true, it won't be long until some start developing here on Earth."

Mordecai hadn't considered that, and Janbi's matter-of-fact delivery made the idea all the more frightening.

"So what's your plan, son? How do you want to proceed?"

"Son. I like that. I never had a father, and you'll do well enough, I guess."

This definitely affected Mordecai, who sat back in his chair and let out a long breath. He and Almira had never had children of their own, raising those of others when necessary and treating the whole planet as their family instead.

I think she'd have liked you, Janbi. I'm sure of it. But you frighten the hell out of me, and I'm sure you know that, too.

"But for now, I'm tired. I think I'll rest for a while."

Janbi stood and started to walk away from the table. Mordecai didn't know what to say to him, and as his universe changed at the will of another for the first time in years, he felt helpless to resist the Beta's pull.

"But, what about the game?"

Janbi turned back, and his crooked nose caught just the right amount of shadow to make his face seem much more mature. The Beta took two quick strides, then used his right hand to tip over first his king, then the queen he'd worked so skillfully to convert.

"I don't understand you, son. I really don't"

Janbi's boyish smile was as wide as ever, but when he spoke it was Mordecai who felt like a child.

"Good. That means we have something to work toward. But as for the game, I already have a queen. I don't need another. I just needed to know how long you'd keep playing after you realized you couldn't win.

"Good night, Mordecai. We'll speak in the morning about damages due my people as a result of the Exile. I think I'd like to speak to the other Reclamation governors as well. Can you arrange that?"

"Yes. Paul will set that up for us."

"Good then. And think about this for tomorrow, if you will: we sent out six other streamships, each with a team a lot like mine. Assuming they didn't also land in the middle of a civil war, that's twelve other Omegas out there somewhere who never met anyone like Mira Harlan, or learned what it means to be truly human. If all went according to plan, they're already dug in, and prepared to hide for a few hundred years and build up colonies with no outside influences whatsoever.

"What do you think they'll have in mind for the rest of us, when they finally do come out? I think we need to go to that ice planet as soon as possible, and find out what made that ship crash, and why. Because there's nothing I've ever heard of that can stop an Omega from getting what it wants, other than a kind word and an open heart."

Mordecai Harrison watched the young man who'd just destroyed his life's work walk out of his office. He felt old, and worn out, but for the first time in many months, he had something to look forward to with the dawn.

I only hope that you kids know what you're doing. Because if you can't help us fight whoever unleashed the virus on us centuries ago, the human race might be doomed after all...

SDF INDOMITABLE

In the command center's dim emergency lighting, nothing was moving save for thin wisps of smoke, falling down like ribbons from a thicker layer gathered at the compartment's ceiling. The ribbons danced and spun at odd angles, like an aurora during a solar storm. To complete the simile, an occasional bright spark popped into life from a ruined console, only to die quickly in the thin atmosphere and add to the cloud of smoke overhead.

The heart of the Home Fleet's newest warship had stopped beating hours ago, with scorched bulkheads and warped deck plates marking the cause of her demise. Charred bodies littered the floor, either pinned in place by ruined machinery or held there by Luna's slight gravity.

The only sound in the compartment was the occasional groan of settling metal, until an overhead conduit burst and belched forth a fine, white mist that froze quickly in the frigid air. As it fell through the smoke, the mist covered a pile of rubble in the center of the compartment with a layer of ice, slowly spilling over onto the rest of the deck. The mist subsided after only a few seconds, but the coating it left behind persisted, giving the rubble a soft, green glow.

Four strong knocks on the other side of the out hatch echoed throughout the compartment, and the knocking repeated a few seconds later. The sound was followed by the slow mechanical grinding of the hatch's emergency release, and when it cracked open a shaft of golden light stabbed through the smoke, followed by a shower of angry red sparks.

A man's voice came in from the corridor, growing stronger as the hatch cranked open another few centimeters shuddered to a halt.

"I'm telling you, it seems like I just did this on *Valiant*, and..." The rest of his response was cut off by the squeal of angry metal when gauntleted hands worked their way into the gap and forced it the rest of the way open.

An armored trooper stepped into the compartment, and the same male voice blasted out from his external speakers.

"¡madre de Dios! ¡Qué en los mundos sucedió aquí!"

There was no audible response, but another armored figure slid into the room seconds later and punched the first in the shoulder.

"Look, I'm sorry, Astrid, but there's only so much more of this I can take! How many more compartments do we have to check before we can clear this..."

The man's voice trailed off as he surveyed the wreckage. His partner tapped him on the shoulder, motioning first to a crumpled form lying against the bulkhead, then making a circular motion around their faceplate.

"I know, I know, I need to fix my pickups. This suit is a few ship-days of hell overdue for maintenance, and the external speakers are the least of my worries right now. Besides, it's not like there's anybody left alive to hear us."

The second trooper...*Astrid?*...shrugged, and waved in more troopers from the corridor. The new arrivals fanned out as they entered the command center, moving and cataloguing debris—and casualties—as they went.

The man with the malfunctioning hardsuit shoved aside a hanging ceiling grate, setting the smoke cloud to circling until the edges started running down the bulkheads. He pulled a cutting torch from his pack, and focused his attention on a long piece of broken conduit wedged horizontally between the pile of rubble and a safety railing. The light of the torch was blinding—even its reflection in his faceplate was hard to look at.

When the torch was almost all the way through, the pipe broke neatly along the cut, dropping slowly to the deck and shifting the wreckage around it enough to free her arm. The man took a step forward, and Caroline grabbed for his boot, wincing at the pain as her fingers closed around the cold armor plating.

"...h...help...m..."

The man's rising scream was the sweetest sound she'd heard since the crash, but even this small effort was too much for her to maintain, and her hand fell limp to the deck.

"Astrid! We've got a survivor!" The man knelt down beside her hand, following Caroline's arm with his fingers until it disappeared under the debris. Uncovering her face, he brushed a frozen sheet of blood-soaked hair away from her eyes. She still couldn't feel her legs, or anything much other than cold. But for the first time in many hours, she had hope, which was probably more than she deserved after all she'd done.

Shipdays in hell, he said. I can relate.

The second trooper—*Astrid!*—appeared at his side, shouldering him out of the way and using her suit's strength to shift the remaining wreckage. A sparkling cloud of condensation rose up as she worked, swirling around all three of them before gently coating both their suits and Caroline's uniform. The moisture stung briefly when it touched the exposed skin of her arm, spreading quickly over her burns and re-opened scars. Caroline welcomed the pain—it was another sign that she just might survive this after all.

"Commander Annahko. Can you hear me, ma'am?" Caroline recognized the voice instantly as Astrid Olvrsdóttir's, which was a bit of a surprise since Caroline had written a letter of condolence to her parents shortly before *Indomitable* lifted from Echo Base.

Sounds pretty good for a dead woman. Better than I do, for sure. Although she's a bit behind the times.

Olvrsdóttir produced an oxygen concentrator from her emergency kit and made to place it over Caroline's mouth, but Caroline shook her head, fighting to draw enough breath to speak.

"capt...captain..."

Olvrsdóttir shook her head, and held the breathing mask to Caroline's face as several other troopers arrived with a stretcher. Her partner was still moving wreckage, and gasped as he shifted the last piece and uncovered her legs. Olvrsdóttir turned her head to see, then quickly returned her attention to Caroline's face.

It was almost a minute before she spoke again, though Caroline noticed her head was bobbing and shoulders shifting the whole time.

"The captain...the captain is dead, ma'am. The gennies killed him, but from the footage I saw it was only a matter of time until we got to him ourselves. Rest easy, we'll talk again when you've spent some time in regen. Alonso, a word?"

Caroline's head was swimming as a new set of troopers lifted her onto the stretcher. Every time she tried to speak, the words swam away from her, until she finally gave up and just watched the smoke swirl overhead. Her skin felt like it was on fire, and the sensation was spreading up her arm and under her ruined tunic.

She didn't notice when the stretcher's AV unit switched on, but when her head rose up to about chest height on the troopers around her, she saw several of them turn their helmets away. One of them collapsed to the floor out of view, but she was too busy enjoying the burning sensation, which was now crawling across her cheeks and the back of her neck.

As her remaining escorts pushed her out of the compartment, Caroline caught one last snippet of conversation before finally surrendering to unconsciousness.

"What do you mean, she's not breathing...."

28 JULY 2640 OER

DEBRA MCCALLISTER

-7.5, -3:26 Roswell, New Mexico
MAH Compound

Deb didn't quite know what to do with herself. She'd been living on adrenaline and mood stabilizers for days now, and keeping herself together for the girls was about all she could manage. But now both her wives were coming home, and her carefully arranged life was about to be blown apart by the twin tornadoes of Marya Andreison and Mira Harlan.

Not that I don't still love them, but all of this works because they spend most of their time away, and I rarely have to see them both at the same time.

In truth, it was Mira she feared more today. Marya had filled her in on the basics of what had happened, but knowing that her childhood friend was now an extraterrestrial and having to live with it for the rest of her life were two different things.

I can do this I can do this I can do this...

Deb rested her hand on the controls to the front door, almost willing them to malfunction so she could have another few hours to prepare. But like everything she designed, she knew they would work as expected, and short of changing the codes there was no way she could avoid reuniting her family.

Pressing her forehead against the warm playaplast of the door, she smiled, feeling the edges of her scar pull on the skin around her left eye and ear. Everything else Tommy had done to her was in the past, but she'd chosen to keep the scar as a reminder of what could happen when you trust the wrong person. The girls didn't know what it meant, and the wives never cared about it anyway.

And if Mira really did find him, after all this time, all the madness is about to start again.

Outside the door was a double perimeter of security, half hers, half Fleet. Her compound was the only thing of interest for a hundred square kilometers, yet there was full battalion of armored troopers protecting every bit of that space. Though the truth was, despite their official mandate, the Fleet personnel were really guarding the worlds against her and her "mad inventions" rather than protecting her from harm.

It doesn't matter. No one can hurt me in here, unless I let them in…

But she couldn't hide forever, and in truth, she didn't want to. Her family gave her the strength she needed to get through each and every day, and shutting them out would put the lie to her fragile fictions.

A buzzing on her right wrist alerted her to the arrival of her visitors at the Fleet perimeter. Her people had judged the transport free of explosives, and had relieved the Fleet of all responsibility for its passengers. Still, everyone had to transfer to a vehicle of her own design to enter the compound, which bought Deb another few minutes to prepare for their arrival.

I can do this I can do this I can do this…

Resting her head against the door, Deb distracted herself by calculating just how much force a projectile would need to breach it, then how to wrap it in an explosive casing that would provide the necessary thrust. Half the North American Reclamation was protected by similar barriers, so she started calculations on how to defeat her latest design with a new ballistic coating that could be applied by an untrained laborer.

Then she started in on defeating the coating, a design problem that occupied most of the six minutes it took for the transport to arrive at the inner compound.

She remembered Marya's face when she got her long delayed deep space posting, after years of discrimination and despite the commendations she had earned, but never received.

She remembered Mira the first time she got leave, and saw what Tommy had done to her face.

She remembered Tommy, as a child, as a man, as a monster, leaving her broken and dying under an open sky because she'd dared to love the same woman he did.

She remembered how grateful she was to see Marya after she got out of the hospital, and how much it had scared her to see murder in Marya's special eyes when the jury returned a verdict.

And what it felt like to see her carted away in chains for giving that son of a bitch what he justly deserved.

Fifty meters away, said her wrist. Seven humans, two of which she'd handpicked for loyalty and marksmanship. Two of which she'd married, and three who were literally out of this world.

Thirty meters…twenty…ten…

The door alarm chimed, and Deb took a step back from the entrance.

I can do this.

Deb swallowed hard, and opened the door to the morning sun. Her protective lenses darkened immediately, and she recognized Marya and her guards standing back from the main party. Standing next to Marya was an impossibly beautiful blonde woman, wearing an ill-fitting coverall and clenching her hands over and over, as if she'd rather be holding something. To their left was a giant with orange skin, tiny eyes, and the most beautiful smile she'd ever seen.

And then there was Mira. Marya's message said the T-virus had changed her, but to actually see her wife's eyes in a new face, one with smooth, unfreckled skin, was a shock nothing could have prepared her for. But it was still Mirabelle Agnes Harlan, still the girl she'd fallen in love with and whose ring she wore proudly on her finger.

Standing in front of her was a little girl wearing Mira's smile. Mira's hands were on her shoulders, but the instant Deb met her eyes the child broke away and ran into her waiting arms, and all Deb's fears drained away.

"Hey, Deb. How've you been?" Mira's voice was still the same, despite her new face. "This is Serene. She's…she's mine. Ours, if you'll have us."

Serene's tiny arms tightened around Deb's neck, and there was only one response she could give.

"Of course she is. Welcome home, my darling.

"All of you, welcome home."

AUTHOR'S NOTE

It's all Ryan Dancey's fault.

I've known Ryan for almost half my life, through both fat times and lean, and one of his core characteristics is a lifetime love and extensive knowledge of science fiction.

We like many of the same things, and differ in opinion on many more. But I know when I ask him to read something I've written, he'll do it, and give me an honest accounting of its strengths and flaws.

Ryan was one of the first people to leave a 5-star review for *Homefront*, one I still look at from time to time for inspiration. In fact, he and I were sharing a cabin on a poker retreat when I put the finishing touches on *Behind The Lines*, and when I offered him the first draft for comment, he gladly accepted.

He didn't like it. But at the same time, he had some critical insights that helped me get the second draft in line. And when my then-publisher (and now-editor) Mark Teppo suggested we turn the two books into a concurrent trilogy, Ryan's suggestions helped me push the book(s) a lot closer to their final form.

Now I'm not saying he's going to come out guns blazing for this trilogy, but I think he'll like what I tried to do with it. And like any true friend, I'm expecting him to tell me the truth about it when he's done.

As I write these words, the ill-defined political structure of my far future no longer seems quite so distant. The ecological and technical disasters I theorized five years ago are now looming much larger on the horizon, so much so that work on these books came to a complete stop in late 2016, only coming back to life last spring as I found more creative ways to express my hopes and fears for our future.

I say ours, because here in 2019 we're all stuck together on Planet Earth, unable to escape the consequences of our actions. There is so much pain in this world, so much I'd like to sweep away with the stroke of a pen.

But instead, I write about hope. About people willing to sacrifice themselves for ideals, for those they love, and for those who cannot help themselves. I try to imagine how those people think, what drives them to make selfless choices when everything around them is going to hell.

I want to believe that there really are Mira Harlans who will always do what's right, that there are Marya Andreisons who will do anything for their families without hesitation. I want Jantines and Janbis in the universe to give us hope for the future, and I want Jasons to remind us of the big picture.

I'd also like for an alien bioweapon to fix up all my aches and pains and give me superpowers, but I'll settle for another 5 star review.

Mahalo.

Scott James Magner

March, 2019

P.S. That retreat I mentioned above was very productive, and before we left I managed to get a good start on the next volume of the Transgenic Wars. Turn the page for a sneak peek of what Marcus Callaway is up to "these days."

From the upcoming ARUS Entertainment release *Red Genesis*, a novel of the Transgenic Wars.

MARCUS

1350 SHIP TIME, SDF NEW ORLEANS

Marcus let out a long, slow breath, steeling himself for the other half of his Fleet mandated rehab. Still seated, he pulled a data recorder from his pocket, and rolled it over his fingers.

The psi-techs at Fleet Medical had let him out of their clutches on the proviso that he would find someone to talk to about what happened aboard *Valiant*, but Marcus was done talking about that. Review boards and head-shrinkers and carefully monitored interviews had teased out every last insight he had about commanding a dying ship to improbable victory, and the thought of doing it some more made him feel even worse.

But during the vetting process, he'd got to know a charming young gennie with the same kind of abilities Mira had. The Gamma "facilitator" had suggested a different kind of therapy, and after a quick review of the regs Marcus discovered that talking to HRL-G243157-T, called Harold, met their threshold of care.

Barely, but I like that kid a lot more than I do any of them.

Harold's specific suggestion had been to record audio journals, and all Marcus had to do was push the button and talk.

OK, here goes.

"I'm not the kind of guy who's into navel-gazing, or introspection, or whatever it is this is supposed to be. But I'm on a spaceship, sitting in a comfortable chair, staring at an image of my house on Earth, and that's as good a place to start as any.

"I don't have what you'd call a normal family, but these days, who does? But one thing I'm fairly certain of is that I'm what's weird about it—my parents, brothers, and cousins down there are the real heroes.

"Five hundred years ago, before the T-virus changed everything, my great-something-grandfather took his new bride to Kenya to study what wildlife was still left there thanks to the human race's many fuckups. He didn't have a lot to work with but good intentions, and I suppose in a way that's all we really have now."

Marcus shifted the image to another part of the estate, an impressive stone mausoleum that had weathered the centuries well. Zooming in to the side, the face depicted on the leaded glass stared at him from another time, and Marcus had no answers to the questions in its eyes.

"But Carl Callaway was a different kind of man than you'll find on Earth these days. They tell me I look like him, but I don't see it. His skin's a different color than mine, his chin is rounder, and so is the rest of his face.

"But none of that tells you who he was, and I guess that's why I'm making this recording today. In Carl's lifetime, he saw the worst parts of humanity get even worse, and he died protecting the one thing he loved most. A patch of land that grew only tall grass and the animals that lived in it. His last words were of forgiveness for the poachers who killed him, and his sons carried on the fight to keep the savannah alive.

"I haven't been back there in a long while, but it looks more or less the same now as it did before the Crash, or the plagues that came after. The AI wars, the Transgenic riots, the Exile, none of that mattered to Clan Callaway, when there was work to be done on the preserve.

"When the sky was full of choking ash and they dragged us away to orbit, lions and elephants looked up to watch us go, and their tenfold descendants were there to greet us again when my father won the resettlement lottery a hundred years ago. We could have lived anywhere on Earth, but we went back to Kenya to honor old Carl and his legacy, and we've lived there ever since."

Marcus switched the display to the station's last overflight of the continent. He knew the blue-green preserve's outline by heart, bordered on the east by the Nairobo Sprawl, and to the north by the ever expanding veldt that was once the Sahara Desert.

"The Reclamation has encouraged the rains, but it's for themselves, not the animals. The poachers burned or drowned or shot each other long ago, and part of me hopes it took them each a long time to die.

"But that's not why I went to space, or why I haven't been back in so long. I'm out here to stop that madness from ever happening again. And despite their best efforts, the Reclamation is as much a part of the problem as all the governing bodies that preceded it.

"Even with the best of intentions, every time humans start tinkering, it's the Earth that suffers. Maybe the Marsborn have the right idea, keeping their planet the way they found it, living in small enclaves of Earth-normal space contained by domes."

Marcus' thoughts, and eyes, turned to the sunken cities of Europe. A swipe of his thumb repositioned the image over the buried arcologies of North America. They weren't that different than the Marsborn Loyalists in their domes. Each group believed their way of life was best for their flavor of mankind, instead of letting the species adapt naturally. And despite their best intentions, the T-virus kept on finding new ways to improve upon baseline homo sapiens, which in turn emboldened the Reclamation government to enact more desperate measures to fix everything their ancestors broke in generations, instead of centuries.

Maybe Janbi Harrison is right. We've failed the Earth, and failed ourselves in the process. If the gennies can help us with that, more power to them. But if we're just going to make the same mistakes all over again, what's the point?

"That's all I have to say for today. That, and I'm sorry. I should have done more, tried harder. But in the end, I did my best, and that's all any of you judgemental pricks have a right to ask for."

Marcus wasn't sure if anyone besides himself or Harold would ever hear these sessions, but he'd added the last bit just in case. He turned off the recorder and rekeyed the display window to set the simulated planet rotating faster. Marcus kept his eyes on the display, afraid to close them and face his own mistakes.

Although the Fleet psychs had cleared him for duty, Marcus still dreamed about *Valiant's* destruction, of tumbling in darkness, seeing her break in two, or flying between house-sized spinning rocks in search of air, propellant, and power. But in the dreams, he was never fast enough to save even a fraction of the lives under his command, and often lost his own in the process.

Watching over the Earth, even this simulation, was the only thing keeping him sane, and even the knowledge that he'd probably saved everyone down there was no comfort once the lights went out.

Okay. Now let's try the other thing the nice gennie doctor who peeked inside my brain recommends for my continued well-being.

After all, he's been right about everything else, why not this too?

Over the next ten minutes he kept watching the big blue planet spin, imagining himself flying over it like a bird, with the upper fringes of the atmosphere playing around his skin.

As each continent passed under his wings, the Marcus-bird dove down to scream at it, cataloging their injustices one by one until he had nothing left to complain about. He even took a few passes over Antarctica, still half-covered by the only remaining glaciers on the planet.

Marcus loved every second of it, and was tempted to take a shuttle over to L1 and check out a grav-glider to try it for real. But the uniform he wore, and the tradition he was desperately trying to uphold meant that sooner or later, he'd have to return to his duties aboard *New Orleans*, and he couldn't do that from the couch.

Yet. It's a new ship, with a new mission. Maybe Mira and I can write some new rules in the process.

Marcus tried to think of the straight-laced, by-the-book lieutenant he'd met when he first came aboard *Valiant* as a whimsical rule-breaker, and failed miserably. After weeks of vetting her for inclusion in Captain Martin's inner circle, the only hint that another side of her even existed was the one night they'd spent together as lovers, and even then her take-charge attitude kept her in complete control.

But I could see it in her eyes, desperate to break loose. Under all her layers of armor is someone who just wants to be free, and now that she's out of the Fleet, maybe she can find that for herself.

And maybe...

Marcus's thought was cut off by a burning pain in his stomach, which was even more enticement to return to his quarters. He shut down the simulation and rolled off the couch, careful not to upset his abused digestive system any further.

A steady diet of stims and a triple lifetime of radiation exposure during the two ship-days he and Alonso kept Valiant's crew alive had done more than earn him a shiny new medal. Were it not for the millions of nano-machines he ingested each day working to keep him alive, Marcus would be in a lot worse shape than the collection of auto-immune disorders the doctors couldn't surgically repair in the hospital.

In fact, he and Alonso had expressed a couple new ones that the Harrison Institute was salivating over, but as long as they kept taking their magic pills and eating out of a tube, the prognosis was favorable. Unless he kept skipping lunch *and* dinner working on the systems integration with Alonso, that is. Missing meals meant he'd also missed out on most of his daily supply of miracle cure, and keeping humans alive in space was the one thing Fleet medical did do better than the Colonials.

Maybe I should start living in my hardsuit like Ramirez, so I can get more regular—and pleasant—reminders than a burning gut.

Marcus took the most direct path he could back to his quarters, and was reaching for a bulb of Fleet Medical's finest almost as soon as the hatch closed behind him. Biting the tip off the bulb, he sucked down the specially formulated machine and medication cocktail he'd come to loathe these last few weeks, along with enough kilocalories to keep him going for a few more hours.

Since the bulb also contained painkillers and a low-level stimulant, Marcus didn't immediately reach for the second of today's missed meals. Instead, he laid back across his bunk with his feet on the floor, and stared at the ceiling until the pain subsided.

After a few minutes, Marcus felt well enough to sit up. There really wasn't much to look at in his quarters besides the blinking message light on his workstation, but Marcus checked every centimeter of it out of habit. After nearly a month aboard, he'd yet to add anything personal to his quarters, a habit that stretched back to his Academy days.

In fact, other than the size of the compartment the only real change from his first duty assignment was the clear box displaying his newly-awarded Distinguished Service Medal. Maglocked to the bulkhead above his bed, the Fleet's highest honor was the only commendation Marcus had ever received that he wanted to refuse. He'd yet to even take it out of the box, even though he was required to wear it as part of any formal display.

Lucky me, I was too sick for Commodore DeMarco to formally award it to me in the isolation ward, and I did most of my testimony during the inquiries from a hospital bed. And since I left the surface, I've spent most of my time in ship's duty uniforms, and with my meals prepared in advance for the next two months I don't have to join anyone in the officers' mess.

Alonso Ramirez and Astrid Olvrsdottir had also received DSM's, but the lanky Marsborn had politely declined. Ramirez was still dazed by how many people now had to salute him, but his fiancee wanted no part of the commendation.

Which is crazy, since she was technically the only officer on Valiant *not committing treason at the time...*

Marcus lay back down, this time properly. Reaching up, he closed his eyes and traced the corners of the box with an outstretched finger, summoning up the faces of the people he'd had to leave behind. With each circuit of his hand, another face appeared, until he'd completed the second of his daily rituals and said goodbye to 173 people he'd barely known, whose deaths were entirely not his fault, yet still haunted his dreams.

Marcus tugged on the case, pulled it down from the wall, and used both hands to hold it on his chest. There was something about the way light played over it that made it seem sinister, and part of him wanted to throw it in the recycler and be done with it. But it wasn't just his to cherish, it was a reminder to the worlds of what happened aboard *Valiant*, and as long as he wore it, those lives would be remembered.

Marcus opened the case, and took the medal in his right hand. He let the ribbon fall over the back of his fingers, turning it this way and that until it was just another piece of metal, something he neither feared or cherished. He brought it close to his face, searching for meaning in the words inscribed on its face.

Omnia Vincit Animo Forti

Courage conquers all.

Odd words to honor a man whose fear now nearly overtook him whenever he was alone, and he closed his hand around the medal to obscure them. Marcus rested his fist upon his chest, and despite still being on duty, closed his eyes and let himself drift off to sleep.

This time, the last face he saw was Mira Harlan's, reaching up to him from the bottom of a deep, dark hole…

ABOUT THE AUTHOR

Scott James Magner has held down many jobs over the years, including circus promoter, warehouse manager, dog-sitter, professional role-playing gamer, and writer. He currently resides in Seattle with his partner of many years and several cats who don't understand why sitting down to write is not an invitation for lap-time.

You can catch up on all things him at his website:

scottjamesmagner.com

www.ingramcontent.com/pod-product-compliance
Lightning Source LLC
Chambersburg PA
CBHW010546100726
47902CB00008B/2105